Hippies

2002

Also by Peter Jedick

LEAGUE PARK

CLEVELAND: Where the East Coast Meets the Midwest

HIPPIES

Peter Jedick

Creative Arts Book Company
Berkeley • California

For information contact:
Creative Arts Book Company
833 Bancroft Way
Berkeley, California 94710
(800) 848-7789

Cover Art Design by Kevin Brown at topdogstudio.net

More information about *Hippies* is available at hippiesbook.com

ISBN 0-88739-381-0
Library of Congress Catalog Number 2001090483

Printed in the United States of America

This book is dedicated to the loving memory of:

sandy scheuer, allison krause,
jeffrey miller, and bill schroeder

Special Thanks

There are certain people without whose help *Hippies* would never have been published, and to those individuals I owe a heartfelt thanks. First and foremost there is my lovely wife, Jamie Quirk, who provided both emotional and technical support. Paul Samuelson deserves special thanks for editing *Hippies*. If you compare my own self-published first edition with this Creative Arts second edition, Paul's knowledge and expertise are self-evident, even though I didn't always follow his recommendations. Thank you to publisher Donald Ellis, who believed in my concept. Patti Clark created a *Hippies* web site for my first edition and the positive comments I received from around the world gave me the incentive to keep plugging away. (It still amazes me that people in places like New Zealand, Uruguay and the Netherlands would want to read my book.) Daniel Ketterick created the web site for this edition, hippiesbook.com. Denise Ziganti and John Scavnicky created the cover for the first edition and provided me with invaluable artistic advice on numerous occasions. Kevin Brown illustrated the new cover. I also have to thank all the individuals and artists in the music industry who helped me borrow the lyrics that give Hippies its historic flavor. Perhaps the most thanks go out to Nancy Birk of the Kent State University Libraries and two former Kent students, John Darnell and John Filo, who allowed me to publish their dramatic May 4th, 1970 photographs.

"Our house is a very, very, very, fine house.
With two cats in the yard,
Life used to be so hard,
Now everything is easy 'cause of you."

Crosby, Stills, Nash and Young

TABLE OF CONTENTS

Hippies

Fall Quarter

"Come mothers and fathers
Throughout the land
And don't criticize
What you can't understand
Your sons and daughters
Are beyond your command
Your road is
Rapidly agin'.
Please get out of the new one
If you can't lend your hand
For the times they are a-changin'."

Bob Dylan

Chapter One:
FIRST DAY OF CLASSES

There it was, the seventh game of the World Series, two out in the ninth, the bases loaded, we're losing by three runs and me down in the count, one ball, two strikes.

The hated Dodger southpaw Sandy Koufax dangled a curve on the outside corner but I laid off it, turned and took a look at the ump.

"Ball two," he screamed. The crowd went wild.

I stepped out of the batter's box, took a deep breath and stepped back in, digging my spikes into the dirt parallel to home plate just like my idol, Rocky Colavito.

"That took balls," Dodger catcher Roy Campanella said softly, trying to set me up for the fastball.

I just smiled. "Give me the blazer," I told him. Koufax shook off Campanella's first sign, shook off another, then finally nodded ever so slightly, his blue cap barely moving. He looked me straight in the eyes as his lips cracked the barest of smiles.

"It's the fastball, I've got him," I decided immediately.

Koufax screwed his body into a pretzel, leaned back and then fell forward, whipping his left arm like the tail end of a roller coaster. I watched the white sphere leave his hand in slow motion. I could see its stitches barely rotating. It's the fastball I'd been waiting for my whole life.

I gripped the bat so hard I felt the splinters in my palms. Before I even began my swing I knew I was going to connect with the sweet spot on the fat of the bat. I could already read the headlines: KUBIK GRAND SLAM IN NINTH WINS WORLD SERIES.

But just as I was about to knock the ball for a loop it disappeared. Instead, I felt a blast inside my skull. I jumped out of bed screaming, patting the sides of my head with my hands, searching for my batting helmet.

Harold, the dog sleeping at the end of my bed, turned his face sideways with a quizzical expression. An American history book was lying on my pillow. Somehow it fell from the desk that acted as a headboard to my mattress on the floor, striking me on the noggin.

I raised my head just in time to see the bushy black tail of the culprit. Spanky, our cat, ran out of the bedroom door with Harold the dog in hot pursuit. I guess I slept in and Spanky, tired of waiting for his usual morning meal, decided to take matters into his own hands. Or should I say paws?

Anyway, that's the way the whole thing started. Senior year. Kent State University. That fateful year of 1969-70.

My roommate, Paul Spalding, never moved a muscle during the entire disturbance. He liked to sleep with a fan clattering over his head to remind him of his native South Florida.

I grabbed my jeans and t-shirt off the floor. Spalding rested face down, spread-eagled on his mattress. Only his curly blond hair and high-instepped feet stuck out from under the covers.

I slowly creaked down the steps trying not to wake my other two roommates, Pat Murphy and Dave Early, who shared the bedroom across the second floor. We had a "First Day Back to School" party the night before and by the destruction downstairs it must have been a far out affair. I could only remember the barest of details.

Our poor house resembled Woodstock after the rock fans went home. Half-filled sixteen ounce Robin Hood Ale bottles covered every square inch of furniture. Roaches and rolling papers overflowed each ashtray. A mountain of paper plates and pizza boxes were scattered over the dining room table. In the kitchen the refrigerator door was still open, a stick of butter melting on the floor.

"We'll clean it up later," I convinced myself, pouring a large glass of orange juice while stepping around the butter. Our stereo system originated in a small storage room behind the kitchen. The turntable and records shared the area with our athletic equipment and other non-essentials. The speakers were strung out into various parts of the first floor.

I dropped "The Rascals Greatest Hits" album on the spindle and waited for the song "It's a Beautiful Morning" to begin my wakeup process. Harold waited patiently by my feet. Spanky sat on the kitchen counter.

"What? Now I should feed you?" I asked the killer cat before opening him a can of liver-flavored Puss-N-Boots. Spanky was a long-haired black cat with a white ring around one eye similar to the dog in the *Spanky and Our Gang* or *Little Rascals* comedies, hence the moniker. He purred pleasantly, smelling the liver-flavored who knows what.

Meanwhile, Harold's tail was wagging vigorously as I opened a can of Kal Kan beef chunks. The strange looking tan dog was named after a character in a Bill Cosby comedy sketch, "Weird Harold." Somehow the face of a little German Dachshund became attached to the body of a large English Boxer. Who his parents were I couldn't imagine.

I gulped down my orange juice while watching the animals eat, then let them out the back door. Like teenage kids they were on their own the rest of the day. Meanwhile, I tried hustling for my first class of the new year.

After a shit, shower and shave I went racing out the front door. But my progress was interrupted by a complete stranger sleeping on our living room sofa.

"Who the hell is this?" I asked myself. All I could figure was that he was a leftover from the party the night before. Kent was like that, strangers crashing for the night were not that unusual. But it was our first night in town and I couldn't remember meeting him. I didn't have the heart to wake him, he was snoring so comfortably. I'd leave him for my room-mates to handle.

The new day's sunshine was calling me outside. I stepped through the screen door out onto our little concrete front porch. It took me a moment to absorb the significance of it all. It *was* a beautiful morning and it *was* the first day of my last year in college and it *was* somehow special. I had to face the fact that in nine short months I'd be leaving the cozy Kent campus for the hard, cold world outside. I vowed to enjoy every last moment of freedom.

I took a deep gulp of clean fresh air, whistled "hello" to the scarlet cardinal hidden in the ready-to-turn red Maple tree on the front lawn and stepped out onto the sidewalk.

Then something magical happened. The door opened on the other side of our Depeyster abode. You see, I neglected to mention that we lived on one side of a faded pine green dou-ble, split vertically down the middle. The other half of the house also housed four students and had its own little con-crete front porch. And stepping out into the sunshine was one of the most beautiful blonde coeds a young man could imag-ine. She was extremely tall, her bright green eyes sparkled and she bounced down the steps like a kitten. But best of all, I knew her.

"What are you doing here?" we both asked in unison as I walked up to greet her.

"I live here," we both answered at the same time.

First we scowled, then we laughed. I'd forgotten how gor-geous she was. Too tall to date most men, she wore tight, faded bell-bottomed blue jeans and a flimsy beige peasant blouse that caressed her braless breasts.

Her name was Michelle and we'd broken up the previous spring. It was the kind of surprise that made me want to stay in Kent forever.

"You got an 8:50?" I asked her.

Her nipples were faintly noticeable through the thin material. How could I have broken up with such a lovely creature? Where was my head at?

"Yeah, at Satterfield," she answered icily. Her initial warmth disappeared as she also recalled the previous year.

"I'm going to Bowman," I said and began to walk with her, pretending not to notice her change in demeanor. The two classroom buildings were right next to each other.

"I didn't know we were neighbors."

"Neither did I."

We turned up Summit Street and began the long, uphill trek toward campus. The edge of campus wasn't far, but the two buildings we wanted were quite a distance and almost totally uphill. There was a campus bus stop on the corner of Depeyster and Summit and I was planning on taking it before running into Michelle. Even if she hated me it was still pleasant walking in her company.

We walked along in silence as hordes of students streamed onto Summit from the side streets like cars in rush hour jamming the Interstate entrance ramps.

"That was some party you had last night," she finally lightened up a little.

"You should've come over."

"I wasn't invited."

"We didn't know you were living there."

"You already said that." More cold silence. And I thought this was going to be one of the great days of my life.

"How was your summer?" I tried again.

"Could've been better," she admitted.

"Me too."

"Too bad."

Then she turned, looked me right in the eyeballs and gave me the sexiest smile I'd ever seen in my life. Basically it said, "You don't know what you missed, dummy." For an instant I could have sat down right there in front of the whole student body and pounded my head on the sidewalk. But I didn't. I kept right on walking as if her smile meant nothing to me.

By this time we were near the Dubois Bookstore that had a Campus Loop bus stop in front of it. The Loop circled the perimeter of the campus every five minutes while the Off-Campus bus that stopped at Depeyster came every twenty minutes.

"Want to take the bus?" I asked.

"No, but why don't you take it?" she said.

I may be a bit dense but I can take a hint, especially when I'm hit over the head with a two-by-four.

"I think I will," I laughed and ran across the street. Michelle continued her uphill route toward class. "See ya neighbor," I hollered back over the traffic noise.

I thought she also said "see ya" as she waved ever so slightly but I wasn't sure. What the hell, we had a whole year ahead of us, no need to be bitter.

"Why do these things always happen to me?" I asked no one in particular as I chased a Campus Loop pulling away from the Dubois Bookstore.

Chapter Two:
THE RALLY

Meeting Michelle first thing in the morning ruined me for the rest of the day. During my first class, American History I: The Revolutionary Era, I never heard a word the professor said the entire period. I kept imagining Michelle dressed like Martha Washington, meeting me at the doorway after a tough day at the Revolution. There'd be a hot dinner waiting on the table and I'd sit back and smoke a corn cob pipe while she sewed new flag designs for the young country.

Or was that Betsy Ross? Whatever.

You get the picture.

By the time class ended I had to borrow a classmate's notes, I hadn't written a sentence. My second class went the same way as the first, more flights of fantasy, little retention. I was considering blowing off the whole day when I ran into my roommate, Paul Spalding.

He was walking on the sidewalk in front of me between classes. I was on my way to the Student Union for lunch when I noticed his large frame standing head and shoulders over the crowd. I had thought about going back to Depeyster for lunch but with only an hour between classes the Student Union seemed like a quick alternative.

Spalding was probably thinking likewise. After a year of rooming together we could pretty much read each other's minds.

"Where you off to, buddy?" I asked, catching up with him.

"Same as you, the Union," he answered in his usual short and to-the-point manner.

"Make your 9:55?"

"Yeah, no problem." He kept looking straight ahead as he walked. I knew there was a pair of bloodshot eyes behind his ever-present aviator sunglasses. He wore them not so much because he was an aerospace technology major but because they were a requirement in his native Florida.

I wanted to tell him about our new neighbor but decided it would be worth the surprise when he discovered for himself that our new housemates were of the female gender.

We walked along the sloping, shaded sidewalk from Van Duesen Hall to the Student Union. It was crowded with students making their fifteen minute trek between classes. Although my classes were scattered all over campus, Spalding's were confined mostly to Van Duesen, the Aerospace Building. I could usually find him there if I needed him.

"Dave and Pat get up?" I made a second attempt at jump starting a conversation.

"Early was still in the shower when I left, one of his half hour specials," Spalding replied. Oooh, no wonder the big guy was grouchy. Early hogged the shower and Spalding didn't have time for one of his own.

That always rubbed him the wrong way. "The Murph's still sleeping," he added.

"Think he'll graduate?"

Suddenly the "Fly-Boy", as we liked to call him, turned serious. I'd finally struck a chord. "It don't look good, he's spending way too much time with Mary Lou."

I was about to comment on the Murph's lack of academic vigor when a couple guys with shoulder-length hair, beards and trashy jean jackets walked by, passing a joint as if they were just sharing a Marlboro.

"Did you see that?" I turned my head in disbelief, following the hippies' tracks. Me and Spalding, with our hair just barely over our collars, looked like Joe College compared to this pair. Yet back home over the summer my parents and siblings threw huge amounts of verbal abuse at me for my looks. If my father caught these guys' act he would've popped a blood vessel.

"We've come a long way, baby," Spalding laughed.

That was a fact. When we first met as sophomores in the Wright Hall dormitory, marijuana was shared with ritual paranoia. Students smoked their reefer with select friends behind closed doors, a lookout posted outside like there was a bank robbery in progress. In two short years the drug craze had come out of the closet. Students were openly flaunting the law, pushing the establishment to the limit.

We reached Kent's Student Union before we knew it. The Union was a small, brick two-story building shaped like a box. Its snack bar was the size of a junior high school cafeteria.

Although it was a quaint, cozy, vine-covered meeting place located near the front of campus, it was woefully obsolete. Designed for a small teacher's college built at the dawn of the twentieth century, it was unprepared for the baby boom generation.

The modern university was an ever-expanding monstrosity bulging with over 20,000 students. Three science buildings, a high rise library and a new Student Union were under construction near the new center of campus. In the meantime the old union would have to do.

On pleasant days the overflow crowd spilled onto the patches of grass surrounding the site, similar to Lauderdale Beach during spring break. Spalding, as usual, bought a couple of hot dogs and cokes and wouldn't accept any of my money. He treated me like the kid brother he never had.

We snaked through the sun-worshippers trying to stake a claim. "Radicals" decked out in long hair, beards and dirty jeans worked the crowd, hawking revolutionary literature and underground newspapers. Catch phrases like "The

Vietnam War," "Tricky Dick," and "The Military Industrial Complex" filled the air.

We finally sat down on a little stone wall that overlooked a walkway connecting the ancient front campus with the Student Union. It was the perfect location for girl-watching, especially between classes.

"Did I tell you that I met our new neighbor?" I finally asked Spalding between bites. I could no longer hold the news inside me.

"Which neighbor?" he answered my question with one of his own as our legs dangled over the rocks.

"The other half of the house," I replied.

"Well, what about him?"

"It's a her."

"A her? What her?"

"Michelle."

"Your Michelle?"

"That's the one."

"Living right next door?"

"You got it."

"Far out," Spalding sipped his coke for a second exploring the possibilities. "She got any roommates?"

"I guess so, I didn't see any."

"This could be really interesting," he laughed.

"Senior year." We toasted our paper cups.

As we talked a pair of very similarly dressed brunette coeds approached us. Their green t-shirts were tied just under their braless breasts, revealing suntanned stomachs. The only difference between the two was that one sported granny glasses and a frizzy afro while the other wore contacts and long, straight hair parted down the middle of her head.

"Coming to the rally?" the frizzle-haired one asked first, handing us each a flyer.

"We've got to stop the war," her sister-in-arms added.

"What time's it at?" Spalding asked, searching the flyer for details.

"Noon, it's almost time now," the straight-haired one answered. "Come on guys, we need you."

"Are you going?" I couldn't help ask.

"Sure," they answered in unison, then giggled at their cheerleader-type response. Very un-cool.

"Then we'll be there *FOR SURE*," the girls blushed at the "For Sure," losing their composure twice in a matter of seconds. Very un-political.

Just then the Victory Bell started ringing on the Commons. It was the Kent signal for a rally to begin. Originally the Victory Bell was rung to publicize pep rallies for the football team. The campus radicals had transformed the tradition from sports to politics.

"It's starting," the girls gushed. Now they were really acting like cheerleaders. "You guys coming?"

"Be there in a minute," I held up my half-eaten hot dog.

"Meat, ooooh," they exchanged gross-looking facial expressions.

"Oops." I apologized for being a meat-eater.

"He bought it for me," I pointed at Spalding.

"Thanks." He kicked me.

The girls headed toward the rally and we flashed them peace signs.

"What were you saying about Michelle?" Spalding laughed.

"Michelle who?" I went back to reading the flyer.

"Let's check it out," Spalding jumped off the wall and I followed his lead. We deposited our hot dog wrappers, cups, and rally announcements in one of the nearby blue and gold (Kent's colors) trash barrels.

The Commons is a flat, grassy area between the Student Union and Taylor Hall, the architecture and journalism building. It was designed like a modern version of the Greek Parthenon and looked down on the Commons like Camelot's castle.

The Students for a Democratic Society (SDS), the radical

left's national organization, sponsored the rally. They usually held them during lunch hour to attract the non-political students like us who were basically wasting time between classes with nothing better to do than watch their strange machinations. In other words we were doing a sixties version of "cruising for chicks." It made their following look much larger than it really was and helped them pick up a few converts along the way.

By the fall of 1969, it was hard to find a college student who wasn't against the war in Vietnam. After all we were the ones next in line to tramp through the jungles. Yet political rallies were much more social than political. They were an extension of the previous generation's panty raids, massive events designed to meet members of the opposite sex.

We reconnoitered a spot on the side of Blanket Hill in front of Taylor Hall.

Blanket Hill had a notorious reputation throughout northeast Ohio as a famous make-out spot. In the pre-sexual revolution days, couples spent their evenings there making whoopee under the stars.

By 1969, "free love" had made Blanket Hill passé. We stretched out on the grass, let the sun warm our faces, and enjoyed the spectacle below. The speakers addressing the crowd on the Commons stood on the brick structure housing the Victory Bell. We watched the back of their heads as they harangued the students through a portable bullhorn.

The first speaker was a Vietnam vet wearing his Army uniform and combat boots. This was the required uniform for most radicals whether or not they served any time in Southeast Asia. He related horror stories of Uncle Sam's atrocities in an interesting yet uninspiring manner. His comments were met with frequent polite applause.

We closed our eyes and almost nodded out until a familiar voice stated matter-of-factly, "The war sucks. End it and go home."

Standing before us like a partial eclipse of the sun was the roommate Spalding wanted out of the shower a little faster in the morning, Dave Early. If Spalding was built like a linebacker, Early was designed along the lines of a defensive tackle, large and burly, wider than he was tall. He also had a habit of philosophizing that was legendary. He took complex situations and broke them down to simple solutions.

"Early. What's happening, brother blood?" I raised my hand to exchange a hippie handshake without getting up.

He reached down to shake mine but at the last second pulled it away, pointing his thumb in the opposite direction as if to say "hit the road, Jack." It was one of his favorite tricks and he laughed that after all the years we'd known each other I still fell for it.

"What it is, my man, you diggin' this rally?" Early jested. We often communicated in a pseudo-ghetto lingo we picked up from working in a mostly black railroad laborer's gang the previous summer. "Spot any nice holes?"

I sat up while Spalding remained horizontal, grinning at our repartee.

"Hey, hey broooother," I stretched it out slow and sassy. "There's a fine looking white chick about to be rappin' our way."

The second speaker at the megaphone was a short, blonde coed wearing the same uniform as the Vietnam vet. She was dressed much like the duo that invited us to the rally. The campus radicals tried hard to show what independent thinkers they were yet they all dressed alike.

First she encouraged a round of applause for the Vietnam vet, then slipped into the standard rhetoric, which branded any soldier still over there as a "baby killer" or "napalm murderer." She was totally unaware of the irony of her arguments.

But she did whip the crowd into considerably greater agitation than her predecessor. As for the three of us, we were pretty unimpressed. After a few minutes of half-listening we turned to more urgent matters, like what our fourth roommate, Pat Murphy, was doing in the crowd below.

"Hey, there's the Murph." Early spotted him first, which caused Spalding to sit up and take notice. Pat Murphy was standing in a large group of students, his bushy black hair bobbing up and down as he laughed. Early was as wide as a brick house, the Murph skinny as a toothpick.

The Murph was always laughing, as if he didn't have a care in the world. This was a strange attitude for a college student on the verge of flunking out. A possible two-year hitch in Southeast Asia didn't seem to worry him. Everyone else on campus was trying to prolong their education to extend their student deferment, hoping that the government would come to its senses and end the war before we'd have to go.

"I bet he's laughing at one of his own corny jokes," Early ventured. We watched him play the crowd for awhile, until by combining our powers of concentration he looked in our direction for no apparent reason. We waved and jumped around to catch his attention. Once he noticed us he climbed the hill, grinning as usual, with an unknown companion following in his footsteps.

"Hey, guys," the Murph gave a sweeping wave of his hand like a puppet on a string. We each nodded hello. "This is Artie."

The Murph introduced a shorthaired kid who didn't look old enough to shave. Artie shook everyone's hand hippie style, forearm up in the air, thumb back, as we introduced ourselves.

"Don't I know you?" I asked him.

"I don't think so," Artie said. "I *was* at the party last night."

"You're the guy on the couch." His face suddenly clicked in my mind.

"Artie just got hired to work with me at Captain Brady's," the Murph explained. "He needs a place to crash until he gets his first paycheck."

The Murph gave us a look that begged our approval. We

exchanged glances, first with each other, then with the Murph, then with Artie.

"The sofa's empty," Spalding offered. "But we go to bed late."

"All right by me," Early added. "As long as he don't eat too much." Early was only half-joking. The kid's face turned more pale than it already was.

"It wouldn't hurt you to miss a few meals," I jabbed Early in the side.

The Murph took my comment as tacit approval. "Great," the Murph slapped Artie on his back. "We got to go to work but we'll meet you back at the house later."

"Thanks," Artie did another round of hippie handshakes. "I'll try and rip off some food for you guys."

"You don't have to do that," Spalding quietly lectured the kid.

The Murph led Artie back through the crowd and the three of us looked at each other again.

"I just hope he don't wear out his welcome," Early said seriously.

"Hey blood, don't you want to help out your broooother?" I gave Early another poke, trying to lighten him up.

"He ain't my brother and he best not be helping himself to any of my shit, man," Early's voice rose considerably. He put up his dukes and called me on. We started bobbing and weaving like television's Fred Sanford and his friend Bubba.

"Hurry up, Ali," Spalding said to me as he checked out his aviator watch. "We're going to be late for fencing."

"I give up, you win." I dropped my fists while still dodging punches with my head.

"*OOOOO-EEEEEEE*, I am the greatest," Early raised his fists in the air and jumped around, doing a poor imitation of Muhammed Ali, the self-promoting heavyweight boxing champ.

We tried to disassociate ourselves from Early as unobtrusively as possible. The rally was breaking up, the crowd dematerialized, and the few students who wandered near Early shook their heads in amazement.

"Try to end the war while you're at it," I said to Early as we departed.

"I wish I knew where he bought his drugs," Spalding said.

"He doesn't do any."

"That's what he says."

Chapter Three:
FENCING

Stopping at the rally made us a little late for fencing class. Fencing was the latest in a long line of physical education courses Spalding and I took each quarter. The classes were an ideal way for two friends with different majors to share a similar experience a couple of days a week. We learned a new sport, got a little exercise, and, most of all, met new chicks. All our phys ed classes were coed.

The fencing class was held in Wills Gym, the original Kent Normal College gym behind the Administration Building. It became the girl's gym when a much larger boy's gym was built next to the football field in the middle of campus.

The football field was being moved to make way for the new student union complex but that's another story. Suffice it to say the girls' gym was old and crusty but only a short walk from the Commons.

There was no dress change required, only tennis shoes, so we went straight to the basketball area. The teacher was already checking attendance when we entered.

"Uh-oh, look who's here," Spalding said as we walked across the wooden floor.

"Who?" I asked, surveying the crowd. Spalding motioned toward Michelle, who was talking with a group of girls. The class was split up like a high school dance, girls on one side, guys on the other.

'I don't believe it."

"She's living next door?"

"Uh-huh."

"Wow, she looks even better than last year."

"Tell me about it."

"Names, please," the instructor interrupted us, obviously irritated by our disruptive behavior. She was a short, busty, female graduate student with short, light brown hair held back by a headband. Quite the eyeful. She was wearing a KSU sweatshirt and nylon shorts that revealed the build of a gymnast.

"Matt Kubik, Paul Spalding," I pointed at myself, then my friend.

"Can't your friend speak for himself?"

"Sure he can," I turned to Spalding, waiting for him to say something. Instead he just stood there flashing his big surfer smile, watching me squirm.

"Well…" she said, her sternness melting under his sunny smile.

"What?" he laughed and she smiled with him.

"Never mind," she looked down at her roster and checked our names off.

"Like I told the rest of the class," she looked at us again. "My name's Miss Thompson. Let's try to be more punctual in the future."

"Sure," Spalding smiled again and I just nodded, looking over at Michelle, who was obviously amused.

Our lovely fencing instructor explained the basics of fencing, going over a few of the terms we needed to know. Then she explained the basic stance. "You place your feet this way, like an L, hold the foil with your palm up, put your other arm behind your head, then move forward and backward, keeping your feet in the L position." She demonstrated the movement as she talked. "Now you try it. Pretend you're holding a foil."

About fifteen of us stood in a line and moved up and down the basketball court, learning to advance, retreat, lunge and double lunge, all the while keeping our feet in the tortuous L position. It was hell on the old hamstrings.

As I moved I tried to sneak a peek at Michelle but she looked straight ahead as if I didn't exist.

"Now we're going to try and get a feel for the equipment," Miss Thompson said. "We don't have much time so everyone take a face mask, jacket, gloves and a foil."

After taking our accoutrements, Miss Thompson showed us how to put on our jackets. We had to step into these white outfits that looked like straight jackets with a white ribbon between the front and the back that slipped under the crotch. Very erotic. I enjoyed watching Michelle put hers on. "Have a neighbor zip up the back for you," she advised. "I'll be walking around to see who needs any help."

"Come on," I told Spalding to follow me and walked right over to Michelle.

"Need some assistance with your chest protector?" I asked her in the spirit of reconciliation.

"No thank you." I could tell she didn't appreciate my sexist inference. "How are you, Paul?" she smiled at Spalding.

"Just fine," Spalding smiled, he zipped up my back while one of Michelle's friends did hers.

"Are you following me or what?" her mood changed again when addressing moi, lowering her voice in controlled anger.

"I was about to ask you the same question," I kept my voice as low as hers, put off by her petty attitude.

"This isn't going to work," she whispered as she struggled to fit into the jacket that was a couple of sizes too small for her breasts.

"I agree, why don't you drop the class?" I was enjoying her difficulties. "Take badminton or something."

"Me? What about you?"

As we continued our heated yet subdued discussion, Spalding watched with glee. He knew our routine from junior year. Michelle's friend was also enjoying the show. She walked up to Spalding.

"I take it you know them?"

"Yeah, I'm afraid so," he said. "I've seen all this before."

"Deja-vu?"

"Yeah, that's it. You should hear them argue politics."

"Chris Rogers," she held out her hand like a man. Chris was a petite, classy brunette with slightly frosted hair. She was wearing a plaid skirt, nylons and tennis shoes, a rare sight on a 1960s college campus populated with bell-bottom jeans and sandals, no socks.

"Paul..."

"Spalding," she cut him off. "I heard."

Michelle and I were so involved in our heated discussion that we didn't notice the instructor walking up to us. She listened for a few moments before we saw her and ceased fire.

"Class," she stated loudly. "We have just enough time to demonstrate how we score a match. I need a couple volunteers to do battle. You two will do," she pointed at Michelle and me.

"I didn't..." I wanted to say "volunteer" but chickened out.

Miss Thompson showed each of us how to hold the foil, placed us in the starting position, face to face, then asked four students to be scorekeepers, placing them on the four corners of an imaginary rectangle.

"Two of you will watch Michelle and two of you watch Matt to see if the foil touches them, if it does you raise your hand," she explained. Spalding was one of my scorers, Chris one of Michelle's.

As Miss Thompson manipulated our bodies I could feel my heart racing. She told me not to hold my foil so tightly, let it hang with my wrist, but how could I help it with my dreaded enemy within striking distance. "First I'll toy with her, then I'll slash her to pieces," I decided.

"Keep the foil parallel to the ground and use short, quick strokes like this," she used her own foil to demonstrate. My legs began to hurt as I maintained the position. "Don't slash

20

like you're in an Errol Flynn movie, keep your legs bent and move only a step or two forward and backward. Each time you strike your opponent you receive a point. The first to score five points wins."

I couldn't wait to start. Here was my chance to repay Michelle for all the grief and aggravation from the previous year. I was sure she felt the same way about me. *Take off the safety tips*, I wanted to shout. *Let's really go at it.*

"Oh, I forgot the masks," Miss Thompson said. Paul and Chris handed us each one like doubles in a duel.

This was perfect. No longer could my intensity be softened by Michelle's lovely green eyes. She would become a faceless enemy, the deserving object of my wrath.

"Now, before you start, raise your foil to your face and salute your opponent."

With our free arm raised behind our head we took our foils, lifted them straight until they touched our nose and then dropped them back down.

"All right, put on your face masks." We did. "On guard, ready, fence." We began to do battle. I have to explain something to those who've never tried fencing or watched a "bout." Everything happens very fast. It's not like in the movies where the pirates jump over ladders and treasure chests. One person attacks, the other blocks their move and counter-attacks and then, after a few back and forths, it's over. It didn't take us very long to vent our frustration.

At first we both hesitated, waiting for the other to make the first move, kind of like young lovers unsure of themselves. Finally, she lunged slightly, missing me completely. I backed up, pushing her foil away with a quick parry. Then she backed up. I circled her foil with my own, toying with her. Another parry, thrust, lunge and she would be history. We shuffled clumsily again, our steel blades clashing, then her blade caught my arm. Spalding and his partner raised their hands, I looked at them in horror from under my mask.

"Invalid, no point, you must strike on the chest," Miss

Thompson explained. She was the referee or director who interpreted the hits from the four judges.

Whew, that was a close one, I thought to myself. *Time to go for the jugular*. With a step forward I lunged toward her aorta.

"Ha, try and stop that!"

She did.

Her foil caught mine halfway up, directing it away from her body. I was over-extended. She stepped back, made a little underhand U move off my foil, took a small step and caught me in the right ventricle. Spalding's hand went up again. "You traitor," I thought.

"Point," Miss Thompson shouted and stepped between us. "That's enough for today."

"Stop? That's it?" I couldn't believe it, I was about to begin my counter-attack. "I thought we played till five?"

"No time," Miss Thompson looked at her watch. "Now take off your masks and shake hands. That's how you end a bout."

Shake hands with my enemy? What kind of civilized sport was this?

"Congratulations," I said nobly.

"Thank you," Michelle said with a smirk.

"You may notice," Miss Thompson interrupted, "that Michelle used a disengage to score her point. That's a move we'll teach you later in the course. Class dismissed."

"A disengage?" I asked Michelle, as Paul and Chris unzipped our jackets. "How did you know about that?"

"I didn't," she answered smugly. Her hair was matted down after removing her mask.

It gave her a sweaty, sexy look that I tried not to let cloud my anger.

"I want a rematch."

"Maybe next time," Miss Thompson interjected. She had wandered back to us after seeing the other students off. "I hope by Wednesday you two can leave your personal feelings outside the gym." She took our foils away from us as if she couldn't trust us with them.

"There won't be a next time," I said. "I'm transferring out."

"No, I am," Michelle said.

"Why don't you both stay," Miss Thompson said calmly. "Fencing is a great way to resolve conflict and I think you'd add a little spice to the class." Then she turned to Paul Spalding and said: "You know, I have to teach five of these classes a day."

"I'll see what I can do," he assured her, in an Eddie Haskel suck-up kind of way. I could have killed him.

"I'm getting out of here," I said and marched off.

"Bye," Miss Thompson waved.

I was angry. My whole day was deteriorating at a rapid pace. I just wanted out of there. But instead of following my lead Spalding lingered a second with the girls.

"Nice meeting you, Chris," I heard him say. He shook her hand once again.

"See you Wednesday," Chris smiled.

"Michelle..." he held his palms out sideways as if he did-n't know what to do with me.

"Peace, Paul," Michelle flashed him the peace sign.

I saw the entire scene out of the corner of my eye as I walked out of the gym, pretending not to be interested.

"Et tu, Brutus?" I said to Spalding once he caught up to me.

"Christ, Kubik, you should be grateful I'm even walking with you. You were beat by a girl."

Chapter Four:
THE APPLE TREE

That's how I remember my first day of classes, senior year. It was a real loser. The humiliation of fencing, a new collection of up-tight professors and the after-effects of the previous night's party combined to kick my ass plenty. I couldn't wait for the day to end. As I turned the corner at Depeyster, I remembered the mess inside the house. I decided not to even deal with it. I'd walk right through it with blinders on and head straight for my bed. What I needed was a long nap.

But there was good old Harold sleeping in the sun on the front lawn and when he jumped up to greet me I began to feel a little better. Then I noticed an older gentleman standing on the girl's front porch talking to Michelle. About what I could not imagine. As he started down the steps I tried to catch her eye but she shut the door as if I did not exist. I could only shrug. It was going to be a long year.

The silver-haired gentleman, dressed in a threadbare herringbone jacket, looked like a down and out ex-college professor. At least *he* was happy to see me. He came trotting up to me in a hurry, as if I might disappear on him. Harold gave a little growl that should have made me suspicious but I hushed him up. I was curious to see what the old guy was talking to Michelle about.

Then I noticed the peck basket full of apples.

"Hello, young fellow," he greeted me with a bit of a fake English accent. He wasn't afraid to smile even though most of his teeth were missing and the ones still intact were the color of broccoli soup.

"How'd you like to help out an old man and buy a few apples?"

I wasn't really crazy about apples but at least the old dude was trying to *earn* his liquor money, not just beg for it like the hobos downtown. Kent seemed to have more than its share of down and outers, maybe because of the train tracks that ran through the middle of town.

"How much?" I asked him.

"Two bucks for the whole basket," he grinned again.

That was kind of steep for my modest means. I was thinking more along the lines of three for a quarter. But then he nailed me with the hook, the kicker, the bottom line.

"I pick them myself, you know. It's not easy when you're my age. I'm a dying breed."

There it was, the old "dying breed" routine. Like he was some sort of bald eagle or something. Hey, I've got a heart, I was even environmentally correct early on. How could I not help save an endangered species?

"Here you go buddy," I reached deep into my jean's pockets and discovered I was down to four singles. It doesn't sound like much today but back in the sixties you could live for a week on that kind of stash. And he was asking for half of it. "I might have to join you in the apple business," I tried to joke with him, but once he saw the bills come out of the safe he was a changed man.

"Bless you, my boy," he cradled the two greenbacks in his gnarly hands. I swore I saw a bottle of MD 20-20 reflecting in his deep brown eyes. "Do you mind if I keep the basket?"

"Sure, go ahead," I was feeling generous after doing my part for the homeless population. I stretched out my gray KSU t-shirt and he filled it with the contents of his basket. And he even held the front door open for me so I could ease into the house. "What a nice fellow," I thought. Maybe I was wrong about the dude. Maybe he needed the money to visit his sick mother in Dubuque.

Entering the front door with a t-shirt full of apples, my notebook under my armpit, I was unprepared for the sight before me. The house was spotless. If you had told a complete stranger that the night before a horde of college students held a party in the same household he would have laughed in your face. Only Artie's makeshift couch-bed was left untouched as a testimony to our extra roommate.

"Early," I smiled to myself as I looked around in awe. Early's nickname was "mom." Every college student should have a friend like him. He was everybody's old-fashioned grandmother. He was the "Odd Couple's" Felix Unger. He cleaned the house, cooked our meals and got on our case if we started showing too many Oscar Madison tendencies.

"I hope he likes the apples," I thought, dumping them into the sink to wash off any pesticides. There was no telling where they came from. I wiped them off and placed them in a large bowl in the middle of the dining room table. "Nice touch," I congratulated myself on my little addition to the general sense of homeliness.

I walked into our stereo command center, looking for the perfect album to put me asleep. I munched on an apple as I searched through our community record collection.

I had just dropped the Moody Blues' "Days of Future Passed" on the spindle when I heard Harold barking out back. That damn dog. I needed my nap and I was in no mood for a barking mongrel. I was about to let Harold inside when I heard a crashing sound like a plane landing in the backyard. I looked out the window and there was my old buddy, "The King of the Road," trying to hush up Harold as he bounced a wooden ladder against the tree in the far corner of Depeyster's back forty.

Then he climbed up *our* ladder to fill *his* basket with the apples from *our* tree. I had just paid two bucks for my own apples. I wanted to kill the guy but I was too embarrassed to admit my foolishness. I'd forgotten that we even had an apple tree.

My anger quickly faded. Maybe it was my overall tired condition but I watched helplessly as Harold barked at the old guy's heels. "What a dope," I thought to myself. At least no one else knew what an idiot I'd been.

Suddenly I remembered Michelle. Had she also been duped? I had to find out. I ran out the front door, jumped on her porch and knocked loudly.

"What do you want?" she answered stiffly. Her stereo headphones were drooped over her shoulders.

"Did you by any chance happen to buy any apples off our friendly neighborhood peddler?" I asked.

She looked at me as if she had no idea what I was talking about.

"The dying breed?"

Ah, those magic words. The phrase struck a chord. She couldn't help but smile. "The 'dying breed' bit was a bit much," she laughed.

"Would you mind coming out back for a second?"

"What for?" she was suspicious of my intentions.

"Trust me," I tried to guide her elbow but she pulled her arm away. She did, however, take off her headphones.

"The last time I 'trusted' you, you disappeared for two weeks."

"I'll explain that some other time," I tried to change a touchy subject. "Just take a look out back."

We circled the house and discovered the apple entrepreneur on his way back down the ladder, kicking at Harold and trying not to spill any of his basket full of apples.

"Do you know him?" I asked.

Michelle stopped in her tracks, stared, then laughed. I whistled and Harold came running over. The old man heard us and bid a hasty retreat over the neighbor's fence, clutching his basket like a fullback trying not to fumble the football.

"At least he could have taken the ladder down," I said, as we walked toward the tree.

"Must be the landlord's," Michelle said, instinctively butting the base of the ladder so I could lower it. "How much did he sucker you for?"

"A couple bucks," I admitted, sheepishly.

"I only gave him fifty cents."

"I always said you were smarter than me."

"You said it but you didn't believe it."

We sat on the back porch steps and listened to strains of the Moody Blues filter through the screen door. The back porch, unlike the front, stretched from her back door to ours. The wooden steps were much more comfortable than the concrete ones in front.

We gazed at the large gravel parking lot bordered with railroad ties and the lawn stretching out behind it. There was a dilapidated brick barbecue grill that we planned to put into service in the near future. The back yard was one of Depeyster's fringe benefits, a major improvement over apartment life.

"So, are we buddies again?" I had to try and break the ice or it was going to be a very long year.

"Depends on what you mean by 'buddies,'" she shot back, still a bit tiffed but I could tell she was softening.

"Not enemies," was the best I could come up with on the spur of the moment.

She looked me right in the eye and I could swear I saw a little of the old spark re-ignite. "Friends," I offered, holding out my hand for a traditional handshake.

She left it hanging out there for what seemed like forever before she took it firmly. "Neighbors," she said and smiled.

What a smile. It felt like the sun just broke through a winter's storm. I was greatly relieved.

"So what do you think about Chris and Paul?" I made small talk and she made small talk and once again I enjoyed the warmth of her company.

Sitting with Michelle under the hot sun, fanned by a cool breeze, it reminded me of old times. For one marvelous moment all was right in the world. I felt invincible, ready to tackle whatever challenges senior year would throw my way, oblivious to the tragedy lurking in the autumn shadows.

Chapter Five:
HOMECOMING

PART ONE: The Idea

After that rough first day of classes things pretty much went back to normal at Depeyster. Life was almost the same as junior year, except now we had a house instead of an apartment. We kind of fell into a routine. Spalding and I usually studied in our room until late in the evening. Then we either went downtown for a couple of beers, or watched the late show on our black and white Philco television.

The Murph was hardly ever home. He was usually out with his girl friend, Mary Lou, the daughter of one of Kent's college professors. He also spent a lot of time working at Captain Brady's, which was kind of a hip restaurant and coffee house, a hangout for the old beatniks and new hippies. That's where he found his young friend Artie. We weren't sure what the connection was between them but we figured he'd tell us when he got around to it.

How the Murph ever managed to stay in school was anybody's guess. We sometimes wondered if Mary Lou's dad was pulling some strings for him. He never went to classes, never did any homework. Hell, he never even bought any textbooks. But he kept pulling Bs and Cs. He was supposed to be majoring in Poly Sci (that's political science for the uninitiated) but you wouldn't know it from talking to him.

His main topic of conversation was partying (i.e. drugs, alcohol or the ultimate buzz). From what we could gather, the Murph's high school career was highly structured. He seemed to be making up for his "lost years" ever since he came to Kent. He was great to be around as long as there was nothing pressing on the academic scene. The Murph's constant temptations were a wonderful exercise in self-discipline. Luckily, we had the specter of Vietnam hanging over us staying in college or we would have given in to his whims more often.

Artie was still living on our couch. He was only there in the evenings. He never ate with us or anything, but we still wondered how long this was going to last. After all, we *were* paying rent for the place and a freeloader was a freeloader even during the hippie years. This especially irritated David T. Early.

Early was about the strangest character on a campus full of freaks. He should have been the ultimate hippie radical but was just the opposite. I already mentioned his aversion to sloppiness. But did I mention that he was one of only about ten students on the whole campus who never used any kind of drugs, even on social occasions? What made his anti-drug posture even stranger was that he played guitar in a local rock band, The Hybirds. How he could jam with a bunch of freaked out acidheads tripping on LSD was anybody's guess. But we heard them and they were cool. Early took "being different" to the extreme. He pushed the envelope to the limit and he never failed to surprise us.

Early was also a bit of a loner. He spent a lot of time in his room studying sociology, his major. Those were the guys and gals who wanted to change the world and sociology claimed to provide the road map. But Early had his own plan. He'd do it through his songs. Sometimes he'd try them out on us, plunking the ivories on the old piano that some previous tenant left in the dining room.

Every once in a while, Early would join Spalding and me for a beer downtown but normally our only social contact with him was when we sat down to our evening meal.

Unlike most college students who ate at strange and varied times, we were still old-fashioned enough to share a nightly communal dinner.

It was a ritual we began our junior year when we first shared an apartment on the other side of campus. And again, we could thank "mom" for making it happen. Early usually cooked a fresh, wholesome meal and if we didn't show up to eat it he got pissed. And since he was wider than he was tall he wasn't the type of guy you wanted to cross.

If Early didn't have time to cook, one of us would jump in and take charge. The food was plain and often experimental but there was usually a lot of it and as growing boys we each had a healthy appetite. Besides, if you cooked you didn't have to clean up afterward. After living together for a year we created a system that worked in an unstructured sort of way.

Fall quarter started out much like the previous year. Go to classes, come home, eat dinner, study on the weeknights, and party on the weekends.

One evening Spalding and I were sitting at our respective desks, studying our respective subjects under the glare of our respective high-intensity lamps. Spalding's desk was in one corner of our room facing the wall, his mattress was on the floor behind his desk chair.

My desk was by the back door, facing the window. My mattress lay on the floor between the desk and the window. The maple tree outside was silhouetted by a nearby street light. Spalding was hunched over his books deep in study. Or so I thought.

"We going to the Donovan concert?" he suddenly blurted out, without looking up from his book. He was referring to the annual Homecoming Concert featuring the popular folk singer.

His question caught me by surprise. I should have known his mind was wandering because he was reading *Papillon* by Henri Charriere instead of his aerospace textbooks. *Papillon* was a 434 page hardcover novel that Spalding read when he needed a diversion from his technical studies.

Spalding wanted to be an astronaut, he wanted to be the first man on Mars. He had the flair for it, and the courage. But the mathematics threw him for a loop.

I was struggling myself. I foolishly signed up for a political philosophy course, hoping to discuss the politics of the Vietnam War. Instead, the prof wanted us to study Kierkegaard, some medieval radical. I welcomed Spalding's interruption.

"You mean Homecoming?" I answered his question with one of my own.

"What do you think I mean, dickhead?" he shot back affectionately.

"What I meant to say is 'are you asking me for a date or are we going to round us up a couple fillies'?"

Spalding stared at the red wall in front of him, took a long drag on his Winston, put it in his Holiday Inn ashtray and turned around, exhaling a long, steady stream of smoke in my direction. "You got a nice ass but you're not my type. I was thinking more along the lines of Chris from our fencing class."

"Right, thinking about yourself as usual," I said sarcastically. "And who am I supposed to take?"

"I'm sure you'll find someone," he turned around and went back to reading *Papillon*.

Now I couldn't get my mind back on my textbook. I opened my top desk drawer and pulled out a bag of weed and a corncob pipe, stored there for just such occasions. Spalding and I owned a bag of communal weed for as long as I could remember. Probably going back to our sophomore year. It was a prerequisite for attending college in the 1960s, sort of like a high school diploma.

Once I packed the corncob and lit it up Spalding could smell the herb. I could almost see him smiling through the back of his head as he raised his head from his book and began searching through the rack of cassette tapes on his desk. Spalding, as usual, had the latest in high tech stereo technology, while the rest of us were still trapped in the world of vinyl albums. He took out Cat Stevens' "Tea for the Tillerman," plopped it in this tape player and closed up Henri Charriere. I took another hit, then walked over and handed him the corncob pipe.

Sitting on the edge of his mattress, I exhaled. He took a hit and handed it back.

"Why don't you ask Michelle?" Spalding wondered.

"We're finally just talking again, I don't think we could handle a real date."

"No one else you're interested in?" Spalding asked.

"Let me think about it," I said. "You think Chris will go out with you?"

"I'm ready to give it a shot," he said. "You know I haven't asked out many girls since I've been up here."

"Just Susan," I could recall. I knew Susan was a sore spot so I stood up and took the corncob back to my desk for a refill.

"Yeah, we're a couple real chumps, huh?" he said, referring to Michelle. They were our girls from junior year. "Here we are seniors and neither of us can get a date."

"There's always Carol."

"Yeah, right. I think we've got an understanding. At least I hope we do."

Carol was Spalding's steady back home in Lauderdale. It was the reason he didn't date much up north. But it looked like he was tired of saving himself for her and with one year left was ready to take a walk on the wild side.

"What kind of understanding?"

"You know."

I could tell he didn't want to talk about it but I felt like teasing him a little.

"No, I don't know. You mean you've agreed to date while you're separated?"

"Kind of."

"Kind of? What's that mean?"

"It means I decided to live a little senior year, all right? Give me a break."

He walked over to my desk and took the filled corncob from my hand.

"Oh, I gotchya, an 'understanding,'" I smiled. He knew I was putting him on.

"It's almost time for 'The Prisoner,'" he said, taking a look at his watch.

"The Prisoner" was a cult television show we watched religiously every week. It was about a prisoner on a fantastic island that escaped every week but by the end of the show always ended up back on the island. It was supposed to be "existential" or something. We didn't really understand it but it made for great programming.

"Okay," I said, following him down the steps to the living room. "But Saturday we go in search of the perfect woman."

"Agreed."

Chapter Six:
HOMECOMING

PART TWO: The Bike Ride

Late Saturday morning, while putting my breakfast scraps in the wastebasket, I noticed Michelle sitting on the back steps. I remembered my vow to Spalding about a date for Homecoming and I half considered asking her out. But first I'd have to feel her out. No use getting shot down if it was entirely out of the question. What better time for a little pleasant conversation.

It was a lovely fall day, cool, crisp air, warm sun, the smell of burning leaves in the air.

The girls had opened their second floor window and placed twin speakers on the sill. Carol King was singing her "Tapestry" album. Two of Michelle's roommates, Renee and Sarah, were sitting on a small patch of grass next to the back parking lot playing euchre.

Renee was a terribly shy nursing major, quite attractive with long shapely legs and straight brown hair. But she hardly ever strung two words together into a sentence. Sarah was a short, stocky, education major, built somewhat like our fencing instructor. A busty, gymnastic type, Sarah loved to blab.

They were as odd a couple as Early and the Murph. Renee

went home to Akron almost every weekend, while Sarah, who was from New Jersey, almost never went home. They shared one of the bedrooms on the girls' side.

Michelle's bedroom mate and alter ego was Jennifer. But she was more of a phantom roommate than the Murph. She only kept a few belongings in their room for appearances. Actually, she was living off campus with her New York boyfriend. She needed a female roommate so her parents wouldn't know about it. Jennifer made dramatic appearances at major parties or other social events like a reigning beauty queen, which she most certainly resembled. We always enjoyed her periodic visits.

I think Michelle missed her since they were close friends in their junior year, like Spalding and me. The previous spring quarter, Jennifer had met Mr. Right, a Long Island native like herself. Thrown into a cultural backwater like Kent, the two socialites became instant heartthrobs. I always wondered how Jennifer's departure affected Michelle, especially back when we were breaking up. But I'm digressing as usual.

I stepped out onto the back porch and posed with my hands on my hips, looking out over the backyard like Ben Cartwright surveying "The Ponderosa." (A popular television show from the era, that was our nickname for the Depeyster ranch.) I pretended not to notice the girls.

"What a day, what a life," I expounded. "A morning like this makes you feel great to be alive."

"What a man," Michelle said in mock admiration. Her roommates giggled.

"Good morning," I smiled. "You don't know how good that makes me feel." I sat down beside her. "Any big plans for the weekend?" I asked casually, trying not to tip my hand.

"No, just my boyfriend's coming up for Homecoming," she looked straight ahead as my jaw dropped six inches.

"Boyfriend?" I stammered. Renee and Sarah hid their faces behind their cards.

"Yeah, I met this guy from Ohio State over the summer," she turned and looked at me with the most innocent of expressions. "He's due in from Columbus tonight."

"A Buckeye. You're dating a *Buckeye*?" I laughed too loudly. I had to attack the guy on some level and since he wasn't around it was the best I could come up with. I was saved from making a total fool of myself by Spalding, who came crashing through the basement door that was located just below the back porch. He was pushing his brown, rusted, fat-wheeled, one-speed Cadillac bicycle in front of him.

"And what's wrong with Ohio State," Michelle was heating up.

Spalding was oblivious to our conversation. "Come on we have to pick up a few things for the weekend," he said. What he meant was for me also to grab my own skinny, red, Schwinn three-speed English racer out of the basement.

"Nothing, nothing at all," I said to Michelle as I stood up. "If you like nuts, Buckeyes are wonderful." I disappeared into the darkness beneath the house.

"The only one nuts around here is you," she hollered after me. Spalding looked at Renee and Sarah for some hint of explanation but only received a couple of shrugs.

I pushed my used bike up the basement incline, hopped on and shot some gravel with my back tire as I sped down the driveway. I was copying the greasers from my high school days who liked to peel rubber for effect.

"What's wrong with him?" Spalding asked Michelle.

"You should know, he's your roommate."

Just then a voice came down from above, like God commenting on the situation. "I like the Buckeyes," Early said from his previously unnoticed perch. Shirtless, he had climbed out his back window and was catching rays on the roof of the back porch.

Everyone broke out into laughter.

By the time Spalding caught up with me I was already a couple of blocks north on Depeyster, heading downtown. The fresh air was caressing my face, cooling my emotions.

"What's with you," he asked.

"Michelle's got some boy friend from Ohio State coming up for the weekend."

"The Buckeye?" he laughed.

"Yeah, where we heading?"

"You tell me," he said. "I thought we were looking for the perfect woman?"

"That's a contradiction of terms," I smiled at my own wit. The bike ride was already making me feel better.

"Well, I'm going to Cucumber Castle," he said.

The Cucumber Castle was the local head shop on the corner of Willow and Main Streets. We began pedaling faster and without a word broke into a race, standing up off our seats, swerving to miss pedestrians.

Halfway down Willow, I tried grabbing a Frisbee in midair that a couple of hippies were tossing in the middle of the street. Instead, I dropped it and splashed one of them by accident as I swished through a puddle.

"Peace," Spalding flashed the two-fingered V sign at the irritated victim. "Who covers your ass when I'm not around?" he asked, passing me once more.

On Saturday afternoons, off-campus Kent was a peaceful kingdom. Everyone was about the same age, college students sitting on their front porches, reading, talking, making music, playing stereos. We slowed down our pace as we neared the Castle. Just ahead of us a pair of coeds were jumping, laughing and kicking up piles of leaves along the sidewalk.

Instinctively, like a little kid, I rode up on the sidewalk, came up behind them and hollered "*BEEP-BEEP*" like the Road Runner. They jumped out of the way in fear of their lives. Once again Spalding followed my wake, flashing a peace sign and saying "Sorry."

"What do you think of them?" I asked Spalding as he pulled up next to me like a cowboy on horseback.

"Look like a couple a mighty fine fillies," he said.

We pulled up to the Cucumber Castle and left our bikes unlocked in the metal bike rack. Who'd want our beat-up, second hand bikes anyway? Besides, we were a pair of naive college kids. I mean, we never locked anything. We didn't even have a key to Depeyster. There was some kind of combination code on the front door but we forgot it about a week after we moved in.

The Cucumber Castle was an old wooden office building that the current owners painted a dull green to match its name. The windows were painted to look like stained glass except instead of pictures of saints they depicted hippies and peace signs.

As you walked in there was a clear glass counter that spread lengthwise like a bar. Behind it sat a slightly older lady, maybe a graduate student, with long, straight brown hair that fell lower than the stool she was sitting on. She wore granny glasses and a mini-skirt that showcased her tanned but hairy legs, easily seen through the glass display case. We tried not to stare.

The cases were filled with all the latest drug paraphernalia needed by the hip college student of the times: rolling papers, hash pipes, water pipes, screens, automatic rollers, you name it and they carried it. If they didn't, you could order it through *The Whole Earth Catalog* or *Mother Earth News*.

There were also displays of pottery, posters, books, records, tapes, art, mobiles, calendars and underground publications. The Saturday afternoon browsers featured various campus freaks and straights. Some of them looked totally out of place in a head shop, like the football player sporting a crew cut and a varsity letter jacket. You had to wonder if he might be a narc. What better place to find out who was using illegal substances?

"I'll take a couple packs of Zig-Zags (rolling papers) and could I see that little hash pipe?" Spalding forced the clerk to reach under the counter, her long hair touching the ground as she bent over. Her firm breasts almost popped out of her v-neck blouse.

I stood near an open window, hoping to catch a glance of our two coeds as they walked by. My heart skipped a beat as they stopped to look at our bikes, then climbed up the steps to the Castle.

They were a strange pair. The taller one was a hippie chick with class. If there was a Vogue Magazine for hippies she could have been their model. She wore all the right anti-establishment clothes: bell-bottom blue jeans with a colorful plaid border on the cuff, a red flannel shirt, sandals, and a rope belt. But they were all tight enough to fit her curvy figure like a coat of paint. Her jet-black hair was pulled behind her ears with a bandana, revealing peace sign earrings. Heavy mascara highlighted her soft violet eyes. All in all, she was strikingly beautiful.

Her shorter friend wore much the same outfit in different colors and a much plainer, baggier style. She hid her true figure more in line with the feminist mantra that deplored dressing to please men's eyes. Her tanned, freckled face was surrounded by a reddish-brown frizzled hairdo that framed her blue eyes like a halo. She was cute and sexy despite her clothes.

I positioned myself by the underground newspaper rack as they came through the door. I watched them sneak up behind Spalding at the front counter. Tall, tanned, and good-looking, Spalding was the perfect bait. He'd hook them and I'd reel 'em in.

"*BEEP-BEEP*," the tall beauty said with a laugh.

Spalding turned around, speechless.

"Why didn't you tell us you were coming in here?" the freckle-face added. "You could have given us a ride on your handlebars."

"Uhhh," Spalding stammered. He was unused to such a direct approach from members of the opposite gender. He looked to me for help but I covered my face with a copy of *Rolling Stone*.

"We didn't have much time to talk," he apologized.

"You're buying a hash pipe?" the tall one continued the inquisition, examining the object sitting on the counter.

"Don't you know drugs are illegal?" freckle-face teased. They were paying him back for our near accident and enjoying every moment of it.

"Oh, it's not for me," Spalding turned immediately defensive.

"A present for a friend?"

"She smokes a pipe, does she?"

Even the girl behind the counter was beginning to enjoy his dilemma. Flustered, Spalding pulled a fin out of his wallet and gave it to the clerk.

"Hey, I didn't run you over, he did," Spalding pointed me out.

I folded my newspaper and slowly sauntered over. "Sorry about that," I said in my best Maxwell Smart imitation. "Allow me to introduce my friend, Paul Spalding."

"Elizabeth," the tall beauty smiled.

"Donna, pleased to meet you Paul," the freckle-face held out her hand and Spalding shook it with great vigor.

"And you're...?" Elizabeth asked me.

"Matt," I answered. I felt like kissing her hand, she seemed to exude royalty.

"And I'm Gail," the clerk interrupted. "I love it when people meet in here, great Karma, you know." She handed Spalding his change and his pipe in a little brown bag. We all laughed.

"You guys about done?" the football player asked. He'd been standing behind Spalding holding a large bong like a Rawlings football. His patience was wearing thin, especially when I cut in front of him to pay for my *Rolling Stone*.

"One second," I interrupted, giving the clerk a dollar.

"Do you read that?" Elizabeth was impressed.

"When I have the time," I tried to put on an intellectual air.

"They have good articles," she said.

"Do you mind?" the football player had enough of us.

"Sorry," I said.

"I guess we'll be seeing you," I said to Elizabeth.

"Sure."

"Of course."

The two girls smiled uncomfortably as we exited.

"Why'd you let those two get away?" Spalding asked as he climbed back on his Cadillac.

"Did they go anywhere?" I asked as I began letting the air out of my front tire. "Imagine that, I've got a flat."

"You rascal," Spalding smiled.

We took turns examining the tire with various degrees of curiosity and concern until the two coeds came out of the Castle.

"What's wrong?" Donna asked.

"Matt has a flat," Spalding explained.

"I guess I'll have to push it home to Depeyster," I looked sadly at Spalding.

"Tough luck, buddy," he said.

"We could take turns if you get tired," Elizabeth offered.

"Thanks for the offer, but I think we can handle it," I smiled in appreciation as we all started walking together. "Where do you guys live?"

"Right up College," Donna answered, and Spalding snuck me a smile as we became a group.

"What'd you buy?" Spalding asked Elizabeth, noticing her brown bag from the Castle. "No drug paraphernalia, I hope?"

"A mobile for my bedroom," she pulled it out. It was a bunch of different colored eyes hanging from different lengths of string, glittering in the sunlight.

"You're going to feel like someone's watching you while you sleep," I said.

"At least I won't be lonely," she smiled coyly.

Talk about your attention getter. The hairs on the back of my neck began to tingle.

Elizabeth lonely? I knew right then that I wanted this girl badly. I kept pushing my bike up Willow Street. Spalding pedaled slowly in circles to match my speed.

"Where do you guys live?" Donna asked.

"South Depeyster," Spalding answered.

"Just a little bit of heaven," I added.

"The Ponderosa," Spalding said and the girls looked at us funny.

"An inside joke," I explained.

"How about that ride?" Donna suddenly asked Spalding.

"All right, let's give it a try," Spalding agreed. Donna eased onto his handlebars as Spalding struggled to keep his balance. After a few anxious moments he pedaled harder and then pulled away from Elizabeth and me. Alone at last.

"Is Donna always so friendly?" I had to ask.

"No, she's really kind of shy but we did some mesc just before we left the house," Elizabeth confessed. "I think it kicked in about the time we were entering the Castle."

"Are you buzzing right now?"

"Can't you tell," she laughed.

"And I thought it was us."

"Maybe you had a little help but I am having a nice time. You want me to push for awhile?"

"No thanks, I'm fine," I looked straight ahead watching Paul and Donna do circles in the street.

"It's the first time Donna's ever done mescaline," Elizabeth continued. "I hope she's all right."

"She's in good hands," I assured her, then paused for a second. "As long as you're in such a great mood I have to ask you something."

"Yes?"

I stopped pushing my bike. "How'd you like to go to the Homecoming concert tonight?"

"You mean Donovan?"

"I know it's the last second..." I tried to explain but she interrupted.

"We're already going."

"Oh well," I began pushing my bike again.

"But it's just me and Donna," she continued. "You could join us."

"Great."

We turned the corner on College Street. Paul and Donna were headed back our way. I had to talk fast.

"But I think Paul already has a date."

"Then why don't you call us," she wrote her phone number on my *Rolling Stone*. "This is where we live."

Their student quarters were much classier than ours, at least from the outside. They lived in a two-story yellow colonial with a large front porch. Spalding pulled up his bike and Donna jumped off.

"That was great," she said. "Thanks."

"How was it for you," I asked Paul in jest.

"A workout," he puffed, feeling his Winstons.

We said good-bye and headed home. Spalding pushing his bike for awhile.

"Well, how'd it go?"

"Can't you tell," I smiled.

"You're in love."

"You got it."

"What else is new?"

"Except I don't know if it was me or the mesc."

"She was tripping?"

"They both were. We ran into them at just the right time. I asked them to the concert but they were already going."

"Bummer."

"With each other," I laughed. "We can take them unless you already have a date."

"Yeah, I asked Chris."

"Well, maybe we can all go together, you know, friends."

"Yeah, friends, my eye. I know you," he laughed and jumped back on his bike.

"What?" I said as he left me behind. We were nearing the

corner of Depeyster.

"Ah, see you soon," he took off like the Cisco Kid did when saying good-bye to his sidekick, Pancho.

He headed home while I pushed my Schwinn to the near-by Marathon gas station in search of an air pump.

Chapter Seven:
HOMECOMING

PART THREE: The Brick

By the time I pushed my English racer to the nearby Marathon station, filled the tire, and pedaled back to Depeyster, I was beat. "Was she worth it?" I had to ask myself. At least I had a semi-date for Homecoming.

I planned to spend the rest of the Saturday afternoon vegetating. Maybe watch a college football game, any team but Ohio State.

There were rumors that Kent had a football team but they were unconfirmed. We almost went to a game once during sophomore year but came to our senses and went to happy hour at the Loft instead. I appreciated Kent's attitude toward college athletics more as I got older. Like most things on campus they weren't taken very seriously.

In fact, about the only things Kent's students took seriously were our parties. We had a reputation to uphold. Ohio State was known throughout the Midwest as a football powerhouse, Kent was famous for its parties.

It was a tough tradition but someone had to maintain it. We had high standards to meet. And when I say "high," I mean "high."

Drugs were the 1960s college student's passports to popularity. Nice clothes, a flashy car, and a wallet full of green-backs might attract a few campus cuties, but a dependable Columbian connection was worth more than all the sports letters you could collect. It was almost as impressive as playing guitar in a rock and roll band. If you could get your hands on some primo weed, suddenly everyone wanted to be your friend.

So you can imagine my surprise when I got back to Depeyster only to discover Spalding and the Murph engaged in a shouting match over drugs. A broken kilo of marijuana, a package of plastic baggies and a chemistry lab scale sat on the dining room table. The Murph's buddy, Artie, stood silently in the background as the two friends argued.

"Hey guys, keep it down, I can hear you on the front sidewalk," I tried to break up the fight.

"Look what your burned-out pal is up to," Spalding lowered his voice a notch, pointing at the table. "He's turned our house into a drug store."

"We're just breaking up a brick," the Murph rolled his eyes at me.

"Well, do it somewhere else," Spalding said. You could tell he was angry by the pulsing blood vessel in his temple.

"Where? Captain Brady's?" the Murph laughed. "The library?"

"You guys smoke it, don't you?" Artie piped in.

"You don't even live here so shut your damn mouth," Spalding turned on Artie.

"I don't like this either," I sided with my Florida friend. "I like to smoke but I never wanted to be a dealer."

The Murph knew he was outnumbered. He shrugged his shoulders and gave us his Alfred E. Neuman "What Me Worry?" look.

"All right, it won't happen again, but we got to finish breaking up this brick."

"Fine," Spalding said, walked into the living room and turned on the television.

I sat down with Artie and the Murph. It was kind of fascinating watching them break up the compressed grass, weigh it and put it in plastic baggies.

"Spalding has a point," I said to the Murph. "It's senior year, we don't need to get busted."

"It would have been better last year?" he laughed.

"You know what I mean."

"Hey, everybody does it," the Murph said. "It's easy money."

"A lot easier than working at Captain Brady's," Artie said.

"As long as you don't get caught," I said.

"They don't care about us, just the big guys," Artie said as he took a bag off the scale.

"You're not filling a full ounce," I told him.

"Profit's not a dirty word," he smiled. Spalding walked past us into the kitchen, acting as if we didn't exist. He put an Arlo Guthrie album on the turntable. I could hear the refrigerator door open. The Murph lit his newly rolled joint, took a hit and handed it to me. I took a hit and began to cough.

"This shit's rough," I said.

Spalding walked past again, dropping off a Robin Hood Ale for me and the Murph. Nothing for Artie. I tried handing him the joint but he pushed it away. That was a first.

"Just try one hit, let me know what you think," I asked. His cigarette abused lungs were a better quality indicator than mine.

He took a long hit, then spit it out and smiled at the Murph. "You've been had, buddy," he said between coughs.

"Let me try it," Artie practically ripped the joint from Spalding's hands. Spalding really didn't like that.

"It's not so bad," Artie said after a little hit.

The Murph grabbed it back and hit it again, real hard this time. "You asshole," he told Artie. "Where'd you get this shit?"

"Smells like oregano," I said, passing the joint under my nose.

Spalding just laughed.

"It's supposed to be top-of-the-line Mexican," Artie said, acting puzzled.

"You better get our hundred and fifty bucks back," the Murph told him.

"No problem," Artie had the look of a frightened dog on his face. He began repacking the weed in a large plastic bag. "Here's one for your trouble," he took one of the little baggies and threw it at the Murph.

"No thanks," the Murph threw it back in the middle of the table.

I grabbed it before it got back to Artie.

"We can use it in our spaghetti sauce," I ventured. Even though it was unsmokable it was the first time Artie contributed anything toward his adopted home.

"Maybe brownies," Spalding suggested.

"No, you need Columbian for brownies," the Murph said.

"Listen to the head chef at Captain Brady's," Spalding laughed. "You have a secret brownie recipe or something?"

It was a relief to see Spalding and the Murph joking around again. We went into the living room to watch the tube. Artie was left to pick up the weed.

Later on I put the baggie filled with whatever in the kitchen spice rack. Big mistake.

Chapter Eight:
HOMECOMING

PART FOUR, The Concert

Once Artie left and the Murph and Spalding nodded out in front of the TV, it was a good opportunity to give Elizabeth a call. So I jumped in the bathtub and dialed her number. If that sounds a little strange you have to understand our weird but functional living arrangements. When we first looked at the Depeyster house the previous spring, the landlord, who had just bought the place, promised to replace the antiquated bathtub with a modern shower stall more in tune with a contemporary college student's lifestyle. Early, thinking as usual, asked the landlord to save the tub.

"We'll find something to do with it," he predicted.

And we did. We put it in the dining room, next to the dinner table, filled it with cushions and used it as a telephone booth. There was something erotic about lying in an old fashioned cat's paw bathtub and talking on the phone. Even if you did have your clothes on and there were no soap or bubbles.

Elizabeth and I ironed out the details of our first evening together. She agreed to let me escort both her and Donna to the Donovan concert. I was in heaven.

Spalding would meet us at the concert after he picked up Chris, who lived on the other side of campus. I would walk since "my girls" lived so close. Spalding would use the family vehicle.

Like I explained before, everything back in the 60s was kind of communal: our weed, our food, our albums, even our automobile. The vehicle of choice was purchased the previous spring from the Murph's older brother for $25, $6.25 apiece. Not bad, huh?

So what if it was a huge rusted out '59 Chrysler New Yorker. The price was right even though its V-8 engine sucked up gasoline like an elephant drinks water. What the hell, gas was only a quarter a gallon.

The Chrysler did look a little out of place on a campus filled with hippie vans, Corvairs, and Volkswagen beetles. We tried to compensate by decorating it with those yellow plastic stick-on flowers that were in vogue at the time. We put them on the door panels, the trunk, the hood, even the roof, but all it did was make it look even more obscene.

Did we care? Hell, no. We were trendsetters, not slaves to the fashion dictates of the age. We were confident that once our contemporaries saw the advantages of our ride they would want one themselves.

After all, the Chrysler seated six comfortably, ten if necessary, started on a dime and best of all, no car payments. What more could a college kid ask for?

The plan was Spalding would take the Chrysler and I would stretch my legs. But as they say, "the best laid plans never seem to work out right." Or something like that.

What we hadn't counted on was the weather. After a fair, dry fall most of the quarter, suddenly the rains decided to appear just in time for Homecoming weekend. As soon as I heard Harold barking at the back door I realized something was up. He came running into the house, soaked, jumping on me with his wet paws. Spanky, the cat, was right behind him.

It was time to change the game plan. No way was I going to escort two lovely ladies to a major event with a long walk in the rain. We'd share the New Yorker whether Spalding wanted to or not.

But how was I going to break this to Spalding?

He was sitting comfortably in the front room's prehistoric Lazy-Boy. His legs were stretched out on the raised footrest, a Robin Hood Ale between his legs and an ashtray with a lit Winston on the armrest. The college football game on the Philco was coming in a little fuzzy.

"Looks like a storm brewing," I walked to the front window and pushed back the flowered drapes, left there by a previous tenant. I figured I'd warm him up to the subject.

"Uh-huh," he said, paying me no mind.

"Nasty night for a concert," I added, sitting on the hand-me-down sofa Artie was using for his bed.

"Guess so," he agreed, taking a sip from the big sixteen ounce bottle.

"Maybe we should make a few changes in our itinerary," I suggested, throwing a little pilot talk at him.

"Like what?"

"Like maybe we should share the bomber."

"No way," he snubbed out his cigarette. "This is my first date with Chris and I don't want you screwing it up with one of your hair-brained schemes."

"Moi?" I was taken aback.

"Yeah, you're always pulling some shit. But not this time."

"You don't want me to walk with Elizabeth and Donna in a downpour, do you?"

"I don't want Chris and Donna anywhere near each other. I don't even like the idea of meeting you there."

"What's wrong? The more the merrier." I meshed the knuckles of my two hands together like revolving gears. It was a code we used to show that everything was in synch. "You know, friends."

"Friends, my eye. I just want to get to know Chris, all right?"

"Okay, okay. How about if you just drop us off, then pick up Chris? We won't even sit together."

"Promise?"

"Right on, brother," I gave him the raised fist salute.

That evening Spalding and I put on our hippest outfits for the big concert. He was wearing a turn-of-the-century three button t-shirt, looking like Paul Newman in *Butch Cassidy and the Sundance Kid*. I was sporting a yellow t-shirt with a sunburst on the front that came out of the rock musical *Hair*. We both wore the required bell-bottomed blue jeans. He had brown deck shoes and no socks. I had black Converse tennis shoes and white socks. I wore a jean jacket to keep off the rain. He had a brown zippered suede. We were on the cutting edge of hippie fashion, dressed just like every other college kid our age.

Spalding took the car keys off the beat-up piano in the dining room. Another hand-me-down from a previous tenant, it provided a convenient shelf for our books as well as a source of relief for Early. It was a bit out of tune but the ivories still worked.

As we stepped out the back door, into the elements, we paused a moment to bundle up. The rain was pelting the back yard with great authority.

We were just about to step out into the night when a strange car came pulling up our driveway. A little red Datsun with an Ohio State Buckeyes decal on the back window. It parked right next to the New Yorker. We watched as a guy big enough to play tackle for Woody Hayes' football team came running up to the porch. He had hair longer than Jesus and a flowing beard to match. A real hippie, he was Sgt. Pepper to our "I want to hold your hand" imitation.

"Does Michelle live here?" he asked very politely.

"That side," I answered gruffly, pointing to the girl's door. We went out into the rain as he knocked.

Spalding was forced to steer the Chrysler around the Datsun like a boat pulling out of a marina.

"Inconsiderate lout," I said, trying to size up the prophet through the rain streaked car window. "There's something about that guy I don't like."

"For Chrissake, you just met him," Spalding laughed.

"I know, but I can usually tell a lot about people when I first meet them."

"Like when you first met me? You thought I was a real jerk."

"There, that proves it," I laughed.

"A little jealous maybe?"

"Just keep driving."

We picked up Elizabeth and Donna. They were both wearing flower print dresses and sandals. Elizabeth was protecting herself from the elements with a knee-length button-down sweater. Donna wore a slick yellow raincoat.

I eased them into the backseat so as not to appear too forward.

"Guys in front, girls in back," I joked. "Just like in high school."

"I never did that," Elizabeth said from the back seat. "Did you Donna?"

"Not me," Donna agreed.

"Me neither," Spalding added. Talk about sucking up to the chicks.

The traffic was already congested as we pulled onto Main Street, thanks to the weather and the concert. "You going to have time to drop us off?" I asked Spalding.

"He's dropping us off?" Elizabeth asked.

"He has to pick up his friend Chris."

"Let us off here, we can walk," Donna suggested as we came to a standstill.

"We're in good shape," Spalding said, suddenly making a u-turn right in the middle of Main Street. Drivers in smaller cars cringed at the sight of the Chrysler spinning like a top.

"Where you going?" I asked him.

"The back way, to pick up Chris."

He finally gave up to the inevitable. We picked up Chris at a little house north of campus. Spalding went inside to explain the new arrangements to Chris while the girls and I discussed the Donovan concert.

When Paul and Chris appeared, I jumped in the back seat, hoping to sit in the middle. Instead Donna just slid over. I was disappointed but knew better than to complain.

Spalding stepped out of character to make all the necessary introductions. He even asked Elizabeth if she liked to be called Beth or Liz. She said she was partial to Liz. Why hadn't I thought of that?

As soon as they said "hi," Chris and Liz looked at each other for a second.

"Beall Hall," Chris laughed.

"Freshman year," Liz smiled.

"Far out," Donna said.

Spalding's uncomfortable situation was instantly vaporized. These three were old friends. They passed dorm stories back and forth from front seat to back all the way over to Memorial Gym. At least it kept the pressure off me.

By the time we parked in the construction area for the new Student Center the rain had lightened. We joined a colorful crowd of crazies, passing joints and pipes under their umbrellas or out in the elements.

Inside the gym the crowd grew wilder. The students sang and danced to pre-taped music blaring out from a reel-to-reel on the stage. We found our seats in the upper deck, on long wooden benches, no backs.

Since we were a little early I offered to go buy some Cokes. As I stood in line at the concession window in the corner of the gym, admiring the spectacle around me, I noticed our present, but soon-to-be former, roommate Artie huddled in deep conversation with a middle-aged man wearing a suit and tie. Something was wrong with that picture. I even thought I recognized the guy but I couldn't place him. One of my profs? He didn't seem the type to be watching a Donovan concert. After collecting five Cokes in a box I decided to follow him. What was Artie up to?

It wasn't a pretty sight. Artie was working the crowd, selling what looked to be hits of blotter acid. I'd never done any myself but I'd seen it before. "That's all we need," I thought to myself. Grass was bad enough. Even though it was still considered an evil weed to the outside world, it was somewhat accepted in the college community. LSD on the other hand, while popular with a few college students, was considered a downright threat to national security. It was supposed to both make you crazy and scramble your reproductive genes, thus making us a nation of loonies. The authorities would really hammer us for dealing acid.

That was the nail in Artie's coffin. He'd have to go and the sooner the better.

By the time I found my seat, the gym was completely dark. Then psychedelic lights showered the back of the stage. A lone spotlight revealed Donovan, sitting cross-legged near the front of the stage. A single accompanist sat next to him playing a flute.

Donovan's sweet romantic lyrics were the perfect vibes for a first date. When he sang about taking his true love to "a beach that never ends," Elizabeth took my hand and squeezed it.

I was falling head over heels for her. I just hoped it wasn't the mesc again.

Chapter Nine:
HOMECOMING

PART FIVE: The Hot Dog Inn

After the concert experience we were all in a pretty mellow frame of mind. We didn't want to take the girls back home right away, but it was kind of late to head downtown to the bars. So we opted for Kent's other late night option, The Hot Dog Inn.

The Inn was one of the few "Open 24 Hours" joints around. And it was conveniently located right across from front campus. It was a Kent tradition to top off an evening with a couple of dogs.

As such it attracted a weird clientele. You had your freaked-out hippies sitting next to your straight townies. You had your motorcycle gangs and college professors, cops and students pulling all-nighters, space aliens and vampires. Just kidding, that was only on Halloween. But you get the picture. Anyone with a late night attack of the munchies could be found sitting in one of the orange, tacky, plastic 1950s era booths shoving a hot dog with the works down his throat.

Much of the after-concert crowd was already in place by the time we arrived. All the booths were taken but we found three empty stools by the counter and, being the gentlemen that we were, of course, we let the girls sit on them.

Eventually a few more stools would vacate and we'd be in Fat City (a Spalding term for utopia).

We discovered the girls were Hot Dog Inn virgins so Spalding gave them a lecture on the various accoutrements available. That was the Inn's mystique. It was amazing how many options were available for dressing up a plain hot dog. As Spalding pontificated, I surveyed the surroundings.

A longhaired hippie and his shorthaired girlfriend were swapping spit in a corner booth as if they were in their own living room. A Harley-Davidson biker with his hair in a pony-tail, an earring and biceps covered with tattoos was catering to a Vietnam vet in a wheelchair. A college professor and his wife were each reading their own novel. They ate their hot dogs, flipped pages and adjusted their glasses without saying a word to each other.

"That's probably me and Elizabeth in a couple years," I looked over at her. She caught my gaze. I looked away, my eyes returning to the Vietnam vet. You could tell what he was because it was printed on the back of his jean jacket. "Or maybe that'll be me," I shuddered.

Donovan had mixed a few protest songs with his love tunes and his lyrics were still rattling around my psyche when my eyes landed on a longhaired youth who somehow looked familiar. Since few of our friends had taken the fashion plunge yet I wondered were I knew him from. He was sitting at a booth with a pair of friends, one of whom also looked strange-ly familiar. I couldn't figure it out so I nudged Spalding.

"What?" he asked, irritated by my intrusion.

"See those guys in that booth, next to the bikers," I tried not to point, just sort of pushed my head in the general direc-tion. "The ones wearing shades."

"Yeah, what about them?" The girls also took notice.

"Do we know them?"

"You think you know everybody," Spalding gave me a shot and the girl's were amused by his comment.

"Isn't that Donovan?" Elizabeth suddenly blurted out, her

voice squeaked from excitement so it was barely audible above the general din. I did notice, however, that one of the three freaks we were staring at stopped mid-bite and looked our way.

"And that's the guy with the flute," I agreed with her observation.

"I'd know him anywhere," Elizabeth put her head down and whispered.

The three hippies became a tad anxious, looking in our direction, as if they were caught with their hands in the cookie jar.

"You know, I think you're right," Donna agreed with her friend. Liz seemed to be the rock and roll expert among us so we deferred to her opinion.

"I told you we knew those guys," I said to Spalding with a certain degree of smugness.

"If you know them why don't you go over and talk to them?" Spalding challenged me.

"Maybe I will." I never turned down a dare.

"What if it's not Donovan?" Chris asked.

"Only one way to find out," Spalding said. "Hey Kubik, your friends are leaving."

They did seem to have cranked up their departure a notch after Liz's remarks.

"Come on," I took her gently by the arm.

"Wait a minute," she put up a slight struggle but gave in easily.

By the time we reached their table, Donovan was already standing up.

"I don't know how to say this," I approached him, "but my girlfriend thinks you sing for a rock band." I put my arm around her. "You know, ballads and love songs." I lowered my voice considerably.

He put his head near ours and whispered, "Arlo Guthrie?"

"No, Donovan," I laughed, almost adding "you dummie."

"You got it," he said with a smile, giving us both hippie handshakes.

I snuck Spalding, Donna and Chris a thumbs up.

"Nice meeting you," his flutist interrupted, politely easing Donovan toward the door.

"Wait a minute," I was trying to stop them from leaving. "How about we buy you guys a couple beers across the street," I pointed through the window toward the Robin Hood Tavern.

"Thanks, but we have to go," the flutist was speaking for Donovan, protecting him from his over-adoring fans.

"I thought you guys liked to party?" I threw down the gauntlet, challenging their egos like Spalding had done mine.

"We do," Donovan came to his own defense.

"Listen, we have a lot to do before we leave, all right?" the flutist was becoming angry.

"Sorry," I backed down just as Spalding arrived with reinforcements.

"I'll tell you what," Donovan fished a piece of paper from his jean's vest pocket as more interested spectators began to crowd around us. "Do you know where this place is?"

He showed me an address on Vine Street that I instantly memorized. "We're going to a party there later on," he continued. "We can talk then."

Donovan put the paper back in his pocket, shook hands with Paul, Donna and Chris, who he knew were with us, and slipped out the door before the rest of the Inn could mob him.

"Was it really him?" Chris asked.

"I hope so," Liz said.

"You should have asked for his autograph," Donna added.

"Did I make a big fool of myself?" I asked Liz.

"No more than usual," Spalding said.

"We going to the party?" Liz asked.

"Why shouldn't we?" Chris asked.

"Maybe he was blowing us off," I said. "You know, groupies."

"I think he was for real," Liz seemed hurt at my suggestion.

We were blocking the doorway, so we had to make a quick decision.

"Well, we going to eat or go to the party?" Spalding asked.

"Eat," I said, my stomach usually ruled my decision-making process.

"Party." Liz said.

"Party." Donna and Chris agreed.

"Let's go," Spalding gave in to the inevitable.

"But I'm hungry," I protested.

"You're always hungry," he said, escorting the girls out the door. "You can eat when we get back home."

"How about if we get a couple dogs to go?" I suggested but no one paid me any mind.

It was already a long night and I hated drinking on an empty stomach.

You didn't need the address to find the party on Vine Street. The driveway and front yard were filled with cars and the music could be heard two blocks away.

We walked through the front door and mingled as if we had a personal invitation. Not just because Donovan had invited us. It was just always easy to crash a Kent party. We'd been doing it since freshman year. In the first place, no one cared, which kind of took the challenge out of it. In the second place, you usually ran into someone you knew, which made it seem like you were invited anyway.

We found the girls a seat on the couch by muscling a couple of freshmen out of the way. I have to explain something about my personality. I like to wander. I've been doing it all my life. I used to leave home when I was three years old, walk out the door, disappear, drive my mother crazy. So if I'm at a party or a concert or a bar I like to mingle, check out the crowd. My friends are used to it, but it's tough on new acquaintances. So just like at the concert I volunteered to search for the keg and bring back some beers.

How did I know there'd be a keg? It was Kent State. There was always a keg. I also knew that it would either be on the back porch or in the basement.

"Keg?" I asked the first drunken fraternity brother I encountered.

"Basement," he mumbled and stumbled.

What'd I tell you?

I gave him a secret fraternity handshake I'd picked up freshman year and continued my quest.

I found the basement stairs, jockeyed around a group of students arguing politics, requisitioned five paper cups from a nearby table and took my place in the keg line. There was an art to my maneuvering that took years to develop. A couple of freshman, barely old enough to shave but with hair longer than mine, were standing in front of me, passing a joint.

"You want a hit?" the one asked me.

I was about to answer "sure" when his friend cut him off.

"Hey, you don't know him," he intercepted the joint. This was definitely not Kent State etiquette but I let it slide due to their youth.

"So," the other one responded, looking stupid as if to ask, "what's your point?"

"What if he's a narc?" the freshman looked me up and down. Now I have a long temper and I can excuse a lot of misguided behavior but calling someone a narc in the 60s was like calling someone a Nazi during World War II. Not only did it piss me off, it made me feel old.

Fortunately, the freshman handed me the joint. "He's just paranoid," he apologized for his friend. I took a long hit, then exhaled into the face of the rude one.

"If I was a narc you would have been busted an hour ago," I told him. Then I cut in front of them to fill up my cups. "Freshmen," I muttered as I walked away.

"You won't believe it," I told Spalding and the girls once I found them. "A couple of freshmen called me a narc."

"So?" Spalding gave me the same look the freshmen did.

"How do we know you're not?" Liz joined in the fun.

"You guys want these beers or should I give them to some real friends?" I passed out the brews. "Speaking of narcs, we better watch out for Artie."

"Who's Artie?" Chris asked.

"The Murph's buddy," Spalding answered. "I told you it was time to throw him out."

"I saw him selling acid to an old guy at the concert. He's either a narc or being set up."

"Why didn't you tell me?"

"I didn't want to spoil the concert," I slapped Spalding on the back but he wasn't too happy with me.

"We could be getting busted right now."

"You want to go home?" I asked him.

"What about Donovan?" Liz asked. She was worried we might bail out on her one opportunity to meet a real, live rock star. The other girls shared her dismay.

"I don't know," Spalding's anger was melted by the girls' concern. He checked his aviator watch. "We'll give it half an hour, but I'm getting more paranoid by the minute."

Three beers later we were all fading fast. The half hour was more than over.

"He's not going to show," I proclaimed.

"He said he'd be late," Liz argued.

"He probably had a lot of packing," Chris rationalized.

"It don't look good," Donna agreed.

Liz was on her own this time. I raised my paper cup and made a toast. "To Donovan, wherever he is." We touched cups, drank them down and slid out the front door, thanking someone who was supposed to be our host.

As Spalding pulled out of our parking spot on Vine Street I watched a white van slipping into it. If it wasn't for the slight rain I might have noticed the California license plates. It was filled with professional rock and rollers ready to party. I know it for a fact because the *Daily Kent Stater* had a story about Donovan frequenting a party on Vine Street as part of their special Homecoming Weekend issue.

The girls probably never would have forgiven us except Spalding, as usual, was right on the money. It turned out we had more important problems to worry about.

Chapter Ten:
THE BUST

The morning after the Homecoming concert Depeyster was a bit too quiet, even for a Sunday morning. It felt sort of eerie. When I awoke, I vaguely remembered dreaming about a thunderstorm, a lot of crashing and smashing, but I just chalked it up to the rock concert.

I stumbled downstairs to find Early hogging the shower as usual. Spalding was still asleep so I jumped into the cushioned bathtub to wait my turn. By the time Early appeared I was sleeping again.

"Morning," he greeted me, all bright-eyed and bushy-tailed.

"Morning," I muttered back.

I hurried through my morning stint, realizing that Spalding would be up at any moment. My next move was to the kitchen for a glass of orange juice. But when I looked for a glass I discovered the cupboards were totally empty. Not a cup, glass or plate anywhere.

My first reaction was one of disbelief. Who would want to steal kitchen utensils. Especially ours. None of them matched, the silverware was lifted from the dorm cafeteria and the pots and pans were bent out of shape. Suitable for our humble needs but hardly of any value.

Of course, my initial reaction was to blame Artie. He stole them for drug money. Then I heard Spalding pounding down the stairs like a rhino. Wait until he discovered the dastardly deed. I decided not to say a word until he at least showered.

Spalding gave me a gruff "morning" as we passed in the dining room. Early was already reclining in the living room, watching one of our favorite Sunday morning shows, mouthing the words to The Monkees' theme song.

"Notice anything strange in the kitchen?" I asked him once the show's introduction ended.

"Like what?" he asked back. His answer reminded me of the cartoon character Sylvester the Cat, when he was caught with Tweety-Bird in his mouth.

"Like we don't have no dishes," I said, playing along with his little game.

Before Early could react, a great roar came out of the kitchen.

"Where the hell's the cups?" Spalding hollered. He postponed his shower in favor of a cup of java.

Early gulped. I could tell something was up.

"You know anything about this, Early?" Spalding's frame filled the archway to the living room, standing with his hands on his hips.

"About what?" Early's answer was timid this time, the swallowed-the-canary look was replaced by one of fear.

"Where's the coffee pot, the cups, all our shit?"

Early jumped out of the easy chair to face us in a less compromising position. "I hid them," he confessed, raising his out-stretched palms high in the air like a prisoner surrendering. "I'm tired of cleaning up after you guys."

We both instantly realized that Early had a legitimate beef. It was the only thing that kept Spalding out of his face. Yet I was a bit defensive. I had always tried to pull my weight in the cleanup department.

"I clean up all the time," I countered.

"Bullshit," Early said. "When was the last time you cleaned the bathroom?"

"Just the other day, in case the girls came over." It was our one incentive to keep the place halfway livable.

"Well, you do a shit job. I spent a half an hour just on the shower stall."

"So did I."

"Bullshit," Early said and walked past us toward the kitchen. We followed him.

"You saw me, Spalding. Wasn't I in there about an hour?"

"More like fifteen minutes," Early continued. "The legend grows."

"I don't care who was where for how long. Just crank up the coffeepot," Spalding demanded.

Early took a paper bag full of utensils out from under the sink and pulled out the electric coffeepot.

"When's the last time you guys did the dishes or cleaned out the sink?" Early handed the pot to Spalding who immediately began spooning coffee out of a large can.

"You don't give us a chance," I apologized.

"I thought you liked doing them," Spalding said. "Give me a cup."

"Here," Early reached into the same grocery bag, pulled out four white cups and placed them on the kitchen counter. Each one had a different label: LOVE, PEACE, HAPPINESS and MINE. "Take one."

Spalding took LOVE, I took PEACE and Early took MINE. "That leaves HAPPINESS for the Murph," Early explained. "From now on its one cup each and you clean it yourself."

Then he proceeded to take four pie tins, four knives, four forks and four spoons out of the same bag. "The same goes for the plates," he added with a certain smugness. "You might want to mark yours."

Spalding took the pie tin in his large hands, held it up like a Frisbee, pulled his Swiss Army Knife from his pocket and, with a few quick strokes, changed the empty circle into a peace sign. Then he threw it into the empty sink. "I feel like

The Prisoner," he said. That made Early smile. Despite the gruffness of his manner, Spalding's tacit approval marked an unstated acceptance for the new system.

"Not funny," I said, borrowing Spalding's knife to carve my initials on the back of my pie tin. "Tell Early about our friend Artie."

"You tell him, you're the ace spy,"

Spalding stood above the coffeepot catching a rush off the aroma.

Early was carving "Dave" on the back of his pie tin. The Murph's would be the one without the mark. "Tell me what?" he asked.

"Artie's either a narc or about to be busted," I said.

"Either way, we better clean up this place," Spalding said.

"Then what are we waiting for?" Early gave Spalding back his knife.

"Breakfast, mainly," I said.

"You guys clean up your weed and I'll take care of breakfast," Early offered.

"I thought you were tired of doing all the housework," Spalding said.

"I said I'll cook," Early said. "You guys clean up. But first get your drugs out of the house. I'm not taking the fall for your addictions."

"Can I borrow your bag?" I was trying to keep the peace. It was an old-fashioned brown bag with string handles attached, the kind Early's grandmother probably took to the market.

"Sure," Early handed it to me. "Check our room first, see if the Murph left any goods in there."

I began my search mission as Spalding waited for his coffee and Early started cooking. But first he hooked up the earphones to the back room stereo so he could groove as he worked.

I felt strange entering Early's room. It was almost sacrilegious. Early and the Murph were roommates out of necessity, not choice. Spalding was Early's roomie their junior year and it almost made him crazy.

Since the Murph was seldom home the room was a total reflection of Early's personality. It didn't look like a college room out of the 60s. More like the 20s.

There were no piles of dirty clothes. No scattered books or papers. No unmade beds. The only sign of life was Early's electric guitar and Fender amp in the corner. He also had a telescope but we didn't know if he used it for peering at the stars or coeds.

I made a thorough search of the Murph's desk and dresser drawers, all in the name of justice. There wasn't a trace of any illegal drug, just a few prescription pills. And there was no reason to check Early's side since he did not partake. Besides, if I disrupted his perfectly folded clothes or moved a pencil out of place there would be hell to pay.

"Your room's clean," I hollered down to Early.

"He can't hear you," Spalding said, ascending the stairs with a steamy cup of coffee. "He's got his earphones on."

Me and Spalding attacked our room with a vengeance, moving the furniture, picking up every seed and roach. I threw our communal bag in the paper sack. "Where should we put this stuff?" I asked Spalding. "I hate to pitch it."

Spalding didn't answer, he just shrugged his shoulders. We let the matter lie as we proceeded to search the downstairs area. It was amazing how much drug paraphernalia we had sitting right out in the open.

I was lying on my back, looking under the sofa when Early came bursting into the living room. He was talking real loud, unaware that the headphones were still on his ears. The long cord reached its limit and snapped his head back just as he entered the living room.

"YOU GUYS WERE RIGHT," he said loudly.

"What are you hollering about?" Spalding asked.

"I just heard it on the news," Early panted. "Artie was

busted last night at Brady Lake. And he used our address as his place of residence."

"That son of a bitch," Spalding said.

"Great," I said.

We moved our search and destroy mission into high gear. Early even turned off his bacon to join us. In about five minutes we were done.

"Where should we put this stuff?" I asked, placing the brown bag on the dining room table.

"Burn it," Early said. "Give up your evil ways. Alleluia. Praise the Lord." He went back into the kitchen.

I looked at Spalding. He shared my feeling that maybe we were being a bit too paranoid. Why dispose of such good shit?

"Hide it," he said.

"Where?" I asked.

Early came back from the kitchen. You could smell the bacon burning. He knew we wanted to keep our stash. "Put it down the basement," he suggested, against his better judgement. "On the girls' side."

Brilliant. Why hadn't I thought of that. There was a door in the basement wall separating the two halves of the house that we never locked and no one ever used.

I went over to the girl's side and hid the grocery bag under some old tires. As I came back up the basement steps I noticed a big cardboard box stuffed into a crawl space under the front of the house. I didn't remember seeing it before. When I tried to grab it I could hear the rattle of glass and plastic. It was Early's stash. His hidden cups and plates.

No wonder he thought about hiding the drugs in the basement. He'd used it himself.

I decided to keep my little secret to myself. There were more important matters at hand.

The crisis over, Early filled our pie tins with scrambled eggs, bacon and toast. We took them into the living room to watch television. The Monkees were done.

"What's on?" I asked as Spalding spun the channel selector.

"How about Earnest Angsley?"

"We could use some religion."

"Did the radio mention the Murph?" Spalding asked Early.

"No, just Artie Baker, residing on South Depeyster, Kent, Ohio," Early said.

"That asshole," Spalding said. "I wonder if anyone else heard it."

"It was on the Akron channel," Early said.

"That's good," I said, since all my friends and family lived in Cleveland.

"Maybe we'd better call the Murph. He's probably at Mary Lou's."

But before we could act there was a loud knock at the front door. I jumped up so fast I knocked my plate of scrambled eggs on the floor.

"Holy shit," Early said.

Harold barked. Spanky jumped down from his favorite spot on top of the television. Spalding peeked behind the curtains covering the front window.

"Relax," he said. "It's only Skerl."

Tom Skerl was our landlord. The last time we'd seen him was the day we'd moved in.

He was the recent graduate of some southern university so he spoke with a slow drawl. His blond hair was slicked onto his head with a generous portion of Vitalis. Despite his youth, he represented a generation that was on its way out. Only a few years separated us but there was already a huge gap between our generations.

Spalding opened the front door as I scraped my eggs off the carpet.

"How y'all doing this morning?" Skerl asked. He was carrying an open wooden toolbox.

"Fine," I said. "We just finished cleaning up the place."

"Just like we do every Sunday," Spalding added.

"I hear y'all have a toilet that needs fixin'."

"I called him," Early pointed at his own chest.

Early escorted Skerl toward the bathroom. "Like the bath-tub," he pointed at our telephone booth, flashing his goofy grin.

"I hear you're buying up the neighborhood," Early asked him.

"I'm thinking about it," he answered.

"Whew," I said.

"Did you ever get the feeling that Skerl is stoned all the time?" Spalding asked.

"That goofy grin?" I was just about to make fun of him when the front door opened without a knock.

"Don't move, this is a police raid," a plainclothes detective stood in our doorway holding up a badge. A uniformed sher-iff's deputy stood behind him with a rifle resting on his open hand like a baseball bat. "We have a search warrant if you'd like to examine it." He waved a piece of paper with his other hand.

A piece of toast froze in place, halfway between the pie tin and my mouth, scrambled eggs dripping from it in mid-air like yellow snots. I was never going to finish breakfast. Spalding choked on his cup of coffee. Early, who had just re-entered the living room after leaving Skerl in the bathroom, pushed his back against the wall with his hands in the air, spread-eagled, waiting to be frisked. Harold and Spanky ran out the opened front door.

None of us dared ask to see the search warrant. Another plainclothes detective had entered through the back door in case we tried to escape.

"Remain seated," the uniformed cop told us. We looked at his rifle and said nothing.

Escape was the farthest thing from our minds. The two detectives went straight upstairs to the Murph's room, as if Artie had told them where he stayed. Skerl was laying under the toilet with the door half closed and the water running. He had no idea what was going on in his own house.

As the detectives searched upstairs I tried to make conversation with the deputy.

"Do this a lot?" I asked feebly.

If looks could kill his stare would have cracked my skull open.

"We're not criminals, you know," Early said casually. Surprisingly, he seemed the least afraid of the three of us.

"What's going to happen to us?" Spalding asked.

"It depends on what they find," he lightened up a little. "Probably one to twenty with good behavior."

I hoped he was joking.

One of the detectives came downstairs. He was carrying the small hash pipe that Spalding had just bought, a bottle of pills and some marijuana seeds. He placed them on the coffee table.

"Any of this look familiar?" he asked gruffly.

"Yeah, that's my asthma medicine," Early pointed at his pills.

The deputy took us into the dining room so they could lift the couch cushions and search the living room. They added rolling papers and a couple roaches to their collection, now on the dining room table.

"Great job, Kubik," Spalding said under his breath.

"It's your hash pipe," I countered.

"What's this, fellas?" the detective came out of the kitchen with the plastic baggie of bullshit weed that Artie had given us. "Found it in the spice rack," he said to the uniformed cop as if he'd struck gold.

"Oregano," Early said with the most serious face he could muster.

"They must use it make those funny brownies," the deputy laughed. He did have a sense of humor after all.

At that exact moment Skerl sauntered out of the bathroom.

"Who's he?" the detective asked.

"Our landlord," Spalding said.

"What's going on here?" Skerl asked.

"You ought to be more careful who you rent your property to," the detective told Skerl.

The other detective started to read from his list. "One plastic bag full of green vegetable matter, one pack of cigarette papers, two small pipes, numerous roaches, brown seeds, unknown pills, who wants to sign for this stuff?" he looked at the three of us. "We're taking it downtown."

We looked at each other in silence.

"I need my pills, man," Early said.

"If they're prescription, you can refill them, sign here."

Early did as he was told.

"See you boys in court," the detective with the search warrant said, as they went out the front door.

Skerl tried to follow them, dragging his toolbox along, hoping to plead his case.

"You boys can fix your own toilet," he said as he exited. "And you better shape up or I'm evicting you winter quarter."

Skerl slammed the door. We let out a collective sigh of relief. But before we could relax we heard a loud commotion out on our front lawn.

We squeezed out onto the porch as three hippies from the house next door, who we'd never even met, were screaming obscenities at Skerl and the cops.

"Get lost pigs."

"Go back to jail where you belong."

"Fascists."

They were your classical hippies, extremely long hair, barefoot, bell-bottomed jeans, headbands and tie-dyed t-shirts.

And they seemed to slightly rattle the uniformed officer who was driving. The cops jumped into an unmarked car while Skerl was still trying to talk to them. The deputy punched the gas pedal, spun his tires on some gravel and almost rammed a passing vehicle that beeped loudly.

"Yeah, all right, hit 'em," the three hippies were cheering

wildly and giving each other high fives as if Kent's football team had just scored a touchdown.

Skerl gave them a dirty look, glanced back at us in disgust and jumped into his own car that was parked in our driveway. We wondered if he owned their house too. The three hippies came over and introduced themselves.

"We heard about you guys on the radio," they exchanged hippie handshakes with us.

"Yeah, we figured the pigs were coming," another said.

"What'd they find?" asked the third.

"Just a lid," I said.

"And some pipes and papers," Spalding shot me a look.

"Not to worry," the tallest of the trio said. "If it's under a pound they won't even prosecute."

"Really?" Spalding's spirits instantly lifted.

"Yeah, they busted us last year," the short one boasted.

"It was great," the one with the pony tail added. "I loved the rifle routine."

"What happened?" Early asked them.

"Oh, nothing," the tall one said.

"Well, we did get kicked out of school," the short one said.

"We flunked out," the pony tail corrected him, much to our relief.

"What are you doing now?" I asked them.

"We got jobs," the short one said.

"But guess what?" the tall one laughed. "We're criminals, they won't draft us."

All three of them laughed loudly and we laughed with them. It was contagious.

"Yeah, if you smoke dope you can't kill babies," the pony-tail said.

"Ain't it a bitch," the short one said.

"We'll catch you guys later," Spalding turned to go inside. He felt a little better but was still worried about the repercussions.

"Stop over sometime," the tall one offered.

"Yeah, we got some dynamite shit," the short one said.

"Great," Early said sarcastically, as we re-entered our humble abode.

We sat around the dining room table, silently wondering what was going to happen to us. Then I looked up and noticed the water pipe Michelle gave me our junior year was still resting on the old piano. It was so obvious the cops overlooked it. We practically considered it a piece of furniture.

"They missed the hooka," I pointed.

Spalding and Early both turned their heads. Then Early did a strange thing. He stood up, grabbed the hooka in his meathook hands and placed it in the middle of the table. I don't think he ever touched it before, even when he cleaned the house.

"Where'd you hide that stuff?" he asked me.

"Downstairs, like you told me."

Spalding looked at him mysteriously.

"Go get it," Early ordered. "Since I'm already busted, it's time to see what this shit is all about."

Chapter Eleven:
HALLOWEEN

The *big* question on our minds after the drug bust wasn't "Are we going to jail?" or "Will we graduate?" No, our great concern was "Where's the Murph?"

We wanted to kill him. And we were also a little worried about him.

Calls to Mary Lou's went unanswered. Captain Brady's said he wasn't due to work until Tuesday. Was he in jail with Artie? No, he would've called us for bond money, he couldn't tell his parents.

We decided to just wait until he showed up. He always did.

Monday night it was my turn to cook, Early had a late class. I thought I'd surprise the guys with a new experiment in culinary delight: Spanish rice. It was kind of a spicy spaghetti sauce over rice instead of noodles. Most of our homemade dishes were variations of ground meat and tomato sauce.

I was just piling the sauce on Early's pie tin when the Murph came sauntering through the front door. He looked like a lost dog, entering with his tail tucked between his legs. Harold was the only one who greeted him.

"Hi, guys," he gave us his customary circular wave of the palm of his hand. His smile was obviously forced. We weren't as angry about the bust as we were about not hearing from him.

"Pull up a seat." I tried to make him feel welcome.

"Sorry about Artie," he said as Early brought out a set of our newest utensils and placed them in front of him. "Nice plates," he picked up his pie tin and admired it.

"Get used to them," Early said.

"Where the hell you been?" Spalding asked.

"Honest. I didn't know about the bust until I stopped by Brady's this morning to pick up my check," he apologized. He was admiring his HAPPINESS cup as Early filled it with milk. "Me and Mary Lou were visiting my parent's house in Eastlake. They were out of town," he smiled.

"Oh great, you're getting lucky while we almost go to jail," Spalding said.

"He's lucky they didn't find anything in our room," Early said. "I'd have killed you."

"Don't worry," the Murph said, after swallowing a mouthful of red rice. "I went down to the prosecutor's today and took the rap for the lid. They said they found it in the kitchen. Artie's shit?"

"The same," I said with a sigh of relief.

"You didn't have to do that," Spalding said, changing his tune.

"Yeah, well, I brought him here," the Murph kept his head down, eating. "I'm flunking out anyway."

"No, you're not," Early said.

"Wanna bet?"

"You say that every quarter," I said.

"I haven't been to a class all year," the Murph looked up. "I don't think they'll prosecute, they just wanted Artie. I guess he's a bigger dealer than I realized."

"That's what our neighbors said," I took seconds of my concoction.

"The girls? They know Artie?"

"No, the hippies on the other side," Spalding explained. "You should talk to them before you drop out. They have to work for a living."

"There's probably more opportunity in the restaurant biz than political science."

"You should try cooking around here," Early said.

"Is that an insult to the chef?" I asked.

"He's right, this shit sucks," Spalding said.

"I like it." I put another big mouthful on my fork.

"You'll eat anything," Spalding said. Both Early and Spalding rose from the table at the same time, their plates still half full.

"I'm working tomorrow, I'll cook Wednesday night," the Murph promised. He kept eating, probably out of pity for me.

"That's Halloween," Early said.

"Shit, I forgot, me and Mary Lou have plans. You guys should come along."

"Where to?" Spalding asked.

"The haunted house downtown," the Murph answered.

"What haunted house?" Early asked. He had begun sweeping the dining room floor as Spalding began clearing the table.

"You never heard of the psycho house?"

We stared at him, dumbfounded.

"There's this big house on a hill, just off downtown. In fact, I think it's down the other end of Depeyster."

"And it's haunted?"

"The story goes that Alfred Hitchcok was passing through town, saw it, and patterned his *Psycho* movie after it. Now it's a big SDS hangout."

"And they're using it for a Halloween party?" Early asked.

"They do it every year. It's far out."

"There's an SDSer who comes in Brady's all the time. He invited me."

"What about us?" Spalding asked.

"It's kind of word of mouth, everyone tells everyone."

"Like Early's 'Everything is everything,'" I said.

"You got it."

"We need some cool costumes," Early said.

"Go to the Goodwill in Ravenna, they got everything. Sorry, Early."

"Cool, dude," Early said.

It sounded like he was joining us, which was unusual. First he sampled some weed, now he was ready to party with the guys. What next?

By Halloween evening we were hot stuff, courtesy of the Ravenna Goodwill. Early put together a football uniform: old jersey, shoulder pads, knee high pants and high top sneakers. He even dug out his old West Tech high school helmet.

Spalding fashioned a doctor's outfit: green medical top, hospital pants and a stethoscope he borrowed from Renee, the nursing student next door.

Me, I decided it was probably my last chance to cross-dress before I entered the real world. I was striking in a cheerleader's ensemble: Ravenna high school varsity sweater, pleated skirt, bobby socks and underneath a 38D cup bra that I borrowed from Michelle. Of course, I had to stuff it with Kleenex tissue, a popular ruse of the day.

Before we left, we wanted to try out our costumes on the girls next door.

"Trick or treat," we yelled, knocking on their front door.

"Trick, definitely, trick," Michelle smiled. "Come on in guys, you can help us carve our pumpkins."

"That's what we forgot," I said to Spalding.

"You can have one of ours, we have plenty," Michelle offered. "By the way, nice tits."

"Watch it lady, I don't put up with that kind of talk," I said as I adjusted my bra.

"Oh, excuse me. How about if we draw 'em and you cut 'em?" Renee and Sarah were already putting the finishing touches on their pumpkins with a magic marker.

"Fine, but we can't stay long," I agreed. "We have a party to go to."

"Oh yeah, where?" Sarah asked.

"The Psycho House," I said smugly, hoping to impress them.

"I went last year," Michelle immediately did me one better. It was her habit.

"What's it like?" Early asked. Now he was the one impressed.

"Definitely cool," she said. Then she went back to drawing on her pumpkin, leaving us hungry for more info.

Early and Spalding took Renee and Sarah's pumpkins and began carving them. Michelle kept erasing her designs with a wet paper towel.

"You're sort of a perfectionist, aren't you?" I asked her.

"I guess so," she admitted. "Like your hair. You should definitely do something with your hair."

"I have a wig," Sarah offered.

"I don't know…" I hadn't thought of that.

"Go get it," Michelle enjoyed toying with me.

Sarah came down from her room with a dark haired wig. Peer pressure forced me to wear it against my better judgement.

"You look great," Spalding laughed.

"You could be my date," Early said.

"I already have one, thank you," I said.

"The bike ride beauty?" Michelle asked.

"Where do you get your information?" I asked. Now I was really impressed.

"The walls have ears," she laughed.

As we made small talk, the pumpkins were scooped out, seeds splattered everywhere and faces magically appeared.

"Does Early really need a date?" Michelle asked me quietly, under the general din.

"Sure," I was suddenly jealous. "What happened to your Buckeye?"

"Not me, you ninny, them," she moved her head toward Sarah and Renee. I was instantly relieved.

"Both of them?"

She nodded.

"I didn't know Early was so popular."

"You'd be surprised."

"Sarah, Renee, would you like to join us?" I spoke much louder.

"We don't have any costumes," Renee looked at Sarah for direction.

"You don't need them," Early said.

"Half the people never wear them," Spalding added.

"How about you?" I asked Michelle.

"It wouldn't work," she said. "You two go."

They agreed, quickly got ready as we finished the pumpkins, and were out the door by the time we lit them on our front porch.

"Watch out for the trick or treaters," I told Michelle as we left.

"I'm ready for them," she held up a box of candy.

Walking up Depeyster toward the Psycho House, I looked back at Michelle standing alone in the doorway. Suddenly I didn't want to go to the party. I wanted to stay with her and pass out candy to the neighborhood kids. I guess it was that evening that I realized that I wanted her back.

But once we picked up Elizabeth I forgot all about her. Liz was a knockout in a Samantha witch's outfit, a slinky black dress with a slit almost up to her waist. It made me want to sell my soul to the devil.

We met Chris at Captain Brady's. She was a cowgirl with knee high leather boots, a jean dress, and a plaid blouse that opened almost down to her navel. I'd forgotten why I loved Halloween. Chris had made Spalding a "Dr. Death" smile button for his lapel.

The Murph had already left for the party but his co-worker gave us directions. We walked back down Main Street and took a right on Depeyster. It was supposed to be close by but we still couldn't see it. I began to wonder if both the Murph and Michelle were jiving us. Some sort of elaborate practical joke. I'd walked these streets with Harold but never remembered seeing a ghost house.

Then suddenly Early pointed at it. You actually had to

crane your neck toward the stars to see it. Surrounded by trees, it was easy to walk past if you didn't look for it.

The stark Victorian structure had long church-like stained glass windows lit up in the evening light. The ornate woodwork, chimneys, and dormers on the roof were classier than the insides of most houses. It was foreboding. And it did look like the Psycho House. You half-expected Dracula or Frankenstein to live there.

As we walked up the long gravel driveway the music, chatter and laughter could be easily heard. The front porch was already spilling over with partyers coming outside for fresh air. What looked like a horse trough sat on the porch. It was filled with four kegs of beer and a ton of ice.

"Looks like they have enough beer," Early said, trying to entertain Renee and Sarah with his wit.

"I thought you're a druggie now," I teased him.

"Nope. Had to try it, but it didn't do a thing for me."

"Didn't do a thing?" Spalding laughed loudly. "You were wasted."

"You played the piano half the night," I added.

"That was you?" Sarah asked.

"We couldn't sleep all night," Renee added.

"They drugged me. What can I say?"

"Say you're sorry," Sarah teased.

"All right, I'm sorry. I'll never touch the stuff again. Let's go inside."

"Looks like a lot of freaks to me," Spalding said.

"How will we know who lives here?" Elizabeth inquired. As a political activist she was dying to meet a real live revolutionary.

"We have to find the Murph," I said.

We grabbed some beers before entering the house like cautious tourists, waiting for some wild knife-slasher to attack us. The first thing we noticed was a table hanging upside down from the ceiling, supported by chains.

"Is that for Halloween or do they eat off it?" Early asked.

"Who wants to know?" the Murph snuck up behind us. He was dressed in a double-breasted pin stripe suit like a gangster. Mary Lou, who we hadn't seen in ages, was wearing a loose fitting flapper dress, the mini-skirt of the Roaring 20s. Her formerly straight brown hair was frizzed like an afro.

"Hey roomie," Early shook his hand straight style (he never did the hippie thing) and introduced his entourage.

"Looks like you struck gold," the Murph laughed. He introduced Mary Lou to the four girls.

"How's your head?" he asked Early.

"He's already swore off the stuff," Spalding said.

"I would too, if it made me that crazy."

"Enough already," Early was becoming irritated. "Let's mingle with the real druggies."

The crowd was overwhelming. If it had been a bar the Fire Marshall would've closed the place down. We tried pushing our way inside when a clown came sliding down the spiral staircase, falling on the floor right in front of us.

"Are you all right?" the Murph picked him up.

"It only hurts when I laugh," the clown smiled, then grimaced. "Don't I know you?"

"Captain Brady's," the Murph pointed at himself. "You invited me."

"Oh wow, you're right."

"These are my friends. This is Al Bernstein, campus revolutionary, charter member of the SDS."

"You live here?" Elizabeth was immediately impressed.

"Great place, huh?"

"Wild," Chris agreed.

"Are you really in the SDS?" Elizabeth whispered.

"Sure, it's no secret," Bernstein said with a sense of pride. "Ask any of the narcs who are here tonight."

"Narcs?" Early asked.

"I'm out of here," Spalding added.

"Not to worry," Bernstein said. "The Murph told me

about Artie. They don't care about you guys. They're after us. Have a good time. Gotta go."

"Wait a second," Elizabeth took him by the elbow. "Wasn't SDS kicked off campus last year? After the Music and Speech protest?"

"Yeah, but we don't have to go on campus to get our message out," the clown was enjoying his notoriety. "If you're interested you should come to Washington for the Moratorium."

"When's that?" the Murph asked.

"In two weeks. I'll call you about it. I've got to check on the kitchen. They're probably making LSD."

"Bring your girlfriend with you," he alluded to my cheerleader's outfit and disappeared into the crowd.

"Don't even think about going," Mary Lou told the Murph. "You're in enough trouble already."

"She's right," Early agreed.

"You don't know the half of it," the Murph grinned sheepishly.

We all stared at him, waiting for the other shoe to fall.

"Mary Lou's pregnant," he finally blurted out.

Our jaws collectively dropped open. Then we began to shake the Murph's hand and hug Mary Lou.

"You old stud," Spalding laughed.

"It wasn't something we were trying to do," the Murph put his arm around Mary Lou's waist. They made a strange couple, surrounded by the freaks in Halloween outfits.

"It was sort of an accident," she added. "I forgot to take my pill."

The music and crowd were so noisy that we couldn't talk very well. So we made our way back outside.

"We should do something to celebrate," I said.

"This is party enough," the Murph said. "You guys should think about going to Washington."

"Why?" Spalding asked.

"Do as much as you can before you get old and have to settle down like me," the Murph laughed.

"Listen to you," Spalding said.

"You're really going to have a baby?" Early asked seriously.

"Are you going to get married?" Elizabeth asked.

"We haven't set a date yet," Mary Lou answered.

"I'd have an abortion," Elizabeth told her.

"I'm Catholic. I don't believe in them."

"It's your decision," Elizabeth said.

"Our decision," Mary Lou put her arm around the Murph's waist.

I knew Elizabeth was a radical, but I didn't realize until just that instant exactly how radical. Abortions were illegal back then, though you could find some doctors who would perform them. There was a big difference between discussing abortion on an abstract level and suggesting it to a pregnant woman.

"This place is too crowded," Early changed the subject. "Let's go downtown."

"JBs?" the Murph asked.

Everyone agreed.

The times were definitely a-changing.

Chapter Twelve:
THE NOVEMBER
MORATORIUM

A couple of weeks after Halloween, on Friday afternoon, November 14, 1969, Spalding and I should have been heading into downtown Kent for happy hour. Instead, we were in our room rolling up our sleeping bags for the trip to Washington D.C. with super SDSer Al Bernstein. The decision to take the trip was enough of a surprise. Now Spalding added another one.

"I've been meaning to give you this all quarter," he said, taking a faded green Army fatigue jacket out of his closet and handing it to me. "It's getting cold out there."

"Thanks," I looked at it in shock. In the 1960s an Army jacket was as cool as a leather motorcycle jacket was in the 50s.

They were hard to come by.

"Try it on," he said. "I found it along the side of a road in Florida. I guess the guy wanted to forget he was ever in the Army."

The fatigue jacket was functional and warm. It had buttons over the zipper front, was tight on the wrists and included a light hood zipped inside the collar until needed. There were also more pockets than you could imagine.

"Just what I need for the demonstration," I looked at

myself in the dresser mirror. "I'll blend right in."

The name "CARTER" was stitched above the front pocket. I wondered who was this guy and what gruesome memories made him want to throw away his army souvenir.

"Definitely a fashion statement," Spalding smiled.

"BEEP, BEEP." We could hear a car blasting its horn outside. Spalding looked through the upstairs window. "It's Bernstein," he said. "I can't believe you talked me into this."

"It'll be great," I said, not wanting to admit that I also had my doubts about the trip.

Early was sitting in the living room when we came downstairs. He was watching *The Little Rascals*. "Nice jacket," he said, checking out my new look. "It's really you."

"Coming with us?" I asked him.

"Not me, I'm a long distance demonstrator. I make my protests with my music."

"It's just a road trip to Washington," Spalding said.

"Yeah, right. Remember that when you're sucking in tear gas." Early turned his attention back to the television set.

"He just wants the girls next door to himself," I laughed.

"He has been helping out over there a lot," Spalding added.

"You got it," Early agreed.

Bernstein hit the horn again. "Why don't that guy just knock like everyone else," Spalding picked up his sleeping bag.

We went outside to look at our transportation. Bernstein was driving a converted bakery truck, kind of an oversized van with its shelves removed. On the back was a "NIXON/AGNEW 68" bumper sticker, placed upside down. "Great coat," he said to me as he opened the back doors. They flew outward like a school bus. The floor was covered with old mattresses.

"Thanks," I said, a bit irritated. My new Army jacket was already drawing too much attention. Were people going to start treating me different because of what I wore? I wasn't sure if I wanted to dress like an anti-war protestor.

"What's with him?" Bernstein asked Spalding.

"He's just sensitive," Spalding said.

After throwing my sleeping bag in the corner I hollered "shotgun" like a little kid going on vacation with his parents. I took the seat next to the driver, smug in the fact that I beat Spalding to the only other seat in the van.

"Where's the rest of the protestors?" I asked.

"It's an apathetic campus," Bernstein stated matter-of-factly, with a hint of a Woody Allen dialect. In fact, he looked kind of like Woody with 1950s black rimmed glasses perched on an oversized nose. But he dressed like Fidel Castro. Short in stature, he wore the traditional protesters uniform: green Army jacket like mine, blue Levi's, a work shirt and black high-topped Army boots. His long hair was pulled back in a ponytail.

The frozen ground was lightly covered with snow as we pulled out of the driveway. I cranked down the window to wave good-bye to Early, who watched us leave from the front porch.

"Give Nixon the finger for me," he said.

"Peace, brother." I flashed him the peace sign.

"You better keep that window closed," Bernstein cautioned as we pulled away. "We don't have any heat."

"No heat," Spalding gasped. "I'm from Florida."

"It's the revolution," Bernstein lectured. "You have to learn to do without."

Meanwhile, I was trying to turn on the radio.

"That doesn't work either," Bernstein said.

"There's no music after the revolution?" Spalding gave Bernstein a shot that he chose not to answer.

"Is this thing going to get us there?" I began to question our decision. We weren't even out of Kent yet.

"No sweat," Bernstein said.

Big soft flakes of snow began falling, melting when they hit the window.

"Here," Bernstein handed Spalding a large windshield

wiper that was laying between our bucket seats.

"What's this for?" Spalding asked.

"They don't work either, you might have to help me out."

"You're kidding me," Spalding said. "No wonder you asked us to come along."

"Actually, I just needed the gas money." Bernstein took back the wiper, opened his window and tried to clear off the windshield with one arm and steer with the other. We almost swerved off the road.

"You must not work either," Spalding took the wiper again, scrunched up between Bernstein and the window, and cleared the windshield as he drove.

"Someone has to lead the masses," Bernstein said. "I don't have time to work."

"What do you do for cash?"

"My parents help me out, just like yours do you. And I pick up food stamps and things. I don't need much."

"I'm paying for my own education. How about you Spalding?"

"Me too," he said. We were purposely trying to embarrass Bernstein. "I'm not doing this all the way to Washington."

"I'll help out when you get tired," I said.

"It's supposed to clear up when we get out of Ohio."

"We may need to expand our minds just to put up with you," Spalding said.

"I don't do drugs," Bernstein said. "I get high on politics."

"That's a new one," Spalding said, moving his arm back and forth outside the truck, a cold wind blowing in his face.

"You ought to try it."

"We're better off without drugs," I interjected. "We don't want to get busted in Washington."

"Oh yeah, sometimes they try to set you up," Bernstein said. "I heard about the Murph."

"Well, can politics keep you warm? I can see my breath in here." Spalding blew out a stream of cold air.

The big empty truck was like a refrigerator. Its metal sides were uninsulated, so it seemed even colder inside the truck than outside. By the time we approached the entrance to the Ohio Turnpike I wanted to relieve Spalding just so I could move around and warm up.

A couple of hitchhikers were standing on the entrance ramp holding a cardboard sign that read "D.C."

"There's our answer," I pointed to the hitchhikers. "Body heat."

Bernstein pulled over and Spalding swung open the back doors. The first hitchhiker handed Spalding his backpack, jumped in and then turned to help up his companion, who was holding a guitar case.

"Thanks," the first hitchhiker said.

"Yeah, it's cold out there," the second one added in a feminine voice. That was a surprise.

"It's just as cold in here," Spalding warned as he locked them in. The girl pulled down her sweatshirt hood. Long dark hair fell to her shoulders. Her rosy cheeks smiled.

Bernstein pulled up to the tollbooth.

A young brunette dressed in a green Ohio Turnpike uniform handed him our ticket. She peered inside the truck to check out our passengers.

"Better be careful who you pick up," she cautioned. "Smokie don't like hitchhikers."

"You can tell Smokie to kiss my ass."

The girl looked at Bernstein in horror.

"Don't mind him, he's an asshole," I hollered over from my navigator's chair as Bernstein pulled onto the highway.

Bernstein shot me a dirty look, but I let it ride. Our visitors were beginning to thaw out.

"We're from Indiana U.," the male hiker said, unrolling a sleeping bag to sit on.

"Kent State," Spalding pointed at the three of us.

"Penn State?" the girl asked.

"No, *KENT* State," Spalding laughed. "The largest unknown school in America. It's right down the road."

"What state are we in anyway?" she asked.

"Ohio," I answered.

"Any of you guys get high?" the IU male asked. Spalding and I looked at each other as he pulled a plastic baggie from inside his socks and began rolling a joint. So much for our paranoia.

"We're going to the Moratorium. I'm Cindy, this is Ray. We're just friends," she added for some unknown reason. I guess she was trying to tell us they weren't dating or anything, just partners for the trip.

Ray just nodded as he licked the rolling paper.

"You caught the right ride," Bernstein turned around to check them out, trying to decide if he was being set up. "That's where we're going."

Before long we were one big happy family, passing joints, swapping anti-war stories, mocking out Bernstein and singing ballads with the female guitar player. As the miles sped by, we kept picking up more hitchhikers who doubled as windshield wipers, radios and heaters. We stacked them in the back of the truck like loaves of bread.

I was glad to be riding shotgun. Each time we had to open the window to clear the windshield the whole group groaned, cursing Bernstein for his incompetence. It was great fun. Before everyone started crashing I took a head count. We'd collected twenty-three students from eight different states, all going to the Moratorium.

Bernstein drove all night. I tried to keep him company, but crashed myself somewhere in Pennsylvania. When I awoke, the sun was rising over the rolling hills of Maryland.

Most of the students were still asleep, twisted in various forms of repose. The Indiana coed was wrapped in Spalding's arms. *You old devil*, I thought to myself.

I looked at the scenery and began to think of Elizabeth. This was more her kind of trip than mine. I should have asked her to come along. I just wanted to visit Washington. She would have made a political statement. I really enjoyed her company, but she was a bit too radical for me. I was against the war but so was everybody. That didn't mean I hated America. I kind of liked my life, my freedom. But she was steeped in the radical left's rhetoric just like Bernstein. They wanted to overthrow everything but didn't know how to do it or what to replace it with.

"We probably would've argued the whole trip," I decided. "Want me to drive for awhile?" I asked Bernstein. "You've been driving all night."

"No, I'm fine," he said.

"You sure you don't do drugs?" I laughed.

"Did you say 'drugs?'" he smiled. "I thought you meant like medicine. I dropped some speed before we left."

"Remind me never to believe anything you say."

He just laughed. "You know what I need? A pit stop."

"Want me to keep my eyes open for a gas station?"

"What for?" he said and pulled the van over to the side of the highway. "Everybody up," he hollered to the back before jumping out of the driver's seat. "Last stop before the nation's capital, home to Tricky Dick and company."

There was little traffic on the new interstate in the early morning hour so Bernstein relieved himself on the front tire.

The students jumped out the back door and staked out various sections of turf like wild dogs, the guys going along the side of the road while the females climbed over a little hill to squat in private.

The countryside was quiet and peaceful and it felt wonderful to stretch out in the fresh air after a long drive. As the students began to regroup near the van we heard a low rumble far off in the distance. It was coming closer and closer. Suddenly a string of green trucks matching the color of my coat appeared out of nowhere.

It was a truck convoy and it wasn't carrying frozen foods. They were Army vehicles and they were loaded with soldiers on their way to guard the government from the violent demonstrators threatening the national security.

HIPPIES

Us.

Bernstein immediately jumped into action. Standing so close to the road he could be ticketed for jay walking, he gave the troops the finger. A couple of the other students joined him. This was not met kindly by the soldiers. The first trucks must have radioed back to the others because each ensuing troop vehicle began throwing things at us from their open back ends: belt buckles, tin cans, K rations. A few even took aim at Bernstein with their rifles.

"Go ahead and shoot," Bernstein taunted them, holding both middle fingers high in the air as they drove by. "No guts, no glory."

Spalding and I were not so brave. In fact, I was a disgrace to my Army jacket having retreated into the company of the women on top of the hill.

"He's nuts," Spalding said.

"He's wonderful," a tall blonde next to me said. She reminded me of Michelle.

"We'll see you pigs in Washington," Bernstein screamed at the last Army truck. By this time he was standing in the middle of the highway, defying them with a raised fist. A passing semi came out of nowhere, blasting Bernstein with its horn. He was forced to jump for cover, the trucker had less sympathy for him than the Army and seemed less concerned with running him over. It was a scene right out of *Easy Rider*.

We ran over to pick Bernstein off the berm, spitting up bits of gravel. "Great theater, eh?" he was smiling ear to ear.

"Souvenirs," he added as he picked up the Army junk thrown at him.

We piled back into the van.

"That was some show," I said once we started again.

"It only gets better." Bernstein smiled, invigorated by the incident.

On the outskirts of Washington, we picked up our last two hitchhikers. Their hair was extremely long, even for hippies. It hung down almost to their belts. They wore Harley-

Davidson motorcycle jackets and leather pants.

We let them in through my door as not to disrupt the crowd in the back. I moved my seat forward and they squeezed in behind me, kneeling in a little area that cleared out for them. We were already overloaded but felt guilty passing up anyone.

"You got any drugs?" they asked before we even pulled out into traffic. The speaker definitely had a New York accent.

I was instantly paranoid. Who were these guys? Narcs? FBI? CIA? After all, we were almost in Nixon's backyard.

Bernstein seemed to share my concern and answered "No" for the rest of the passengers.

"Then maybe you need some?" the other biker asked. He opened a large gym bag for inspection by the masses. "You need it, we got it."

These guys were New York big city hustlers, hippie entrepreneurs. They could care less about protesting the Vietnam War. They were out to make a buck like medieval merchants working a country fair.

"Hash, speed, grass, coke, whatever tickles your fancy."

Money started changing hands like the win, place and show windows at the Kentucky Derby. These guys hit the jackpot.

"How much for a hit of acid?"

"Got any window pane?"

"What kind of hash is this?"

They were overwhelmed with requests. They worked the student crowd relentlessly.

By the time the Big Apple professionals finished their wheeling and dealing, Bernstein had pulled the van onto the lawn in front of the Lincoln Memorial.

"Here we are," he announced. He got out of his seat, walked around to the back of the van and swung open its doors. The smoke from the lit pipes hit him like a dirty hurricane. It almost knocked him over.

The passengers were equally struck by the remarkable

sight. Throughout their windowless ride they were not pre-pared for what Bernstein and I were witnessing, the slow growth of a pedestrian nation of freaks.

The panorama the open doors afforded them was like watching Woodstock in a movie theatre. The doors framed the colorful masses. Even the New Yorkers were silent, held in a state of suspended amazement.

Spread out on the grass surrounding the Washington Monument was the largest crowd in the history of the nation's capital. By the end of the day it would number a quarter of a million citizens. If you stared, it resembled a three-dimensional moving multi-colored abstract painting.

I was in a state of shock. I never dreamed there were so many freaks or hippies or whatever you called them.

"I'm going to leave it parked here," Bernstein explained to the troops. "If any of you need a ride back home, meet us here after the rally."

The passengers emptied out, giving the three of us hippie handshakes and a "thanks," then losing themselves in the crowd. The protest was beginning and everyone was in a hurry to be a part of it.

"I've got to report to the National Committee of the SDS," Bernstein told us as he locked up the truck. "I don't suppose you'd like to join me?"

"Naw," Spalding said.

"We're amateurs," I admitted. "Where should we meet you?"

"Right here, tomorrow morning," he slapped the side of the truck. "We should be back in Kent by tomorrow night."

"What about tonight?" Spalding asked.

"You can crash at any of the local universities," Bernstein explained. "They're ready for you. I like George Washington myself."

"Well, make sure you don't get arrested, we need the ride back."

"Don't worry about me," Bernstein smiled his all-knowing smile. "Call me at SDS if you need to make bail."

"Not funny," Spalding said.

"We're peaceful protesters," I added.

"That's what they all say," Bernstein laughed, flashed a peace sign and disappeared into the crowd.

We were left like orphans in a storm.

"I can't believe it," I said to Spalding, soaking in the sights. The Washington Monument was on one side of us, the Lincoln Memorial on the other. There was music and chatter and the smell of marijuana in the air.

"I can't believe you talked me into this," Spalding said, as we went with the flow of the crowd. Everybody seemed to be heading in the same direction so we just went with them.

"What's wrong? I thought you wanted to come."

"I have a bad feeling about all this, like I'm never going to graduate."

"What about that Indiana chick?"

"Her? She was nice. She said she'd visit us in Kent, even if she misses the ride back."

"She going to bring her friend?" I teased.

"Give it a break, will ya? That's all he is, a friend, a travelling companion, like you and me."

"Do you think I'd dump you for a cheap thrill?"

"In a second."

"What if Bernstein's right?" Spalding asked. "What if we get arrested, if only for a couple days. Then I got a record and I'll never get a job with an airline."

"You're paranoid."

"Damn right I am. You don't worry about anything. Look at Artie. We got less than a year to go, I don't want to blow everything on a trip we didn't even have to take."

"Look at all these people. They can't arrest all of us."

"That's what you said about Artie."

"Do you have to keep mentioning him?"

That was the end of that conversation. We walked along in silence, lost in our own thoughts. The air was crisp and cold but I was cozy in my new Army jacket. The sun felt great on my face. For all the serious talk about ending the war the crowd was festive, like at the Mardi Gras in New Orleans.

Music blared from hand held radios and open car windows. Sidewalk musicians played guitars and bongo drums on the street corners. Kites flew overhead from the grassy commons surrounding the Washington Monument. Frisbees whirled by like the spaceship in *The Day the Earth Stood Still*. There was dancing in the streets.

"Thanks for the jacket," I tried warming up the conversation.

"Forget it," Spalding said. "Check out that sign."

A tall, lanky kid who looked like he was still in high school was carrying a large "STOP POLLUTION-GAG AGNEW" sign. The kid was struggling to hold his sign up against the wind.

"Just trying to get on television," I said.

"Shit, that's right. What if my parents see me?" Spalding said.

"They'd cut you off."

"Not funny, buddy."

"I hope we are on television. We'd be heroes back in Kent."

"Great." Spalding was angry again. It was going to be a long day.

Eventually we found ourselves among a great pool of people being directed by the DC cops through a funnel of barricades. The crowd stopped for about fifteen minutes, organizers giving various orders on megaphones, most falling on deaf ears.

"Keep it orderly, keep your drugs out of sight, don't offend the folks back home."

Fat chance.

I never saw so many drugs used so openly in my life. The police didn't seem to care. I didn't know if it was because they were outnumbered a thousand to one or they were afraid if they arrested anyone it would start a riot.

Actually, the DC police were quite friendly. It was as if they hated Nixon as much as we did. Once we started marching, one of them even gave me the peace sign.

We walked down Pennsylvania Avenue like we were in a parade. Local residents brought out their children, watching us from behind the barricades along the curbs.

The television cameras began to whirl as various groups began their chants. "One, two, three, four, we don't want your goddam war." And "Ho, Ho, Ho Chi Min, NLF is going to win."

We didn't chant. We didn't carry a sign. We just walked and stared, adding our bodies to the critical mass of citizens that was the largest protest against the U.S. government in the nation's history.

We were sending a message to President Tricky Dick Nixon. The message was simple. End the war in Vietnam now. Forget the politics, admit it was a costly mistake and bring the troops home right away. It was a war that wasn't worth dying for and we shouldn't have been involved in it anyway.

And, most importantly, end it before we were forced to go ourselves.

Eventually, we even walked past the back of the White House. We could see the famous Rose Garden. It was pretty well barricaded by our Army buddies, the ones who passed us on the highway. I wondered if they were looking for Bernstein. And I wondered how the Prez felt watching the demonstration out his back window, sipping scotch with Spiro Agnew.

Agnew had called us "a bunch of bums" a few days earlier. Did he feel at all threatened by the number of bums who showed up?

Lost in my thoughts, swept by the tide of humanity, I wasn't paying much attention to where we were going. We were in sort of a daze. One moment we were walking down

Pennsylvania Avenue like celebrities, the next, we were at the end of the route being ordered to disperse by the police. I figured our fifteen minutes of fame were about over.

"Where to?" Spalding asked.

"Washington U.? Or do you want to see the sights?"

"I could use some eats," he said.

"Me too."

We bought a couple of hot dogs from a street vendor, sat on a bench, and rested in one of those little parks that are all over Washington D.C. We had no idea where we were.

"I wouldn't mind seeing something, maybe the Smithsonian," Spalding admitted between bites. "You ever been here before?"

"Once, when I was a kid. How about you?"

"This is my first time. It's a long way from Florida."

"Everything's a long way from Florida. And everything here's pretty far apart."

"Maybe we should ask a cop for directions."

"I thought they were the enemy?"

"Maybe yours, not mine."

And then it happened.

It sounded like the crowd at a football game, hollering jaunts and cheers. But it was coming toward us and it was peppered with the sound of breaking glass. We stood up.

An unruly mob, right out of the French Revolution, was coming our way. It was nothing like the orderly protest we'd just left. We dropped our hot dogs and tried to outrun the pack, but it caught up to us. Overwhelmed us.

We ran like hunted animals. The National Guard was hurling tear and pepper gas at us. We learned later that the Yippies, Jerry Rubin's self-proclaimed anti-war activists, had broken some windows at the Justice and Labor Department buildings.

A tear gas canister rolled under my feet. My eyes began to swell. A student wearing a blue Levi jacket took a bandana off his head and used it to pick up the canister. He hurled it back at the guardsmen but the smoke hit me right in the face. I looked for Spalding. He also took a hit. My whole face stung, as if a firecracker blew up in my face. I grabbed Spalding's arm for support. We moved sideways, away from the crowd, toward a nearby house. One of the National Guardsmen followed us up the stranger's lawn. The mob swept past us but he decided we were his prey. He pointed a .45 automatic at us. We cowered in fear. I thought all of Spalding's premonitions were about to come true.

"Let's go, my lovelies," he ordered. "You're coming with me."

Just then the door to the house opened. An elderly man, noble in stature stepped outside.

"What are you doing in my yard?" he asked. I thought he was going to help the officer throw the book at us. But he was shouting at the National Guardsman.

"This is private property," he walked over to the guardsman and addressed him in no uncertain manner. "These boys are under my jurisdiction. Do you have a search warrant?"

"Uh, no." The guardsman was flustered.

"Then be gone with you!" he shouted.

The guardsman looked at us, then at the elderly gentleman. "I'll deal with you two later," he said, then walked off to catch up with his unit.

"Thank you, sir," I said. So did Spalding.

"That's all right boys," he winked. "In a pinch, it's best to try a little bullshit."

He flashed us a peace sign then went back into his house. I never did find out who he was. I've always fantasized that he was a Supreme Court judge or senator. Whoever he was, he saved our asses.

"I need some water," I rubbed my eyes, trying to make out Spalding's familiar shape.

"Me too. How's your eyes?"

"Not so good. So much for asking for directions."

"Screw the cops," Spalding said.

"You've changed your tune."

"Let's find George Washinton U. or somewhere. I'm burning all over."

Somehow we found the university. We were amazed that complete strangers welcomed us with open arms.

"Gassed?" a male student in John Lennon glasses, asked us.

"Yeah, we're hurting," Spalding admitted.

"You look it, follow me to the gym."

The gym was set up like an hospital emergency room. A short coed, almost dressed like a man in military garb, guided us to a showering area, where we were instructed to go behind some curtains, disrobe and hand over our clothes. We obeyed with pleasure.

"We'll wash them for you. Here's your numbers." Mine was 171, Spalding's 172.

"You're doing a booming business," I had to laugh, sticking the top of my naked torso through the curtains.

"Nothing but the best for our guys," she answered like a nurse in a MASH unit. She handed us a pair of GWU gym shorts and a couple of towels. "The showers are on the other side of the curtain. We'll be waiting for you when you come out."

The showers, four of them, consisted of hoses hanging from a metal framework surrounded by plastic shower curtains. If you looked hard enough you could see the outlines of our naked bodies but we didn't know that until we came out.

Despite the crude stream it was the most wonderful shower of my life. I stepped out, dried off, put on the gym shorts and came out of the holding area onto the gym floor. My eyes were finally working again. It seemed like there were a thousand freaks crammed in the gym, but none of them paid us any mind.

Our coed slash nurse returned with a sheet to wrap around ourselves. I felt like I was at a toga party. And now that my eyes were finally working I realized our helper was beautiful, or at least would be if she took off the uniform and put on a mini-skirt.

She took us over to a volunteer doctor, who looked into our eyes with a pencil-sized flashlight and pronounced us fit as a fiddle.

"No damage," he said. "You boys were pretty lucky."

"You're telling us," Spalding said.

"I can't believe how well organized this all is."

"We've been hosting demonstrations here in Washington for over a hundred years. They just keep getting bigger."

"You're doing a great job. We owe you a debt of gratitude," Spalding said in his best Southern hospitality accent.

"You can thank the student volunteers," the doctor said. "They make it all possible."

"I'd like to thank the one who took our clothes," I said to Spalding.

"That's my daughter," the doctor smiled and I was ready to swallow my shoe. "Thanks for the compliment," he shook our hands.

We were directed back to a little holding area by another lovely volunteer who wore a black t-shirt with a big peace sign on the front. Her braless tits bounced when she walked, reminding me of Michelle.

"You can sit here for awhile, have some soup and wait for your clothes," she instructed us.

"Can we spend the night?" Spalding asked her.

"Pardon me?" she responded, misunderstanding his intentions.

"Not at your place. Here," I clarified his question.

"That's what everyone else is doing, even me," she answered sweetly.

"But we lost our sleeping bags in the riot," he added.

"I'm sure you'll find someone to share with," she smiled coyly at Spalding. I was already jealous even though I never met her before and would probably never see her again.

"You wouldn't be from Indiana, would you?" I asked as Spalding gave me a dirty look.

"No, why?"

"Just wondering."

The doctor's daughter returned with our clothes and we thanked both of them. I didn't want to take off my toga, I was having a great time but we had to follow the program. They smiled good-bye and went on to make the next helpless victim feel at home. There was an endless stream of stragglers and they made each one feel like family. Clara Barton would have been proud.

After changing back into our original duds we found some hippies from Pennsylvania who had their sleeping bags stretched out like sheets. They invited us to share their space and we swapped war stories for awhile.

Then they gave us a hit of something. I think it was mescaline. Whatever it was, it worked wonders. Suddenly we forgot all about our close call with the law.

In fact, we forgot just about everything that happened from that moment on, until we were halfway back to Ohio. I've quizzed Spalding on this a number of times but his brain cells were similarly damaged.

I also remember very little of the ride back home. Except Bernstein did say something very interesting before dropping us off.

"You know, Kent State's a powder keg, ready to explode."

"What are you talking about?" I asked him. I'd never felt that way about our campus.

"There's a lot going on behind the scenes that other colleges would kill for."

"Like what?" I asked.

"Little things, in a lot of different areas. Maybe nothing will happen until spring when the weather warms up, but we're making a lot of progress."

"I thought you said this was an apathetic campus."

"It is," he smiled. "But not for long."

Chapter Thirteen:
THE LOTTERY

We didn't know it at the time but our experience at the November Moratorium changed us. We'd become more political. More open to the arguments of the New Left. Subconsciously, I even thought about growing a beard.

Then, a couple weeks after the Washington demonstration another event cemented our political views for the next decade. President "Tricky-Dick" Nixon announced that the federal government was "reforming" the draft. It was no coincidence that it came on the heels of the largest demonstration in the history of the country.

The government was scrapping the old draft system that gave great leeway to local draft boards. It would be replaced by a national lottery.

The "new" idea to reform the draft was actually the resurrection of a system used during the Civil War. On Monday, December 1, 1969, all 366 birthdays, leap year included, would be drawn from a fishbowl. You would be drafted in the order your birthday was chosen. The earlier your birthday was picked, the greater your chances the government would come calling.

The Nixon argument was that the national lottery would take favoritism out of the hands of the local draft boards. Often, especially in small towns, rich and influential parents made sure their sons didn't go to war. Instead, the poor and disenfranchised were hauled overseas.

There was some truth to this argument. There was also the argument that the current system draped uncertainty over every youth's life. It was difficult for us to consider a career or marriage with Uncle Sam breathing down our necks.

The new system would let everyone know exactly where they stood so they could begin planning their future. There was some truth to this argument.

But we knew our fearless leader better than that. We knew he wasn't doing us any real favors. What he was really doing was trying to fragment the anti-war movement. He hoped to buy off half the so-called "baby-boomers."

He knew we were basically a spoiled, selfish bunch. His vice-president, Spiro Agnew, constantly reminded us of it. If we no longer had to worry about going to Vietnam, why protest? We must really have shook him up trooping past his back yard.

The Big Drawing was held on prime time television. And since it was a subject close to our hearts, graduating in June and all, we prepared for it like any other major social event, the World Series or the Super Bowl.

We chilled a case of Robin Hood Ale on the back porch, pre-rolled a couple joints, popped some fresh popcorn and invited the girls next door over for moral support.

To make it interesting, we each threw a fin ($5) on the living room floor. A little side bet. The first guy whose number was drawn might end up tramping through the jungles of Vietnam but at least he'd have enough money to buy himself a lid for the road.

The black and white Philco never broadcast a clearer picture even though Spanky was sleeping on top of it, curled around the rabbit-eared antenna. Spalding, sitting in the Archie Bunker easy chair, took a pencil and wrote our four birthdays on the wall, next to our American Indian poster.

It seemed appropriate. The poster was one of the few items leftover from our apartment days at College Towers.

It was a close-up of a longhaired American Indian chief named Ishi. He looked like the model for the hippies of the 1960s.

It was titled "ALMOST ANCESTORS: The First Californians." And there was a quote on the bottom from Saxton T. Hope, whoever he was. It read:

> He looked upon us as sophisticated children
> Smart but not wise.
> We knew many things, and much that is false.
> He knew nature, which is always true.

Like the poster, the birthdays would become a fixture on the wall.

Early, meanwhile, turned the sound off the television and cranked up a series of protest albums on the back stereo. Bob Dylan, Phil Ochs and Donovan joined the Beatles and Country Joe for an all-star lottery concert.

As each plastic capsule was drawn from a huge fish bowl, the birth date was flashed on the screen with its corresponding number.

I sat at the end of the davenport between Harold and Michelle, bracing myself for the worst. It was comforting being surrounded by two of my favorite mammals.

Renee and Sarah sat on the couch's arms. Early sat next to Michelle on the other end of the couch. I could tell he was enjoying the company of his Halloween dates. Spalding and I wondered if he'd seen them while we were in Washington.

The Murph was standing under the arch separating the living room from the dining room.

"Sit down, buddy," I suggested.

"Pull yourself up a chair," Spalding added.

"We can make room," Early squeezed closer to Michelle which did not escape my notice. I also squeezed over, crowding Harold off the couch so Michelle could move closer.

"Naw, I'm going to take off," the Murph said to everyone's surprise. "I'm supposed to meet Mary Lou at the Kove."

"Hey, this is your life," Early said.

"You guys can tell me what happens. I can wait." He laughed and headed toward the door, taking his Navy Pea coat off the tree stand. "Don't let your meat loaf."

"Or your pussy willow," Spalding gave him the response he expected.

"Peace," he flashed a peace sign and went out into the cold, bitter night.

"Mr. Carefree," Early said. We turned our attention back to the talking box.

The room was quiet. Number after number was lifted from the fishbowl, like trinkets in a carnival game. We listened to the music and let out a sigh of relief each time our small circle of friends was excluded.

The numbers shot past fifty and still no direct hit. Our collective anxiety increased exponentially.

The Robin Hoods went down in larger gulps, the joints were passed around faster and the popcorn was devoured by the handful.

Finally, the little numbers on the tube told the gruesome story. Draft Number 61, August 29th. My birthday. My goddam birthday. Why couldn't my mother have held out a little longer? I didn't notice any August 30th yet. How could she do this to me? I was doomed. Doomed.

"Shit," I said.

Spalding double-checked the wall behind him. "You're it, buddy." He put my number next to my birthday with an asterisk to indicate I'd won. Or lost, depending on how you looked at it.

"An asterisk, no, not an asterisk," I stood up pleading with him. "You can't do this to me. I ain't no Roger Maris."

I was making a fool of myself. All the faces in the room looked at me with pity, as if I'd just been told my parents had died. Even Harold seemed to sense what was happening, looking up at me with his sad brown eyes.

Early picked the twenty dollars off the floor and handed it to me without saying a word.

"Thanks," I said quietly. I'd calmed down. Since my days were numbered it was time to appreciate the little things in life, the small victories, the gentle moments.

Spalding was the next to go. Number 102. August 15th.

"You and me," I said. I could tell it hurt him to write his number on the wall.

"Maybe we could join the Army on the buddy system."

"What's that?" Sarah asked.

"That's what they did in all those World War II movies," Michelle explained.

"I don't know if you can do that anymore," Early said.

"You don't have to worry about it," Spalding was more than a bit jealous that Early's number hadn't come up yet.

"You wouldn't really go, would you?" Michelle asked me.

"Not if I can help it," I heard myself saying.

The numbers kept rolling by. 200, 225, 250. Early was still high and dry.

"What's with you, Early? Who do you know?" Spalding asked.

"When you live right, everything falls your way," Early gave a big grin and held his large palms out sideways, like an archbishop giving his blessing.

"Here we go," I interrupted. Early's jellybean came up. Number 254, October 16th.

Spalding wrote it on the wall.

"What about the Murph?" Early asked.

"He's the winner and still champion," Spalding admitted reluctantly.

The Murph was almost one of the luckiest young men in America. They finally called his number at 360, June 20th.

"A toast," Early held up his bottle of Hood after the last number was picked.

"To the Murph," I said.

"To Kubik," Spalding said.

"To America's fighting men," Early said.

"May they all go to Canada," Michelle said and we clinked bottles and laughed.

"Then who'd be left for us?" Sarah asked.

"Me," Early beamed.

"You shit." Spalding gave him a playful shove.

They started to wrestle but I turned up the Philco. "Turn down the tunes," I said to no one in particular.

The network commentator was asking a member of the Defense Department what it all meant. The best I could make of it during the commotion was that if the draft continued at its present pace of 250,000 men a year, the first hundred numbers should begin ordering their uniforms. The second hundred were on the bubble, they could go or they could stay.

Of course, those closer to 100, like Spalding, were in the greatest jeopardy. Anyone with a number over 200, like Early, could pretend the Vietnam War did not exist.

Tricky-Dick Nixon earned his nickname with this one. In one swift move he accomplished his objective. He cut the anti-war movement in half. But what he didn't count on was the fact that he lit a fire under the other half. From now on their fate was sealed so they'd be running scared.

I was one of the honored ones, the brave, the few, the freaks. I immediately decided I'd never get another haircut. It was time to tune in, turn on and drop out of society altogether. I'd grow a beard, move to Haight-Ashbury and make a living selling pottery.

I held up my ransom, my four crisp five dollar bills, and made an important announcement:

"The Venice anyone?"

Chapter Fourteen:
THE VENICE

If there was a bar in Kent that we called our own, it was the Venice. We'd discovered it one strange fall afternoon after walking the railroad tracks that bordered the Cuyahoga River in downtown Kent.

We were thirsty from a long hike but first stopped at the abandoned Kent railroad station on Franklin Avenue. For decades students had left their homes across the state and traveled to college by train, arriving at the quaint brick station downtown.

Many of the numerous downtown bars owed their livelihood as much to the trains as to the college. Kent was also a major railroad intersection and that contributed greatly to its growth.

The automobile age changed all that. Trains were now viewed as a nuisance. The tracks ran right through downtown and often caused major traffic backups. Students' only contact with them were on weekend evenings when they'd often jump on a slow moving freight for a free ride from one bar to another. It was amazing that you never heard about a drunk freshman being run over by one.

We rummaged through the old station looking for souvenirs. Since both Early and I worked on the railroad summers to finance our education we appreciated the rugged beauty of the rails.

The station was pretty much empty but Early somehow opened a jammed closet to discover an old kerosene switch lamp. We knew they were going extinct so we grabbed it. He painted it up, put an electric light in it and it became another fixture at Depeyster.

What does this have to do with The Venice?

I'll tell you. Every time I see that old light I recall our first visit there and it makes me want to go back. That's probably why I wanted to go there the night of the lottery.

The Venice was a townie bar as opposed to a student bar. The owners didn't want the headaches that came with big crowds. To enter, you had to first pass the little old Italian lady with a flashlight who guarded the entrance. She didn't care if you were fifteen or fifty, but you'd better have a valid ID or you could take your business elsewhere.

This discouraged a lot of students right from the git go. Fortunately, in Ohio at the time if you were eighteen you could drink something called 3.2 beer. This is back in the dark ages before Light Beer. At twenty-one you could drink the high powered stuff, about seven percent alcohol content. This simple fact rubbed a lot of our generation the wrong way. Once we were eighteen we could be drafted, asked to carry a rifle and kill gooks, but we couldn't vote or drink regular beer. Something seemed wrong somewhere.

The atmosphere inside the Venice was very un-Kent like. There were no neon lights, no beer posters, no blaring rock music. The only sounds were from a television set above one corner of the long wooden bar.

All the lights were turned on like in an English pub. The only decorations on the wall were murals of Italian scenery, reproductions of the old country.

The bar was filled with tables and chairs, a few booths lined one wall and two pool tables took up most of the floor space. Two elderly gentlemen, obviously of Italian descent, sat at the bar and a young couple snuggled in the corner booth. They were the only patrons on the cold December night.

Our appearance doubled the Venice's population. I approached the bar with my blood money while the others pushed a couple of wooden tables together near the pool tables.

The bartenders were a couple tiny Italian guys who looked like they just came over on the boat. They seemed more interested in watching "Dragnet" with their compadres than serving me.

"Could I have a couple pitchers of 3.2 and six glasses?" I finally said loudly, hoping to draw the attention of at least one of them.

"Sure thing, kiddo," the nearest one said, trying to act hip with an Italian accent that matched the lady bouncer's at the door.

He poured from memory, letting the tap run as he turned to watch Joe Friday browbeat a criminal into a confession.

"You watch the lottery?" he asked while handing me the pitcher.

"Yeah, that's why I'm down here."

"Number not so good?"

"Sixty-one," I rolled my eyes toward the ceiling as I handed him one of the fives.

"You keep," he pushed my money away. "American GI's, they come to my village during World War II. They kill Mussolini. I follow them here."

"Thanks," I said, taking the pitchers over to our table.

When I returned for the glasses he added: "You be a good boy. You do us proud."

"I'll try," I said. I wanted to tell him there was no Mussolini in Vietnam but I wasn't in the mood.

"These are on the house," I told the group as I filled their glasses. "The bartender thinks I'm already in the Army."

"It's probably your jacket," Michelle said.

"I took off my Army jacket and put it on the back of the chair. "This is your fault, Spalding. You jinxed me."

"At least you got a free pitcher," he laughed.

"They take care of you GI's," Renee teased.

"Even your roommate's taking a shot," I told Michelle.

"You love it," she smiled.

I put the lottery money on the table for anyone who wanted a refill. Early put a quarter in the pool table to release the balls. Spalding walked over to the jukebox to play a few Beach Boys tunes. I sat back, sipped my beer and enjoyed a few quiet moments of domestic tranquility.

"You ever play?" I asked Michelle.

"No."

"You want me to show you how?"

"Sure."

"First you have to find the right stick." I took her over to the pool cue rack. "One that feels right in your hands."

"How do you know which one's right?"

"Whatever feels good."

She started fondling them in a most erotic manner. It was making me hot until Early interrupted us.

"Roll them on the table to see if they're crooked," he suggested.

"Maybe I like crooked ones," she teased.

"Oops, did I interrupt something here?"

"Guys versus girls," Spalding said, before I could answer Early.

"That's not fair," Sarah said without thinking. She liked to use her diminutive size to feign persecution when she was really setting you up for the kill.

"Yeah, we don't know how to play," Renee added.

"I thought you guys were women's libbers?" Early picked up on Spalding's major tease.

"*She* is," Renee nodded toward Michelle as if she and Sarah didn't buy into their roommates program.

"That's right. Anything a guy can do a girl can do better," Michelle boasted.

She picked up the wooden triangle that hung from the bottom of the pool table.

"How do you start this game? Don't tell me. You put the balls in this thing, right?"

"Right," Spalding said. We three males admired her spunk. We watched as she filled the triangle with loose balls.

"Put the tip of it on the dot," Early slid the filled triangle into the proper location. "We'll play eight ball. It goes right here." He moved a few balls around.

"You break."

"What?" Michelle stammered.

Early lifted the triangle and took Michelle to the other end of the table, placing the cue ball on the green felt. He took her hand and showed her how to hold her fingers so the cue stick slid through them.

Spalding and I stared, admiring Early's technique. We knew he was the best pool player among us. He grew up with one in his basement. But we never realized he could be so smooth with the opposite sex.

"Hit it as hard as you can," Early told Michelle.

She whaled on it. The balls scattered in all directions. Then the seven ball plopped in the corner pocket.

"Nothing to it," she snapped her fingers and handed the stick to Renee.

"I think she's hustling us," I said.

We gave her a silent applause, clapping our hands politely as if we were at the opera.

"Go again," Spalding said.

"Oh," she looked surprised.

"Try to knock in another solid one," Early explained. "You keep going as long as you keep sinking them."

"I knew that," she took the stick from Renee.

She tried again but to no avail.

"All yours, Early," Spalding said.

Early proceeded to put on a masterful display of pool prowess that clearly amazed me, Spalding and our feminine observers. In a few minutes he completely cleared the table of striped balls.

"Eight ball, side pocket," he declared and sank it. He put his stick on the table and smiled with a shit-eating grin. "That's the game."

"Huh," Renee said, her mouth hanging open. She had been patiently waiting her turn.

"There's still a lot of balls left," Sarah said.

"Only solid ones," Spalding explained.

"The object of the game is to sink the eight ball," Early said.

"We won," I said.

"You cheated," Sarah objected. "I don't know how you did, but you did."

Everyone laughed, including Sarah.

"Early, why don't you explain to the girls what happened? I want to talk to Spalding."

Spalding was filling the glasses from the second pitcher. He gave me a quizzical look when I motioned for him to join me at an empty booth.

"What?" he asked, sitting sideways towards the girls with his legs hanging over the end of the bench.

"What are we gonna do?" I asked him.

"About what?"

"Vietnam, asshole."

"Keep talking like that and you won't have any friends left."

"Hey, you're in this too."

"By the time they get around to drafting us it'll probably be over," he said nonchalantly.

"I wouldn't bet on it. I can't believe how calm you are."

"Hey," he leaned over his beer glass. "I'm scared shitless. But what am I supposed to do, riot?"

"No, but we could look at our options."

"What options? Army," he held out one hand. "Jail," he held out the other. "Army, jail. Army, jail. How complicated is it?"

"How about the Air Force? You're a pilot. I could be your navigator. We could napalm the shit out of them."

"You're talking crazy. That's six years. And I don't like flying over anti-aircraft fire."

"Six years? You're right. We'd be twenty-six by the time we got out. That's almost thirty. Our lives would be over."

"Either way we're screwed. Let's shoot some pool. Save the theatrics for Bernstein."

"Who?" Michelle asked. She'd walked over to join us. "You guys look pretty serious."

"Matt wants to napalm babies," Spalding said as he got up and joined the pool shooters.

"You what?"

"He's kidding. I just said we should look at our options, like joining the Air Force."

"And drop napalm?"

"It's better than marching through the jungle with a rifle on your back."

"I know you. You wouldn't drop bombs on innocent people."

"It's either them or us," I said with all the seriousness I could muster. I couldn't believe I was talking like this. That lottery number must have really affected me.

"You don't have to go, you know."

"If they draft me, it's either do what you're ordered or go to jail."

"You could be a conscientious objector."

"I think you got to be Amish for that. Or maybe a Mormon."

"What about Canada?"

"And never see my family again."

"They could come visit you." She suddenly took pity on me, coming over to my side of the booth. I slid over to make room for her. She put her hand on my knee. It was just like old times. I forgot all about Vietnam. We could feel the freight train roaring by outside, shaking our glasses.

"You know, they have draft counselors on campus. Promise me you won't do anything foolish until you talk to them. Promise?"

"Cross my heart and hope to die."

The next thing I knew she was kissing me and all the feelings left over from the previous year came rushing back, filling my chest like an oil gusher.

I didn't want to stop but she pulled herself back.

"We better get back to the others," she said. We could see them looking at us.

"Do we have to?" I was beginning to enjoy her pity, like a World War II GI hoping for one last fling before being shipped overseas. I wanted to tell her I might not come back alive.

"I can't," she answered my question before I asked it. I was going to suggest going back to Depeyster without the others.

"Where are these draft counselors?" I asked as we stood up.

"The Student Union, I think."

"We'll go there tomorrow," I assured her.

Chapter Fifteen:
BEATING THE SYSTEM

Bright and early the next morning Spalding and I decided to skip classes and head right to the draft counselors office in the Student Union. I mean, what are a couple of grades when your life's on the line.

On our way we passed the Army ROTC building at the base of the Commons. ROTC (pronounced rot-see) allowed students planning a military career after graduation to begin training early. After graduation they became low level officers instead of infantry grunts like your common draftee. ROTC bribed students into joining the program by paying part of their tuition. Many students who never really cared about the military joined as a way of affording college.

Originally, there were two ROTC buildings, an Army and an Air Force. The protestors had burned the Air Force one during the previous spring riots. No one really cared. After all, they were supposed to be temporary structures built during World War II. The dilapidated one-story wooden box was painted battleship gray.

The Murph worked in one of the buildings sophomore year. It was the supply quarters. It was the perfect job to outfit his friends in trendy Army fatigues. It was where he bought his Navy Pea coat. But he had to quit after feeling the wrath of his fellow students, who claimed he was contributing to the "military industrial complex."

That was a term President Eisenhower coined about the time he left office. A military man himself, he warned the nation about too large a buildup of peacetime arms. He seemed to sense the Vietnam War coming before it happened.

Having ROTC on campus gave the protesters a perfect target. Every year one of their demands was to rid the campus of ROTC, not just at Kent but on all college campuses. It seemed the military and the university mixed even worse than the city folks and the hippies.

"Maybe we should join ROTC?" I suggested as we passed their building.

"I think it's a little too late. We graduate in June."

"What if we just don't graduate?"

"If that worked everyone would be doing it. And I can't afford another year."

"We'll have to ask the guy."

The draft counselor's office was in the basement of the small student union. The hallway leading to it was already crowded with students, the result of the previous night's lottery.

"Hey Tom," Spalding approached another aerospace student in the crowd. "This the line for the draft counselor?"

"Paul," the skinny, dark-haired youth gave Spalding a regular non-hippie handshake, pumping it up and down extra hard. Tom could have been a double for Mister Rogers of PBS fame. "First you go inside, pick a number, then you come out here and wait till they call you."

"Like the doctor's office," I said.

"Worse," Tom laughed. "We're like a herd of cattle."

"I'll get us a number," Spalding said. He worked his way through the crowd.

"What's your number?" I asked Tom.

"Today's or yesterday's?" he asked back.

"Touché."

"Last night I was ninety-six, today I'm fourteen."

"Sixty-one," I pointed at myself.

"Ooooh, you're gone," he shook his head in sympathy.

Tom had a sneaky way of lowering his eyes and looking at you from the tops of his wire-rimmed glasses.

"How'd we do?" I asked Spalding upon his return.

"Twenty-seven," he held up a little piece of blue paper with a number scrawled on it.

"Where are they now?" I asked and as if on cue a loud voice boomed down the hallway: "TWELVE, NUMBER TWELVE."

"Number twelve, number twelve, number twelve," the students passed along the information, mimicking the Beatles song, "Number Nine."

"You're looking good," I said to Tom, meaning his number.

"Oh, thank you," he said. For a second he thought I meant his appearance. "Oh, my number, of course," he was a bit embarrassed. "Listen, I'll tell you what. I really need a bite to eat before I see the counselor. You want to trade numbers?"

"If you really..."

"I do, I do." He exchanged slips of paper with Spalding. "You owe me one."

"Stop over to Depeyster, anytime."

"I will."

"He's a pretty nice guy," I said to Spalding after he left.

"A little too nice." Spalding wiggled his open hand sideways like Archie Bunker did on the television show "All in the Family" when he wanted to signal someone of homosexual leanings.

"He is?"

"I'm pretty sure," Spalding said.

I was shocked. To my knowledge I'd never met a true homo before.

"Wow," I said. "He'll have a tough time in the Army."

"No shit. He probably had to build up his courage before facing the draft counselor."

"NUMBER THIRTEEN, NUMBER FOURTEEN," a voice called out.

We worked our way to the desk just inside the draft counselor's doorway. A pretty redheaded coed took Spalding's number fourteen. She was twirling her long straight locks with her free hand.

"I thought I just gave you 27?"

"We traded," Spalding smiled, honored that she remembered him.

"That side," she pointed to the right half of a divided cubicle. I was surprised she didn't question his explanation.

"Where you going?" she asked me as I began to follow him. "One number per person."

"We're a team," I said. I was suddenly tempted to take Spalding's hand. Maybe that would get us out of the draft.

"It won't work," she was reading my mind. "It's been tried before."

I just kept following Spalding as she shook her head in disgust. I could tell she was having a bad day.

The draft counselor's office was unbelievably small and cluttered. When he stood up to shake our hands, he knocked at least three piles of papers off his desk. We immediately bent down to help pick them up. Each one represented someone's hopes and fears and here they were scattered on the floor.

"There's two of you?" he asked, as we were all on our knees. He was short and stocky with his long hair pulled back in a ponytail. He didn't look much older than us, probably a graduate student, but his face showed traces of a rough life. I figured he was a former drugee. He wore a white shirt with button-down collar and a paisley tie, but I knew it was only for show. After work he was the kind of guy you'd see holding down a barstool at Walter's Cafe, the main hippie hangout.

"We're..." I was going to say "a team" but stopped in midsentence. "It's easier this way."

"We both have a class at 10:20," Spalding explained.

"Joe," he held out his hand and we exchanged hippie handshakes and introductions.

"That doesn't give us much time," he looked at his Mickey Mouse watch. "Most everything you need to know is in this

PETER JEDICK

little packet." He handed each of us one. "Take them home, look 'em over and come back when it's not so crazy."

As we glanced at our flyers someone began crying uncontrollably in the other counselor's office, just on the other side of the partition.

"Someone's losing it," I said.

"He must have a really low number," Spalding added.

"It happens." Joe lit up a cigarette, moving some papers away from his ashtray. It overflowed with butts. This prompted Spalding to light up, too. "So what can I do for you guys?"

"Save our asses," Spalding put it bluntly, putting a match to his Winston.

"Ah, if it was only that easy," Joe blew out a smoke ring. "You don't have a helluva lot of choices. If you did there'd be no one left over there to fight."

"What about conscientious objector?" I asked.

"Are you a Quaker, maybe a Mennonite?"

I shook my head "no."

"Then forget it."

"I could convert."

"It's too late, the draft board won't buy it. There's a lot of bullshit out there on the streets but you really only have two choices."

"And they are?"

"You can go to Canada until it's over and hope the government comes to its senses sometime down the road and lets you back in."

"And the other?"

"Or you can try for a medical discharge."

"Medical?"

"It's the best way to go. The most painless." Joe stood up and tried opening a drawer in his file cabinet. The shelf was stuck, he had to pull hard on it. "You'd be surprised what can keep you out of the Army."

The cabinet suddenly opened and almost knocked Joe over. He took a couple of papers out of it.

"Doesn't flat feet work?" I'd heard stories about that keeping guys out of World War II. Some famous athlete used it.

"How about high insteps?" Spalding asked. His were sky high.

"I'm not a medical expert, but we do have a list of potential defects," he handed us the papers. "A lot depends on how your doctor writes it up. He has to convince the board you're not qualified."

"Know any doctors?" Spalding asked.

"Yes," he smiled. "But you'll have to find your own. See all those students out there, I can't send them all to the same doctor. I will tell you one thing..." he paused for effect. "You'd better do it right away. If the paperwork hasn't gone through by graduation day it's 'Good Morning, Vietnam.' I know, I've been there."

Joe stood up, shook our hands again and began easing us out the door without us even realizing it. I guess he'd become quite adept at the procedure.

"That's it?" Spalding asked, putting his Winston out in Joe's ashtray.

"That's all I can do for you today," he tossed his head in the direction of the crowded hallway. "Make another appointment before you leave. Good luck," he flashed a peace sign.

As I turned to walk away something suddenly struck me. "What's it like over there?" I asked him.

"You don't want to know," he smiled wistfully. "Next."

"Sixteen," the redhead shouted.

"We're supposed to make another appointment," I told her.

"Why don't you call back tomorrow?"

"You too stressed out?"

"I need a break," she admitted. "It's going to be a long day."

"You know, when I said we're a team, I meant buddies, you know, roommates." I was embarrassed trying to explain myself.

"Hey, whatever turns you on," she smiled. "Some guys will try anything."

"Does that work?" I asked her.

"Oh yeah, if it's for real. But it's little rough explaining it to your parents."

"Hey, thanks for your help," I shook her hand, business-like.

"Next time make separate appointments."

"Sure, peace." I flashed her the universal sign. I'd been using it too much lately but thought the occasion called for it.

We walked away more confused than ever.

"The next time we see Joe maybe we should hold hands," Spalding jested.

"That's what I was thinking, but he's not the one we'd have to convince."

"You know any doctors?"

We'd walked up to the Student Union cafeteria. Spalding bought cokes and chips while I studied the paperwork.

"What'd you find?"

"Well, I had rheumatic fever as a kid and it's on here." I showed him one of the diseases I'd circled. "Don't you have an enlarged heart?"

"You say the sweetest things," he snickered in a feminine accent.

"Save it for your shrink. Your heart's on here."

"I'd rather go to Vietnam than let anyone think I'm gay," he said.

"That's what they're counting on."

"What about a doctor?"

"I had one in Cleveland but I haven't seen him in years."

"Is he against the war?"

"He's a doctor, he saves lives, he has to be."

"My, are we testy."

"Just remember, I've got you by forty numbers."

"So what?"

"There's probably a million guys between us. I'm a little more worried than you are."

"You're just panicking."

"Okay, I'm panicking. Let me panic, all right."

"Fine."

"Fine."

We walked back to Depeyster in silence, each of us worrying about our own futures. I called my doctor in Cleveland and made appointments for us for the following day.

Ten A.M. Wednesday morning, we were parking the Chrysler across from the Keith Building in downtown Cleveland.

"Drink enough coffee?" I asked Spalding as we dodged traffic on Euclid Avenue. The girls next store had recommended that Paul take a thermos of coffee for the trip. It would pump up his blood pressure, which was already above normal.

"My heart's jumping out of my shirt," he said. "I still think we should have tried acid."

"I called the redhead, she said it would show up in a blood sample."

The Keith Building was an impressive old office building, early twentieth century. As we waited in front of the ornate brass elevator doors I felt an impending sense of doom.

"I don't know about this," I told Spalding.

"What?"

"I'm starting to remember this doctor."

"Now, you remember?"

We stepped on the elevator and hit the tenth floor button.

"I think he's kind of old-fashioned, a bit of a stuffed shirt."

"Then why are we seeing him?"

"He's the only one I know."

The doors opened and we put on our best behavior as we entered Dr. Stoltz's office. We were practically dressed for church. Dress shirts with button down collars, pressed slacks instead of blue jeans, and penny loafers. They were the clothes we'd put away freshman year and only wore when visiting relatives.

"Matt Kubik," I told the receptionist/nurse at the desk.

"And this is my friend, Paul Spalding. We discussed him on the phone. He's from Florida."

"Of course, right on time," she looked at her appointment book and then her watch. "Please take a seat, the doctor will be with you in a minute."

The nurse had pure white hair that reminded me of my grandmother on my mother's side. But she wasn't that old, maybe in her early fifties. She sat very straight and wore the traditional white nurse's uniform: white dress, white hose, white shoes, even the paper cap sticking out of her hair.

There was only one other patient in the waiting room, an elderly gentleman holding a dark brown cane on his lap.

"How you young fellas doing?" he asked us right away, hungry for conversation.

"Fine."

"Ah, to be young again," he began reminiscing without any prompting. "I used to dance all night," he tapped his knee with his cane as if to say he couldn't anymore.

"Mr. Williams, the doctor will see you now," the nurse interrupted him.

The old gentleman pulled himself slowly out of his seat. I was tempted to offer my help but wasn't sure if it would bruise his pride.

"What happened?" I pointed at his knee as he hobbled past us.

"A sniper's bullet, World War I," he said proudly. "The War to end all Wars."

"Oh great," Spalding said after the doctor's door closed.

"That's a bad omen," I said.

The nurse overheard my comment and shot us a look of pure hatred.

"I don't think she likes us," I whispered to Spalding. I opened a pack of gum and gave a piece to him.

"Let's go back to Kent," he said.

"Please step over here Mr. Kubik," the nurse said. "I have

to check your vital signs before the doctor sees you."

"Call me Matt," I said as I sat next to her. She put two fingers on my wrist to check my pulse and I could feel the hostility passing between us.

"Relax," she ordered.

"I'm trying."

She wrote down my pulse and wrapped my arm with a blood pressure cuff.

"Did you take any artificial stimulants this morning?" she asked.

"No," I said bluntly and shot Spalding a look. "Why do you ask?"

"We have a lot of college students coming in here trying to avoid the draft."

"You don't seem to like college students."

"My son couldn't get in college. Now he's in Saigon."

"I'm sorry."

"Nothing to be sorry about. He's doing his duty to his country."

"Does he like it?"

"What do you think?"

She put the blood pressure cuff away. "Let's have a look at your Florida friend."

Before she could check out Spalding, Mr. Williams came out of the office and the nurse escorted me inside.

"Dr. Stoltz," I held out my hand in a friendly gesture. "Remember me."

The doctor was a tall, stately gentleman with gray hair, closely cropped and parted on one side. The smell of talcum powder emanated from him. If the nurse reminded me of my grandmother, this guy was my grandfather, and he was old enough to fit the bill. The tight starched collar on his white shirt rode up his neck as he spoke. His pinstriped dark suit was tailored to his exact size.

"Of course, I was just looking over your records. When was the last time I saw you?"

"Maybe freshman year," I said sitting across from his desk. If the draft counselor's desk was a magazine ad for a hippie handbook, Dr. Stoltz's would be featured in *Efficiency Today*. It's glass top was perfectly organized, down to each paper clip.

"How have you been doing? Have you been seeing another doctor?" he asked. "Please don't chew gum in here." He held up his wastebasket for me to deposit my gum in.

"No, I've just been healthy, I guess," and I immediately realized that I'd made a mistake.

"Then how can I help you?" He looked at me through wire-rimmed glasses.

"I've been told I might not be able to join the Army because of my rheumatic fever."

"Do you want to join the Army?"

"No, not really, but I might be drafted."

"Then you don't want to join the Army?"

"Not if it's bad for my health."

I tried to stop from laughing. I wasn't answering his questions very well. GI Joe should have rehearsed me.

"Ah, your rheumatic fever, we almost lost you, you know that?"

"You did?"

"Let's see if you have any lingering effects." He rose from his chair and motioned for me to sit on a cushioned table in the corner of his office. "Take off your shirt."

He began questioning me as he held a cold stethoscope to various parts of my upper body.

"What school do you go to?"

"Kent State."

"Didn't they have some trouble down there last year? Cough, please."

I tried coughing and answering at the same time but it didn't come out right. "A demonstration got out of hand, cahh, cahh, and a few students were arrested, cahh, cahh, but it was no big deal."

"Please, be quiet," he listened to my heart for a few seconds then continued. "Didn't they take over a building or something?"

He put down the stethoscope and brought out a little triangular rubber hammer.

"Actually, I think they were trapped in the building by the police." He began tapping my knee. It might have been my imagination, but it felt like he hit it a little harder than he had to. My leg jumped like a frog's in biology class. "I don't know, I wasn't there."

I began to feel like a criminal getting the third degree.

"Do you always wear your hair so long?" He began feeling around my lower abdomen. "Lay down."

My hair was short by Kent State standards. I guess things were different in Cleveland.

"I've been meaning to get a haircut," I lied. I was tempted to ask him if he always wore his so short, but I bit my tongue.

"Turn your head and cough, please." I did. "You can sit up now."

"Have you had any trouble with your heart? Any murmurs?"

This is where I should've lied but I was too angry. "I don't think so."

"You can send your friend in," he abruptly ended the conversation.

I walked out without saying another word.

"Be cool," I cautioned Spalding as I passed him.

I picked up a *Time Magazine* and read the latest war news. After a few minutes Dr. Stoltz called the nurse into his office. She came back out with a urine sample and some papers. She stored the urine and began typing at her desk. I felt like a murderer on death row waiting for a reprieve from the governor.

Spalding finally came out. We were both told to wait a few minutes. The time dragged by ever so slowly. More typing. More notes from Dr. Stoltz. More war news. High anxiety.

Eventually, the nurse called us to her desk. "Here's your letters for the draft board. Do you want us to send them or do you want to take them yourselves?"

"We'll do it," I practically ripped it out of her hand.

"That'll be ten dollars each," she said. "Since you're not regular patients the doctor would prefer that you pay before you leave."

I had to dig deep, ten bucks was more than I usually carried. Spalding once again came to my rescue.

"I'll pay you back when we get back to Kent?"

"You bet you will," he said as we waited for the elevators. His usual response was "forget it." I knew he was stressed.

Once inside the elevator we both ripped open our envelopes.

"You first," I said.

He read it aloud. "Mr. Paul Spalding suffers from unusually high blood pressure. However, I would suggest quarantining him before granting any exemption since his condition seems artificially induced."

It was my turn. "Despite Mr. Matt Kubik's youthful bout with rheumatic fever he seems to have fully recovered. I can find no reason why he should not be able to serve his country in any capacity."

"Shit," we said at exactly the same time. Spalding punched a dent in the elevator door just before it opened. We shoved our way through the business people waiting to enter. They looked at us like we were escaped criminals. At the first trash can we crumbled our letters and pitched them in.

"Any more bright ideas?" Spalding asked as we crossed the street, oblivious to passing cars. We were walking in a mental fog, like lost aliens on a strange planet.

"What's Canada like this time of year?"

"Too cold for comfort," the Floridian said, buttoning up his brown leather jacket and kicking a pile of dirty, gray snow.

Chapter Sixteen:
THE CHRISTMAS TREE

Our visit to Dr. Stoltz's office in Cleveland was the pits. It was probably the low point of our senior year. I mean, we had other difficulties, downright scary experiences, but nothing was as devastating as not having our medical exemption in place for graduation.

What we should have done is gone out and found a more sympathetic doctor right away. Instead we did what most twenty-year-old males do when faced with a dilemma. We forgot about it. We put it on the back burner so to speak. In our naive minds we expected the problem to go away by itself. Something would happen before we graduated and we'd skate. Somehow everything always worked itself out.

Besides, fall quarter was ending. It was time to study for our final exams and make plans for Christmas break.

On the female front, I was in a constant quandary. Elizabeth and I had become an item. I was madly in love with her but wouldn't you know it, she already made plans to spend winter quarter in Switzerland. It was part of some exchange program.

Here it was senior year, the time you're supposed to make plans for life after graduation and the one girl I wouldn't mind settling down with was going away for three months. That was almost a lifetime to a hormone-crazed college senior.

Then there was my next door neighbor Michelle. I loved

her once and could easily love her again. But living right next door was both a convenience and a curse. I always felt funny bringing Elizabeth over. And I couldn't stand seeing Michelle with her Ohio State boyfriend.

Yet it was very pleasant walking to class with her. She hung around us guys like a kid sister, bringing over food, helping us clean up, joking around. It made me really regret ever breaking up with her.

What was a fella to do? I treated it just like the Vietnam War. I tried not to think about it. Something would happen to straighten out the mess. Something always did.

The week before finals all of us were on edge. The pressure of classes, the cold weather, the snow, being cooped up inside, it all combined to make us a bunch of old crabs.

Things came to a head one night after dinner right before finals weekend. It was one of those rare nights where Mary Lou was busy and the Murph was hanging around.

"Look at this place," Early started complaining as he picked up the dirty pie tins we'd left on the dining room table. We had slipped back into our old habits and "mom" was right there to nag. "We don't have any Christmas decorations, no Christmas tree, not even a Christmas album. We're living like a bunch of heathens."

"Right on," Spalding said. "Let's buy an album." It was one of his favorite hobbies.

"An album, you want an album?" Early was almost shouting. "I was *kidding* about the album."

"Then what are you trying to say?"

"We need some Christmas spirit. Decorations, candles, presents under a tree. Have you been over to the girls' lately?"

"That's it, he wants to be like the girls," I said.

"How about some mistletoe?" the Murph teased. He put some dirty pots and pans in Early's dish water without rinsing them first. That really made him mad.

"Then we invite the girls over," Spalding said.

"That'd get me in the Christmas spirit."

"Girls. That's all you guys think about, babes and drugs," Early fumed. He was washing the dishes with great vigor. I dried while Spalding and the Murph cleaned up the kitchen and dining room.

"You're right," the Murph lectured Early. "With the right drugs we wouldn't need any decorations." We all laughed, including Early.

"I'd like a tree," Spalding admitted. "Your trees are different than the ones we have in Florida."

"You know how much a tree costs?" I asked.

"Plenty," the Murph answered for me. As college students it was against our unwritten code to spend money on anything that dipped into our beer fund, even a Christmas tree.

"We could take a ride in the country," Early was serious. He felt that at least the conversation was going in the right direction.

"Lots of free trees out there," I said.

"Let's do it," Spalding made the decision communal.

He took the car keys off the piano. We didn't finish our cleanup chores and Early didn't crab. What a shock.

In December in Ohio it gets dark early. We ventured out into a cold, crisp winter evening. Spalding drove the Chrysler through the back roads south of Kent. One of the pleasures of living in Kent was its proximity to rural America. Five minutes on the road and we were on a different planet. No cars, no streetlights, no salt trucks.

The sky was clear, the stars shone brightly and a full moon lit up the countryside. The glistening white landscape was right out of a Currier and Ives print.

I rode shotgun. The Murph and Early sat in back. We took a certain pleasure in helping Spalding, the Florida surfer, enjoy his last winter up north. He had opened his Lauderdale home to us the previous spring break and it gave us a certain satisfaction to repay his Southern hospitality. It was also refreshing to find someone who relished the cold northern climate most of us natives cursed.

It wasn't long before a likely target presented itself. About an acre of pine trees in various stages of growth appeared on the horizon. The owner was obviously growing them for sale. A modern ranch home sat on a little hill next to the trees, on top of a long driveway. There were no lights on.

"That's our spot," the Murph said. "He won't miss one tree."

Spalding slowly cruised by, surveyed the area, then did a u-turn at the next intersection. As we approached the trees, he cut the engine, turned off the lights and glided up to the trees like he was landing a plane. We snuck out of the car like we were Green Berets raiding a Viet Cong village.

"Got the ax?" I asked Early. He had secured a small ax from the basement of Depeyster.

"Yeah," he whispered. "Which tree do you want?" We all kind of looked at Spalding to make the call.

"This one looks good," he picked one out nearby, about four feet high with a nice symmetrical shape.

"All right," Early said. He kneeled down in the snow, pushed the lower branches away and took a mighty swing. The noise of the hard steel hitting the soft wood ricocheted like a gunshot across the still wilderness.

We all hit the snow in unison as if we were under attack.

"Keep it down," I whispered to Early with great intensity, trying to be forceful and quiet at the same time.

"Here, you try it," he handed me the ax. "Bitch, bitch, bitch."

I took a few chops but couldn't really see what I was doing. It was like trying to cut a steak blindfolded. And with each swing we became increasingly nervous. Except for the devil-may-care Murphster. He thought we were hilarious.

When a light came on in the owner's house, Early began to panic. "Oh shit, someone's coming," he said.

"He's probably got a shotgun," the Murph joked.

"How we doing?" Spalding asked.

"I can't see squat."

Spalding took out his lighter and we all stuck our noses under the tree like hound dogs following a scent. The ax marks were pitiful. No two hit the same location.

"This isn't working," I said.

"We should have brought a flashlight," Early said.

We all looked around nervously. "Let's get out of here," Spalding finally said as a figure appeared at the front door.

We stomped back to the car so fast my head hurt. But as we started to leave the Murph said, "Hold on. Wait for Early."

He'd taken the ax and chopped a small tree the size of an Azalea bush with one firm stroke. Carrying it like a potted plant he threw it in the back seat as Spalding was already moving.

Spalding handled the big Chrysler like a Ferrari, swerving and sliding around every back road turn like a moonshiner with the Feds on his tail. We leaned into the curves, bounced over chuckholes and laughed all the way back.

We didn't slow down until we were safely within Kent's city limits. But just as we breathed a collective sigh of relief, less than a half mile from our Depeyster home, Spalding suddenly pulled over.

"What's wrong?" I asked from the co-pilot's seat.

"We got trouble," he said, jerking his thumb toward the back windshield.

We turned around in unison. Red and white flashing lights filled our vision. A police car was pulling us over.

"Anybody holding?" Early asked.

No one said a word. It was understood that nobody had any illegal drugs on them.

"Just a hot Christmas tree," the Murph broke the tension.

"Not funny," Spalding said.

He stepped out of the car to intercept the cop before he saw the tree in the back seat. The Murph opened the window on his side to eavesdrop on their conversation. We could only catch bits and pieces of information.

"Your taillight's out, do you know that, son?" The uniformed cop was huge.

Spalding was big himself, large enough to play linebacker for the Kent football team, but this guy dwarfed him. He could have picked all four of us up in a giant bear hug.

"No, sir, sorry sir," Spalding knew the routine. "I'll get it fixed."

"That's probable cause," Murph the poly sci major provided us with a color commentary. "It gives him the right to interrogate us."

"Could I see your driver's license?"

"Sure," Spalding opened his wallet.

"He wants to know if he's an outside agitator," the Murph said.

"Florida, huh? Maybe you better come with me."

"Bingo," the Murph smiled smugly.

The officer escorted Spalding into the back of his cruiser, into the land of no door handles.

"Not to worry, Spalding's a pro at this," I said.

"Yeah, he hasn't been in the slammer yet this quarter," Early said.

It was a fact. Paul Spalding, the world's nicest guy, a genuine laid-back Florida surfer, somehow managed to end up in the slammer every quarter since he came up north. If the Kent jail had an Aunt Bea she'd have known him on a first name basis by now.

Nothing serious, mind you. He just had a knack for being in the wrong place at the wrong time. If he took a leak behind a bush walking back from downtown after happy hour, they'd nab him for "public urination."

If he walked out of a bar with half a bottle of beer to watch a fight between a couple coeds, the cops were waiting to slap him with "open container."

He'd already met half of Kent's police department. They should've known by now that he wasn't an "outside agitator," just your average drunken college student.

The longer we waited the more concerned we became. He

looked scared sitting in the cruiser's back seat, behind the plastic divider. What if they'd tied him to our recent drug bust? What if his past records had finally totaled some magic number that pushed him into the realm of felonies? What if the tree farmer had figured we were Kent students, called ahead and the cops put out an APB for a flower-covered Chrysler?

The imagination runs wild when your future lies in the hands of a complete stranger.

Finally, the officer opened the back of the police car and let Spalding out. He returned to us without a police escort. We took that to be a positive signal. But the squad car remained, lights flashing. Were we all under arrest?

"Let's go guys," Spalding said. He stuck the car keys back into their slot in the steering column. "We've got to walk home."

"What gives?" the Murph asked. We opened all three doors simultaneously.

"Can we take the tree?" Early asked.

"Go ahead," Spalding said. "They don't want the tree, just the car."

"The car?"

"It's hot. We've been driving around in a stolen car."

"No shit," Early said. He was kind of turned on by the danger of it all.

"No way," the Murph said. We'd bought the car from his brother.

"He wanted to see some registration," Spalding explained as we began walking. Early was dragging the tree in tow. "I told him we didn't have any. Do we?"

"I think so, back at Depeyster," the Murph said.

"Well, he ran a check on it and it's hot," Spalding looked straight at the Murph.

"Who'd want to steal that hunk of junk?" Early asked.

"Probably one of my brother's friends," the Murph laughed. He was changing his tune in the face of mounting evidence.

"No wonder we got it so cheap," I said. "Why didn't they arrest you?"

"He let me go with just a ticket," Spalding pulled it out of his wallet. "Remember the time we were drinking outside the Loft, last spring?"

"We were just talking about that," Early said.

"He's the same cop."

"I thought he looked familiar."

"How could you forget him?"

"He remembered me being from Florida. I told him we bought it for cheap transportation. He let me go on a personal bond, said I'd have to tell it to the judge."

"That's what happens when you steal a Christmas tree," Early moralized.

"It was your idea, dickhead," Spalding shot back.

"I never thought you'd do it."

"We did it for you," I said.

"Don't do me any more favors."

We finished our walk in silence. Our Christmas spirit had evaporated. It was as if the Grinch had joined us on our walk home. By the time we reached Depeyster we were in a foul mood.

Spalding held the front door open so Early could carry in the tree. He almost tripped over Harold, who was running out to greet us.

"Goddam dog," he said. Early was definitely a cat lover. "Where should we put it?"

It was a pitiful biological specimen. It was only about two feet high, skinny and with a couple of broken branches. The kind of tree only Charlie Brown could love.

"We got to put it on a table," the Murph pulled the lamp off one of the end tables and put it by the front window. "You can see it from the outside."

"That's what I'm afraid of," Spalding said.

"Use these to hold it up," I took a couple of nearby textbooks and used them like bookends to steady the base. "I'm selling them back next quarter anyway."

After it was finally situated in its resting-place we all sat down to stare at it.

For what seemed like an eternity no one said a word. We watched as Spanky jumped on the table to smell its pine scent.

"Is that a tree or a branch?" I finally asked.

We all started laughing.

"All it needs is some decorations."

"Like maybe a hundred dollar bill."

"Or a bag of Colombian."

It became a game of one-upmanship, and with each comment our laughter increased accordingly. It was probably due to relief after another brush with the law but by the time we finished tears of laughter were falling from our eyes.

"What we need is a party, a tree decoration party," the Murph said.

"Invite the girls next door," Early suggested.

"Chris, Elizabeth and Mary Lou," Spalding said.

"Your aerospace buddies," I suggested.

"The Murph's freaky friends," Early laughed

"Artie," I said and everyone stopped laughing. "Hey, it's Christmas."

"Early's rock and roll band," the Murph laughed and we went right back at it.

"The Golden Flashes football team."

"Those losers. I'd rather have the marching band."

"Yeah, at least they're coed."

"Yeah, more babes.

"Lots of babes."

"Two girls for every guy."

"Let's do it."

"Do it."

"Do it."

"Agreed."

Chapter Seventeen:
THE CHRISTMAS PARTY

Our Christmas tree sat bare butt naked for about a week waiting for its decoration party. We planned it for the last night of finals week so we could stage a real celebration. Those fortunate students who finished their finals a bit early stuck around just for the occasion.

As a special holiday treat we decided to put our dining room bathtub to an alternative use. We cleaned it out and bought a wild combination of fruit juices and alcoholic beverages. Early took over as the master mixer, using a large wooden spoon to add various ingredients to taste.

By the time he threw in a few bags of ice we had an unusual concoction, something that the partygoers would remember for quite a long time. Since our bust we kind of shied away from doing drugs in front of strangers, even our closest friends. You never knew who would show up to a Kent party.

I had a more pressing concern than some secret recipe for bathtub gin. This was the night that Elizabeth was destined to meet Michelle. Even though Michelle was dating her Ohio State Buckeye, I felt weird about the whole thing. I guess it meant I still had some feelings for Michelle.

I really didn't know what to make of the situation, so I figured I'd let the chips fall where they may. Que, sera, sera, that sort of thing.

141

Students began arriving late in the afternoon, as soon as their finals were over. And each one brought a unique tree decoration.

The girls next door made colorful paper decorations for the classical touch. They also surprised us with a baked ham and a couple of loaves of bread. We'd only provided the usual party snacks, chips and nuts, being more concerned with the liquid refreshment.

The other students weren't quite as traditional. Our sacrilegious guests loaded the branches with rolling papers, condoms, roach clips, even Playboy centerfolds. I guess it was a sign of the times. By nightfall the little tree was drooping from the weight of its ornaments.

By evening Depeyster was wall-to-wall in students blowing off three months of tension. The conversations ranged from finals to winter break to the Vietnam War to Spalding's latest brush with the law.

He held court while sharing the piano bench with Early. Early tickled the ivories as Spalding faced the crowd.

Chris was seated next to Spalding, listening for the umpteenth time how we were pulled over during the Great Christmas Tree Heist.

Three of his aerospace buddies were sitting around the dining room table picking at the ham and making strange paper airplanes. The aerospace crowd sported shorter hair and neater clothes than the rest of the visitors. Spalding was the only one of them who looked the least bit gruffy. The rest seemed poised for their Future Pilots of America picture. They discussed aerodynamics, hurling occasional shots at their host, Paul Spalding. It was all in great fun. He seemed to be enjoying his notoriety as a wanted criminal. Or maybe it was the bathtub booze he drank out of his LOVE cup.

"Hey Spalding, tell the judge you'll give him a ride in a Cessna if he goes easy on you," Ron, a thin, blue-eyed pilot suggested, twisting his napkin into strange contortions.

"Just make sure the plane's not hot," laughed Tom, our gay friend from the draft counselor's office.

Michelle and her friends were standing around the bathtub, sipping out of plastic cups.

"What's going to happen if you're found guilty?" Renee asked. She was dressed in a short, striped skirt and tight sweater. We were used to seeing her in blue jeans and flannel shirts. None of us realized she had such a dynamite body beneath the baggy exterior.

Chris answered the question for Spalding. "The prosecutor told him he'd probably catch a fine, anywhere from fifty to two hundred dollars, depending on the mood of the judge."

"What if you don't come up with the money?" Michelle asked.

"Then I'll spend Christmas in the slammer," Spalding answered flippantly. "You guys'll visit me, won't you?"

"I'll bring you a doggie bag," Chris patted his thigh. He was drawing a bit too much attention for her tastes.

"With a file in it?"

"If you need some money to make bail, let me know," Tom offered.

"We'll take up a collection," Ron said.

"Thanks, but we're giving blood tomorrow morning," Spalding explained.

"And on Sunday, we have a job cutting wood for the Murph's boss," I added.

"We figure we should raise about a hundred bucks."

"Are you sure that's enough?" George, the third aerospace major asked. They were the first words he'd spoken all night. He seemed like a typical nerd, complete with pen and pencil set in his shirt pocket and dark-rimmed glasses. However, he had muscular forearms sticking out from under his short-sleeve shirt. He reminded me of Popeye.

"If not it'll be Spam for Christmas dinner." Spalding's false bravado was growing thin. Tom threw a paper airplane at him.

Spalding caught it and threw it back. It flew over Tom's head and landed in the bathtub gin.

A nearby freak, probably one of the Murph's friends, picked it out of the punch and sucked it dry like a Popsicle. "Good shit," he smiled. "Where's the Murph?"

"Yeah, where is he?" Early turned around. He'd been playing background music during Spalding's recital.

"He has to work late," I said.

"Where's Elizabeth?" he asked me.

"She'll be late, too," I gulped. Michelle was standing right next to me. I knew she heard about Liz through the grapevine but we'd never discussed her. I shot Early a glance that said "thanks for nothing." He caught my drift.

"How about putting on an album?" he asked. "I need a break."

"I'll do it," George got up from the table. "Where's the stereo."

I was about to show him when I heard the front door open and felt a blast of cold air.

The Murph walked into the dining room, his dark blue Navy Pea coat covered with snow. The freak by the bathtub gave him a hippie handshake.

"Hey guys," he said. "I got something for you, Spalding."

The Murph pulled "The Beach Boys Christmas Album" out from under his coat. "Merry Christmas, buddy. I couldn't pass it up."

"Something to listen to behind bars," he laughed. A big smile broke over his face.

"Here you go, George," Spalding handed him the album.

"The Beach Boys?" the Murph's freaky buddy said in contempt. "They're bubble gum. What're you guys, in high school?"

It was true the psychedelic generation had left the Beach Boys behind, but they still had a loyal following, especially among surfers like Spalding.

"Watch your mouth, boy," Spalding stood up, face to face with the freak, letting his Southern accent roam.

"Don't hassle me, man," the freak pushed Spalding.

Spalding gave him a shove and he ended up in the bathtub, purple punch splashing in every direction.

For a moment it was mass confusion as the hippie splashed around like a goldfish. Tom and Ron pulled him out.

"Wow, what a temper, no wonder you're going to jail," Chris laughed. She was a little turned on by the show of force, pulling him back down onto the piano bench.

"Peace, brother," the hippie flashed him a peace sign as he got out of the tub.

"Come on upstairs, I'll get you some dry clothes," the Murph offered.

"Sorry," he apologized to everyone.

It was definitely uncool for a member of the laid back hippie generation to get angry over anything except the Vietnam War or Civil Rights. But the crowd loved it.

The party continued on track and eventually the freak came downstairs and shared a few cups with Spalding. I even heard rumors that he'd lost a couple hits of acid during his dunk. That made the punch all the more desirable. Early just added a few more bottles of his secret ingredients and everyone drank as if nothing had happened.

Me, I entirely missed the acid-flavored punch. During the post-fight cleanup I wandered into the front room, watching the Philco that was on with the sound turned off. I was starting to worry about Elizabeth.

But just as I'd given up hope of seeing her, she appeared in the doorway as an apparition. Large snowflakes fell around her outline, her long dark hair covered with a fur hat like a Russian noblewoman out of *Dr. Zhivago*.

In the confusion I was the only one who noticed her.

"Sorry, I'm late. A lot of last minute plans for the trip."

"I can imagine."

"I wish you were going with me," she kissed me full on the lips.

"Can I take your coat?" I offered to hang her long maroon

coat on the coat tree. It hung down to her fur-trimmed knee-high black leather boots.

"I really didn't have time to put anything on," she whispered playfully in my ear. With a discreet motion she opened a button about halfway down, revealing her bare navel. My heart about jumped into my throat. "After tomorrow we won't see each other for a whole quarter. Would you mind terribly if we skipped the party?"

"I'll get my coat," I said as fast as my tongue could move, just about knocking over the tree rack.

Putting on my coat was a signal to Harold that I was taking him for a walk so he began jumping on me, making a scene I wanted to avoid. "Down boy," I told him.

"Where you going?" Early asked me out of nowhere. "Merry Christmas, Liz."

"Merry Christmas to you," Liz said.

"It's an emergency, we got to go," I said to Early.

"Aren't you going to introduce me to your friend?" Michelle said. She was following Early into the living room. It seemed like everyone was coming into the room.

"Oh yeah, Liz, this is Michelle, she lives next door. Michelle, Liz."

"Pleased to meet you," they said in unison.

My feet started moving but there was nowhere to go.

"Elizabeth, come on in, have some ham," the Murph said. "Can I take your coat." He was pulling her by the elbow into the living room.

"No, we've got to go. How's Mary Lou?"

"Fine, she'll be here later."

"Elizabeth," Spalding said and planted a kiss right on her lips. "Mistletoe," he pointed toward the ceiling of the arch between rooms.

It was the first I'd noticed it. The girls next door must have brought it. I was about to have a nervous breakdown.

"We've got to go," she explained. "I've got to finish packing."

"I've got to go help her," I stumbled over my words. I tried not to look at Michelle but I noticed her examining Liz's boots.

"Bring us back something from Switzerland," Early asked.

"Yeah, some cheese."

"Or some chocolate."

"How about a watch?" she smiled.

"You're going to Switzerland?" Michelle asked her.

"Yes, I'm leaving in the morning."

"We'll have to talk when you come back."

"I'd love to."

"I live right next door."

I couldn't believe what was happening before my eyes. Liz and Michelle were hitting it off. The next thing I'd know they'd be best friends, comparing notes, and I'd be out in the cold.

"We really have to go," I said, escorting her out to her car.

"Chou," Liz waved goodbye.

"Merry Christmas," they all said as they crowded around the doorway.

And a Merry Christmas it was.

Chapter Eighteen:
DAY IN COURT

Spalding's court date forced us to adjust our plans for winter break. The last couple of years we'd developed a system. Putting the family vehicle to its maximum use, we'd drop the Murph off first since he lived on Cleveland's eastern fringe, Eastlake. Then Early and I would drop Spalding off at the airport on Cleveland's west side, which was by our homes. One of us would keep the car and maybe even go out together once or twice over break.

When school began again, we did the same route only in reverse. Like the rest of our systems it only ran smoothly when there were no glitches. Having our car impounded was a major glitch. My father was going to have to pick us up.

Spalding's court appearance was another major glitch. Luckily, it was scheduled for the Monday after finals week. It would only hold up our break plans for one weekend.

Kent's campus emptied out pretty fast once exams were over. There was a large commuter population that went home every night anyway. Break time was practically deserted and it was peaceful to hang around. The campus took on a very calm atmosphere without the students, kind of like those end-of-the-world movies where all the buildings in a big city are empty.

It took us most of the weekend to recuperate from the tree decoration party. The girls next door went home, Elizabeth was already in Switzerland and Chris was back in Canton. Only the Murph had Mary Lou to visit since she was "a townie."

Despite "mom" Early's nagging we did little to clean up the house. From the looks of us maybe there was some acid in the homemade punch. The bathtub had a permanent purple ring around it.

We put off domestic chores until we returned from break with the usual burst of energy that a new quarter sparked. The house smelled like the inside of a bottle of Robin Hood but we couldn't care less. We had to raise funds for Spalding's bail.

Saturday afternoon we gave blood at the local Red Cross Plasma Center for ten dollars a pint. I felt sorry for whoever received those red corpuscles. They probably got an instant high. I just hoped they could handle it.

That really knocked us out for Saturday. Sunday we spent the day cutting wood for the owner of Captain Brady's. Besides sobering us up, it earned us another twenty dollars apiece.

By Monday morning we'd raised a grand total of $120. Any more than that and Spalding was on his own. Hasta la vista, amigo. Ah, see you soon. Feliz Navidad behind bars.

The Murph was our ride to the courthouse in Ravenna and he was running late. We thought he was borrowing Mary Lou's father's car. Instead he pulled in Depeyster's driveway with a black '57 Chevy.

The three of us piled out the front door, crowding onto the little front porch, dressed in our Sunday best. The Murph stepped out of the driver's side, smiling ear to ear like the Cheshire Cat.

"No, don't tell me," Spalding held out his hands in mock terror. "I don't want to know."

"You want to drive?" The Murph flipped him the keys.

"Hell no," he handed them to me. I gave them to Early and he tossed them back to the Murph.

"Is it ours?"

"Does it have a registration?"

The Murph just nodded. He pulled a piece of paper from his coat pocket and handed it to Spalding.

"How much?" he asked, inspecting the document.

"Fifty bucks," the Murph beamed.

"That's twice as much as the Chrysler."

"Inflation, buddy."

"That's twelve-fifty each."

"Who do we owe?"

"My brother," the Murph said sheepishly.

"No, no way," Spalding said. He walked back into the house. "I'm calling a cab."

"It's too late," Early followed him inside.

"I'll pay his share," I said. "He's always covering for me."

Early coaxed Spalding back outside, convincing him it was better to be on time for court. He could argue about the car later.

"I'll take the ride but I won't pay for the car," Spalding came back out disgruntled and hopped in the back seat.

"Fine," the Murph said. "Let's roll."

As we rumbled down Route 59 toward Ravenna, we witnessed every type of modern American architecture imaginable. It was a real hodge-podge. Our mood was as somber as the weather until the Murph decided to lighten things up.

"Anyone for a buzz?" he asked, pulling a joint from his shirt pocket.

"What are you crazy?" Spalding fumed.

"Throw that thing out the window," Early screamed.

"Just kidding," the Murph laughed, hiding it under the front floor mat. "You wouldn't want me to litter, would you?"

The rest of the trip we just listened to country music on the AM radio but the Murph really had our adrenaline flowing.

Inside the Portage County Courthouse a strange collection of minor criminals congregated. Hippies, townies, cops, bikers, lawyers, prosecutors and students whispered in little circles. They looked like leftovers from the Hot Dog Inn.

There were no felony cases on trial, just misdemeanors and traffic violations. We let the Murph, our experienced amateur lawyer, show us the way.

Despite the crowd we managed to snare a few seats in the last pew. It reminded me of church. Maybe because everyone was dressed in their best clothes. The gorgeous blonde sitting in front of us was a case in point.

I recognized her from campus. She was an art major. I often noticed her and her easel at various campus locations. She always wore a super tight, faded pair of bell-bottoms and a bare midriff top, her long blond hair blowing in the breeze. If you saw her once you never forgot her. I'm sure the other guys recognized her too.

In the courtroom, however, she wore a green cashmere dress buttoned to her neck, nylons, high heels and white gloves. Her hair was piled in a bun on top of her head so we could admire her long, curved neck. And she wore enough make-up and perfume for me to figure she committed a crime of the highest order.

Whatever she had done I was certain the judge was going to go easy on her.

"All rise," the bailiff announced, as the judge entered the courtroom. "Everyone please be seated."

The room was ornate with classical woodwork. It looked like the kind they used for movies in the 1930s. So was Judge Verder. Gray-haired, slight in stature, he could barely hold up the weight of his black robe. It caused his shoulders to droop.

Judge Verder dispensed justice with great dispatch. He pounded his gavel, asked the defendant to step forward, read the charges against him or her and asked how they pleaded.

Then he'd make an instant decision: "Guilty, not guilty, or bring the case back later." He seemed to be in a hurry to do his Christmas shopping, like the judge in Santa Claus' trial in the movie *Miracle on 34th Street*.

I glanced over at Spalding. He was wringing his hands but

he looked completely straight in his dark blue blazer, dress shirt, tie, pressed slacks and penny loafers.

His hair was neatly combed, parted on the side and slicked down with Vitalis. I could tell he needed a Winston.

After fifteen minutes of fidgeting, I couldn't stand it any longer. I tapped the blonde on her shoulder. "Don't you go to Kent?" I whispered.

"Yes," she turned slightly and spoke softly.

My three compadres were watching my every move.

"What're you in for?"

"Speeding. And you?"

She turned her head a little more and we could see her deep blue eyes.

"My friend drives stolen cars," I nodded toward Spalding.

"Ooooh."

Spalding gave a grim smile.

"Know anything about this judge?"

"I hear he's a real bastard," she said out of the side of her mouth but everyone in the courtroom could hear her.

"Can we have silence in the courtroom?" the bailiff shouted, peering over the crowd, looking for the perpetrator. We all sat up straight.

"Thanks," Spalding mouthed the words without speaking them in my direction.

"The case of Portage County versus Paul Spalding," the bailiff announced next. "Operating a stolen vehicle."

Spalding stood up and passed us as if we were in church and he was going to Communion and we weren't.

"Break a leg," the Murph said.

"How do you plead?" Judge Verder asked him in a stern voice. Spalding was standing before him with his hands cupped behind his back like he was at parade rest in the Army.

"No contest, sir," Spalding answered like a buck private.

The Murph had told him this was his best plea. "No contest" neither admitted guilt nor presumed innocence. He was basically throwing himself on the mercy of the court.

"Then I'm forced to find you guilty as charged." The judge pounded the gavel and we gulped in unison. "Do you have anything to say in your defense?"

The Murph said the judge might give him a minute to make his case and they'd prepared a little speech but Spalding became tongue-tied.

"I, uh, well, we, uh, bought this car off a friend of a friend, your honor, and, well, you know, we never thought it was stolen."

"That assumption is going to cost you $100 plus court costs. Next time be a little more careful who you deal with."

"Yes sir, your honor. Thank you sir." The bailiff led him away from the bench.

"You pay at the cashier's window on the way out," the bailiff explained. "I think he liked you."

"He did?" Spalding was surprised.

"Sure, stolen op usually costs a couple hundred."

"Geez, how much are court costs?"

"Seventeen dollars. Good luck," the bailiff said as he opened a side door for us to go pay the fine. "I've got a kid at Kent myself."

"Thanks." Spalding was smiling wide enough to swallow a shoe.

Out in the hallway we crowded around him, slapping him on the back as if he'd just been spared the electric chair. "Let's get out of here," he said.

"Maybe we should stay to see how the blonde makes out?" Early gave me a shot.

"Yeah, Liz probably hasn't even landed yet and you're already hitting on other women," the Murph said.

"I was just being friendly."

"Yeah, right."

"Besides, Liz and I have an agreement," I argued.

"Like what? You can date other people?"

"No, you know, we just didn't make any promises."

"Then you won't care if some Swiss yodeler chases her around the Alps."

"Of course, but she's going to be gone for three months."

By this time Spalding finished paying his fine. "We got three bucks left."

"That's a tank of gas."

"Road trip."

"Yeah, to Cleveland, I've got a plane to catch."

"We could drive you to Florida."

"Come on down. But I'll meet you. I'm flying."

"How about if we stop at the Robin Hood for one?"

Spalding looked at his aviator watch. "Just one. Where's the keys?"

The Murph looked at him for a second and handed him the keys. "Way to go, big guy."

Chapter Nineteen:
AN ETHNIC HOLIDAY

Winter break was always strange and since this was my last one it was probably the strangest of all. Riding back to Cleveland from Kent was like taking the Yellow Brick Road in reverse. I was leaving Oz for Kansas.

I enjoyed seeing my family but the generation gap was growing wider by the month. We were living in two totally separate cultures, not destined to blend together for another decade.

Cleveland was too straight, too middle class, too un-hip. Besides, my sex life always nose-dived the moment I left Kent's border.

The highlight of Christmas with my siblings was our big family dinner at my grandmother's house. She lived in an old ethnic enclave on the city's near west side, in the bottom half of a double home. In a way it reminded me of Depeyster.

There were only two bedrooms, a small living room, a large dining room and a large kitchen, yet she managed to raise eight successful children in the cramped quarters. It was typical of her generation.

The upstairs, which was an exact replica of downstairs, was always rented out for additional income. There were some inconveniences in sharing the same house with strangers, but it helped pay the mortgage during the Depression and supplemented Grandma's social security in her old age.

Those Depression children were now my aunts and uncles. Their sons and daughters were my cousins. I was the firstborn of my generation so I had to be the pioneer of any new fads like Beatles music or bell-bottomed jeans. I took the brunt of the parental attack to pave the way for the others to follow.

I guess I wasn't setting a very good example for the younger set. At least that's the drift I picked up over Christmas dinner. I hadn't cut my hair in a couple of months and it was beginning to look a little scraggly. I already decided I was going to grow a beard winter quarter but was too chicken to start it over break. Why ask for abuse?

The dinner conversation, like that in most American homes that Christmas, turned to the Vietnam War. My uncles had all served in World War II.

They were the stand up guys, the veterans, and I admired them for their efforts in the Big One. I was the only representative of the hippie generation: the college kids, the draft dodgers, the protesters, the bums.

"What are these college kids trying to prove anyway?" Uncle Joe asked, tearing some turkey off a thighbone. He wasn't talking to anyone in particular, just making conversation. "Don't they have any respect for the flag?"

"They're all on drugs," Uncle Ed said. He was the family instigator. I knew he was trying to get a reaction from me by the way he slid his glasses down his overripe nose, looking over them like the intellectual he tried to be. I kept stuffing food into my mouth so I wouldn't put my foot in it. As long as they were talking about "them" and "those" and not *moi*, I tried not to take it personally.

"The kids are all right," Aunt Stephie, Uncle Ed's wife said. "Remember what you were like when you were young?"

"I was in a foxhole in France when I was their age," Uncle Ed said. He almost said "his age" but stopped himself.

"Only because you were drafted," Stephie came and stood behind him. "Didn't you do crazy things when you were in college, like swallowing goldfish and stuffing telephone booths?"

"I was twenty-three and married when I was in college," he muttered with a mouth-full of mashed potatoes. A few of them splattered my way. "And I never used the flag to patch my pants."

That was an opening lob. A signal to let the battle begin. I was waiting for the right moment to fire my initial salvo.

Our conversation was only one of many in an extremely noisy household. Kids of all ages were being chased around by their mothers, some eating in the kitchen, others in the dining room. Only myself and Ed's daughter Barbara, a high school senior, were considered mature enough to share the main table with the adults.

"They don't like the flag because we're fighting a stupid war to defend it," I suddenly blurted out. Uncle Ed's eyebrows raised; this is what he'd been waiting for.

Barbara looked up from her plate and gave me a little smile of encouragement. She was probably dating a longhaired acid-head who she was afraid to introduce to her parents.

"Oh, let's not get into that again," Olga, Joe and Ed's sister, said. She always played the role of peacekeeper.

"You stay out of it, Olga," Joe said. "It's a damn shame how these college kids waste our tax money putting down the very government that's giving them a free ride."

I was about to explain how I was paying my own expenses when Olga cut me off.

"Look who's talking. You went on the GI Bill."

"After I did my four years in the service," Joe explained.

"All you did was hunt and fish in Alaska," my father said. Everyone at the table laughed. They were well aware of Joe's tough stint in the Army.

"Yeah, well you didn't see any Ruskies coming across the Bering Straight, did you?" Everyone laughed again.

The mood had lightened at the dinner table so I bit my tongue. No matter what I said it would fall on deaf ears.

I was glad my father had came to my defense. Of all the relatives he had seen the most battles. Like most veterans, the ones who experienced the worst horrors seemed to speak the least about them. It was the way of their generation.

My grandparents had come to America from Eastern Europe at the turn of the century and appreciated the great liberty we took for granted. All their sons had gone off to war to protect their adopted homeland from the dreaded Adolph Hitler.

These veterans could not differentiate between World War II and the Vietnam War. When your country called it was your duty to serve it. No questions asked. Otherwise you were a chickenshit.

The only one who sympathized with me was my grandmother. Her deceased husband, my grandfather, was the family's original draft dodger.

He came to America to escape the Russian Czar's call to arms in the First World War. They had a much cruder military draft in those days. The Army came to the village one day and took all the young men with them, no ifs, ands, or buts.

He had served once in the Russo-Turkish War and was in no mood for a repeat performance. So he split for the good old U.S.A. and took his wife with him.

He was my trump card, my ace in the hole, but I hated to play it. I felt the arguments against the Vietnam War should stand on their own merits.

Rather than re-open the argument I took my plate into the kitchen. My grandmother was at her usual station, hunched over the kitchen sink, washing dishes.

She was old and wrinkled, a little wisp of a thing, but she grabbed my face with her large farm hands and pulled it down so she could give me a kiss, smack on the lips.

"So's what could youse do?' she asked, wrinkling up her nose with a little smile. Despite the noisy atmosphere she was well aware of the conversation in the dining room.

Nothing went on in her house without her knowing about it.

She had a unique accent that if you weren't familiar with it would be hard to understand. I had to laugh at her comment.

What should I do? I wondered.

"How you doing, Grandma?" I asked her, taking a towel to help her dry the dishes.

"Fine, fine," she said. She had me alone for a moment and it gave her time to quiz me on her favorite subjects, love, marriage and babies. She left the war news to the men.

"So Matthew Michael, do you have a girl friend down there at college?"

"Yeah, I guess, Grandma."

"Then why don't you bring her to see me? I'm not always here, you know."

"You're not going anywhere." I put my arm around her like a fragile china doll. "I think she'd like to meet you, maybe for Easter."

"Let me know when you bring her. I'll bake some Boolechki."

"What about me? I love your poppyseed rolls."

"Oh, I bake you some too," she laughed. She knew I was joking. "You growing into a man, Matthew. Maybe time to marry, make babies."

"Maybe, Grandma, maybe."

I was admitting more to her than I was to myself.

Winter Quarter

"When the truth is found to be lies.
And all the joy within you dies.
Don't you want somebody to love?
Don't you need somebody to love?
Wouldn't you love somebody to love?
You better find somebody to love. Love."

Jefferson Airplane

Chapter One:
MOVING DOWN

The sound in the Rose Bowl was deafening. The crowd was going crazy. But inside the huddle you could hear the big offensive linemen breathing hard.

"This is it," I smiled.

"Give me the ball," Jim Brown, the famous fullback demanded.

"Sorry Jim, but they're gonna be all over you." I was the quarterback and I wasn't about to take any orders from a running back.

"The coach wants Brown off tackle," Gene Hickerson, the future Hall of Fame guard said. He wanted the last play over his number 66.

"Screw him. We're gonna fake to Brown and hit Spalding on the button hook."

I could see Spalding smile behind his face piece.

"On three."

We broke huddle. Third and goal to go on the five yard line. There were two seconds left on the clock in Super Bowl V and the Packers were beating us by four points. We had to go for the touchdown.

I put my hands under the center, my long hair blowing in the breeze just like Joe Namath. I tried to quiet the crowd but it didn't work. They just cheered all the louder.

"*HUT, HUT, HUT,*" I screamed.

I faked a handoff to Brown. He dove into the line. The Packers bought it, swarming all over him. Then I curled to my left and saw Spalding all by himself in the corner of the end zone.

A little feather pass into Spalding's sure hands and the game was over. KUBIK WINS SUPER BOWL FOR CLEVELAND BROWNS, the headlines would read.

But just as I was about to release the football a bell began ringing inside my helmet.

It was the telephone. I ran downstairs to answer it.

"Were you sleeping?" Michelle asked.

"At this hour?" I looked at the dining room clock on the wall. It was already 12:30.

"Well, you sound like it."

"What's happening?"

"I have to go downtown to run some errands and none of the girls are here. I thought you might want to come along."

"Any other time, I'm moving today."

"You are? Where?" she sounded disappointed. It was the first weekend before winter quarter and she thought I meant to another apartment.

"Just downstairs."

"Downstairs?"

"In the basement."

"The basement? Why down there?"

"I need my independence. A place of my own."

"Won't it be cold?"

"The furnace warms it up. I already tested it with a blanket by the back door. It's pretty toasty."

"Okay, good luck."

"Thanks, you'll have to check it out."

"Bye."

I had made the decision over break. I was too old to have a roommate. I needed my own place to entertain members of the opposite sex. Spalding and I had an old fashioned divider that we used if we had company but it didn't really allow for any privacy in the sack.

I only had two quarters left in college and I was determined to make the best of it.

I only wished Elizabeth hadn't gone to Europe. Well, at least I'd have everything ready for her when she returned.

Spalding helped me move after lunch. He was only too glad to have some privacy of his own.

"I hope you don't take this personal, buddy," I told him as I unscrewed the beveled mirror from my grandmother's dresser. "You were the best roommate I ever had."

"Thanks," Spalding said as he popped the Beatles' "Let it Be" cassette into his tape deck.

"Sometimes a man's gotta do what a man's gotta do."

"You sound like Early."

"How about a little help over here?"

He held the mirror while I took out the final screw. Then we started taking it down the steps.

"Only two more quarters," I tried making light conversation.

"Yep," he said as we struggled around some tight curves on both the upstairs and downstairs steps.

"What are you gonna do when you graduate?"

We knew in a vague way what we wanted to do for professions. He was going to be a pilot and I was going to be a journalist. But we'd never talked specifics before. That was one of the trademarks of our generation. Live for today, don't worry about tomorrow. But tomorrow was coming quick.

"I don't know. Maybe get me a ranch in Florida."

"Be a cowboy?"

"Why not?"

"Like Sky Pilot?"

"That'd be perfect. How about you?"

"I think I'll join a hippie commune with Liz. Write poetry up in the mountains."

"Sounds groovy."

We finished with the mirror and went back for the rest of the dresser.

"Why don't we get our own commune?" I asked as we took another crack at the steps. "Buy a farm in the country."

"And raise what?"

"Something simple, like walnuts."

"Walnuts? *You're* nuts."

"I mean, you plant the trees, right? Then you only have to pick them once a year. The rest of the year you party. How hard can that be?"

"You're crazy."

"We could do it. We just need the right people."

"You're a dreamer."

"Yeah. I guess so."

We finished moving the dresser into place against the cold stone wall and suddenly I was depressed. It was the final piece of furniture, making my new digs complete. I should have been happy.

But I had to face the fact that college was going to be over pretty soon and I probably wouldn't be seeing my friends much anymore. In the back of my mind I'd always hoped we'd buy houses in the same neighborhood and keep hanging around together. It'd be great fun. But it was just immature fantasy. The real world didn't work like that. It was disheartening.

"How about holding my poster?"

"Sure."

Spalding held my "Spirit of 76" poster against the metal furnace while I taped it. It was an updated version of Archibald Willard's famous portrayal of Revolutionary War soldiers.

But contemporary characters replaced the Minute Men. A white college student with a bandanna across his forehead marched along blowing a flute, a black militant held the flag and a long-haired hippie pounded the drums as a fallen comrade waved them on.

We hung my other poster over the water pipes with some string. It was a quote from the English writer Edmund Burke mounted on a cardboard backing.

"ALL THAT IS NECESSARY FOR THE FORCES OF EVIL TO WIN THE WORLD IS FOR ENOUGH GOOD MEN TO DO NOTHING."

"That's it?" Spalding asked.

"That's it." I agreed. "Welcome to The Cave."

I put up a sign leftover from a freshman dorm skit.

"The Cave, huh? That's cool. What are you gonna do the rest of the day?"

We headed back upstairs.

"What've you got in mind?"

"I thought we'd go traying. We haven't gone since last year."

"You do like those winter sports."

"Might be my last chance."

"Then we better do it. Let's round up Early."

Chapter Two:
TRAYING

Later that afternoon, Spalding, Early and I found some old dorm cafeteria trays and headed over to Blanket Hill. It was the same place where we sat in the fall to watch the anti-war rally. Except this time it was freezing cold, covered with snow and without a crowd or speaker.

The sun was drooping behind the hills by the time we arrived. There were about a dozen other students already hitting the slopes, packing down the snow. Their laughter echoed through the silence.

"You go first," Spalding said to Early.

"Why me?" he asked.

"You're the trailblazer, the scout," Spalding said.

"Yeah, you check out the trees. If you hit one let us know," I said.

"Thanks for nothing," Early said.

We were at a different part of the hill than the other students. If Early took our bait we would have a steeper run, faster but slightly more dangerous.

He put his rather large behind down on the small tray. It was a Kent tradition to use trays stolen from the cafeteria as sleds. We'd requisitioned ours sophomore year and kept them around for such occasions.

Early barely fit on the slab of plastic. He tucked in his legs, aimed for an open area and Spalding gave him a shove. Down he went, headed for a huge oak tree, then turned over at the last second to avoid a crash.

"You're next," I said to Spalding.

"Why me?"

"This was your idea."

"Let's go over by the others?"

"What's wrong? You chicken? Anyone can be a follower."

"So shoot me, I'm a follower."

Spalding started walking over to the other end of the hill.

"Where you guys going?" Early hollered up.

"Over there," I pointed toward the crowd.

"Sissies," he screamed.

As we approached the other students, hoping to share their ready-made run, one face was familiar.

"Michelle."

"Matthew, Paul."

"I thought you were running errands today," I said.

"Finished," she snapped the fingers on her cloth gloves. "Besides, I'm easily diverted."

"So I see."

"Who're your friends?" Paul asked. They weren't the girls next door.

"Old friends from the dorm."

Michelle was a vision of loveliness in her winter gear. She wore a purple cap that let her long blond hair fall aimlessly. A short leather coat left the shape of her beautiful behind showing. And her tight blue jeans were tucked into a pair of knee-high leather boots, displaying her long legs.

Looking at her, I knew it was going to be a long winter without Elizabeth.

"Going down?" she said to us.

"Sure."

She sat down on her tray. Spalding and I put ours on each side of her. We aimed for an open area, no trees, and went down easily. Early was standing at the bottom, his tray tucked under his arm.

"Thanks for waiting for me."

"You don't make a very good scout," I said.

"We would've got killed if we followed you," Spalding added.

The four of us climbed back up the hill, joining Michelle's friends. We didn't even exchange introductions. We just trayed, taking turns putting our trays behind each others, next to each others and racing each others. More students piled out of the dorms. The crowd grew as the darkness settled in. Someone started a fire in a trash barrel and we stood around it between runs.

"I can't believe it's winter quarter already," Michelle said.

"Spalding's last taste of the white stuff," I said.

"Cocaine?" she teased.

"He's going to miss it," Early said.

"Yeah, like a bad rash."

"You guys didn't have a back to school party this quarter."

"We're getting old," I said.

"Everyone but Early," Spalding said.

"I won't grow up, I don't want to grow up."

"How's the band?"

"We got a gig coming up at the Kove. You should come see us."

"Sure," Michelle said.

"How come you didn't tell *us*?"

"You guys would just hassle me."

"We will now."

Watching Michelle talk with my friends through the sparks coming out of the fire, it all started coming back to me. The reasons I was attracted to her in the first place.

Michelle was one of the guys. She got along with everyone so easily. She was different than other women, even Elizabeth. She was beautiful, she was feminine, but she could also talk football. You didn't have to baby her or suck up to her. You could just be yourself around her.

Why *did* we break up junior year? Oh yeah, I was afraid

of the big C word: Commitment. How could I be chained to a relationship? I wanted my freedom. Yet she wasn't really pressing me, she wasn't asking for anything more than my friendship.

And who was I kidding? Maybe it was all in my mind, maybe she didn't even want me anymore. As I watched her laugh I realized what a fool I'd been.

"We're leaving, Michelle," one of her friends called over.

"I'll be right there," she said. "See you guys at Depeyster."

And just like that she was gone again. The three of us stood around the fire for awhile, just staring at it. I could read their minds. They were all thinking about Michelle.

"Am I the world's biggest fool or what?"

"We've been saying that for years," Early said.

"There you go, tell it like it is," Spalding said.

"Geez, you don't have to be so quick to agree with me."

"Why don't you ask her out again?"

"She wouldn't buy it."

"You never know if you don't try."

"And what do I tell Liz?"

"She's in Switzerland."

"It's a long winter."

"And when she comes back?"

"I'll take her off your hands," Early said.

"I don't know about you." I picked up a snowball and threw it at him. He counter-attacked and we began a full-scale battle, using our trays for shields. By the time we stopped we were halfway back to Depeyster.

Chapter Three:
VALENTINE'S DAY

It was about a month into winter quarter and I still hadn't built up the nerve to ask Michelle out. Part of it was fear of rejection. Part of it was out of respect for Elizabeth, even if she was overseas. But mostly it was just to avoid complications.

On the other hand, I was suffering from a serious case of cabin fever. It was one of the coldest winters anyone could remember and we spent a lot of time inside.

I was walking home from classes one day and noticed that someone had shoveled the sidewalk, probably Early. He'd left the snow shovel sticking out of a dirty snow pile by the mailbox.

I checked for the daily mail and, lo and behold, there was one of those one-page, light-blue folded letters from Europe, only the second one I'd received since Liz left.

I went inside. Spalding greeted me as I put my Army jacket on the coat tree. He was carrying a fried bologna sandwich in one hand and his LOVE cup filled with milk in the other.

"Nice job on the sidewalk," I told him.

"Early did it."

"I figured as much. You also missed the mail."

"What'd we get?" he followed me into the kitchen where I grabbed some Fig Newtons and filled my PEACE cup also with moo juice. "Just a little letter for moi."

"Not one of those Europa mailgrams?"

"How sweet it is," I ran it under my nose searching for a certain feminine scent.

We sat down at the dining room table. I dropped cookie crumbs on the letter as I unfolded it, then spread it out on the tabletop.

Spalding ate in silence as I digested figs and news from our Swiss allies at the same time. The letter started off innocent enough, a few stories about the family that she was staying with, a couple of short trips that she'd made to Germany and Vienna and visits to the Opera and Ballet.

She even enclosed a black and white photo of herself romping through the Alps, her black hair flowing, a long scarf hanging and her legs showing between her coat and her boots. It was the same ensemble she wore the night of the Christmas party.

But she finished with a little note about how she met an American student of the male variety living in the same town of Basel. From Ohio State, no less.

I immediately went into a state of panic. Another goddam Buckeye. Didn't they have any women of their own down there? I was developing an intense hatred for our sister school in Columbus.

She signed it with a couple intersecting Y's, I guess for the Ying and the Yang, and simply Elizabeth. The first letter had been signed Love, Liz.

What was she trying to tell me? I threw the letter over to Spalding.

"Read this and tell me what you think of it?"

"Nothing risqué, I hope?"

"Hardly," I said.

"Sounds like she's having a good time," he said, after reading it.

"Too good a time."

"What?"

"How about her friend from Ohio State?"

"Sounds like you're jealous."

"Just horny. These Buckeyes are really beginning to piss me off."

"Maybe *she's* horny."

"Girls don't get horny. Do they?"

"What planet are you on?"

Spalding took his empty cup into the kitchen. I couldn't sit still.

It was time to take Harold for a walk. It was a technique I'd mastered in grade school whenever I had something serious to consider, like a math test or the senior prom. I'd walk the dog, take in some fresh air, and mull things over in my mind. By the time I returned I'd have my answer. It always worked.

We stayed on the back streets, the off-campus neighborhood surrounding Depeyster. Harold jumped up on snowdrifts and slid on icy sidewalks. I was amazed how the freezing conditions never seemed to bother his bare paws and thin hairy legs. If us humans were so superior to the animals, why did we need so many accoutrements just to go for a winter walk? Maybe I could learn something from Harold.

Number one: I liked Michelle, I always did.

Number two: I was a fool to break up with her in the first place.

Number three: I liked Elizabeth, but she was in Switzerland.

Number four: It wasn't my fault she was in Switzerland.

Number five: Whom did I like better? Michelle or Elizabeth? Elizabeth or Michelle?

Number six: Who was this guy from Ohio State and why were these Buckeyes always attracted to my women?

Number seven: Did either one of them even care or was I just wasting my time?

That was it. It took me all the way to front campus to figure it out but I finally hit on the key to my dilemma. It was time to head back to Depeyster. For all I knew neither one of them still liked me so all this mental anguish might be for nothing.

There was only one way to find out. Ask Michelle if she'd go out with me and if she did and we hit it off I'd have to see how I felt about Elizabeth when she came back. Life was a gamble anyway. Roll the dice, Kubik, and let the chips fall where they may.

I hated to apply logic to love but I had to. I'd taken Calculus freshman year, math was my thing.

Now all I had to do was build up the nerve to ask Michelle out. I couldn't just ask her, that was too plain, too unromantic. I needed a gimmick. By the time I reached Depeyster I was still grasping for straws. I was tempted to ask Spalding for advice but this was too big. If it blew up in my face I wanted to keep it to myself.

Before I walked in the front door I looked up at her room. It was right next to Spalding's and her light was on. She was probably studying. What could I do?

Spalding was taking a shower and Early was nowhere in sight. The Murph was probably at Mary Lou's. It was now or never.

I jumped in the bathtub and picked up the phone. Then I put it back down. I thought about knocking on her front door but decided against it. I was sweating like a high school kid. What was wrong with me? I dialed with trembling fingers.

Jennifer answered the phone. What was she doing there? She's never home.

"Hello, can I speak to Michelle?"

"She's up in her room. I'll get her."

She put down the phone, then picked it up again. "Is this Matthew?"

"Jennifer?"

"Yeah, how you doing? I haven't seen you in a long time."

"Fine, just fine." This was already getting complicated.

"Here she comes."

"Okay, thanks."

"Hello?" a soft, familiar voice asked.

"Michelle, your neighbor to the north."

"Which one? We have lots of perverts in this neighborhood." She recognized my voice but was just playing with me.

"The slow, stupid one in the other half of your house."

"Not Matthew? He lives to the south."

"That proves my point." She laughed. It was just like old times. "Hey, you took philosophy last quarter, didn't you? From Dr. Hoffman?"

"Yeah, it was a great course."

"Well, I got him this quarter and I just realized I'm supposed to read *Siddhartha* by tomorrow. You wouldn't still have your copy, would you?"

At this crucial moment Spalding walked out of the shower with a towel wrapped around his waist. "Who you talking to?" he asked.

I tried to shush him with a finger to my lips.

"I think so, I'll have to go look. How about if I call you right back?"

"That'd be great."

I hung up.

"*Siddhartha*? I think I got a copy of it," Spalding said.

"Thanks, but no thanks."

Spalding stopped for a second before going up to his room. "What are you up to?"

"You'll never know."

"Yes I will. You'll tell me," he smiled and went upstairs.

The phone rang. "I got it," I hollered loud enough for Spalding to hear me.

"Matthew? It's me. I found it. Want me to bring it over?"

"Naw, I'll come over. No use going out on a night like this."

"Okay."

I hung up the phone. "Here we go," I said to myself. "First base."

I was going to go out and knock on her front door when another idea struck me. I went down to the basement and through the door I'd used to hide the dope the day of the big drug bust.

Their side was filled with junk left over from previous tenants. Half of it I put over there from our side when I cleaned out a space for my new room. They didn't complain so I figured they hardly ever went down there.

I stopped at the top of their stairs before opening the door. Maybe I should knock first? I might catch her roommates in a compromising position. All the more reason to surprise them. No, I'd better play this straight. I didn't want to get thrown out trying to steal second.

I knocked on the door. There were a couple of screams, then Jennifer hollered, "Who's there?"

"Neighbor from the north. I mean south."

She opened the door.

"What are you doing down there?"

"You scared the hell out of us," Renee said. She was standing close to Jennifer.

"Sorry, I thought Michelle told you I was coming over."

"Not from the basement," I heard her voice coming down the steps from her room.

"I didn't know you could get through down there," Jennifer said.

"I did, but I thought it was locked," Michelle appeared behind her friends. It was like they were clustered together to protect themselves from the savage beast who invaded their privacy.

"I'm living down there now so I thought it would be easier than going out in the cold."

"Yeah, we heard," Michelle said and the others finally split, leaving the two of us at the top of the landing in their dining room.

I'd always felt weird on the rare occasions when I visited their side of Depeyster. Even though we lived under the same roof, their feminine decor made me feel like I was in foreign territory.

"Is that the book?" I pointed at the small paperback hanging from her fingers.

"Oh yeah, here."

"Thanks. Sorry if I scared you. I won't do it again." I started back down the steps, then stopped. "Turn the light on for me?"

She was standing next to the light switch at the top of the stairs as I began my descent.

She flipped it on. "How'd you get over here in the dark?"

"Slowly, very slowly."

I stopped again at the bottom of the steps. "Michelle?"

"Yes?"

"How about us going out again?"

"Huh?"

"You know, for old time's sake."

We were standing like Rhett and Scarlett in *Gone with the Wind*. Except the bare wooden staircase lacked any resemblance of grandeur.

She hesitated for a second. "Let me think about it."

"Great, I'll call you."

I disappeared into my Cave and heard her turn out the light.

"Safe," I threw Herman Hesse's classic on my bed and made an exaggerated umpire's signal with my arms. "Safe at second."

I didn't waste any time. The longer I waited the more reasons she'd come up with for not going out with me.

I ran upstairs and jumped back into the bathtub. Spalding looked at me from the kitchen like I was crazy. He went back to boiling some hot dogs and beans.

Jennifer answered the phone once more. "Me again."

"I knew your voice sounded familiar. I'll get her."

"Hello?"

"Well, what'd you decide?"

"I told you I'd think about it."

"Let's just go out and then you can think about it."

"That doesn't make any sense."

"Nothing makes any sense. Isn't that what they taught you in philosophy?"

"Not really," she laughed. "Where would we go?"

"We could fly to New York for the weekend or go downtown for a couple beers. What's your pleasure?"

"I already have plans for the weekend, so it'd have to be downtown."

"Eight o'clock tomorrow night?"

Silence for a moment. Then...

"Well, okay. But you'll have to use the front door."

"Agreed."

"See you." She hung up.

I walked on air into the kitchen. "A triple buddy, I'm rounding third heading for home."

"What are you talking about?"

"I've got a date with Michelle for tomorrow night."

"You didn't."

"Well, it's not really a date, date," I used two fingers from each hand to mimic quotation marks like a professor.

"Where you taking her?"

"Just downtown for a couple beers."

"How romantic."

"It's better than sitting at home with Early." I took a hot dog off Spalding's plate and put it on a piece of bread.

"You should go see Early. He's playing at the Kove."

"Good idea, buddy. I'd invite you along but..."

"I know."

Spalding was understanding like that. He knew when something wasn't cool and when it was.

Fortunately, I didn't run into Michelle the following day. I thought that if I did it would be too uncomfortable. I also hoped Spalding wouldn't spread the news all over. Fat chance.

Our date was the talk of Depeyster, both sides of the house. As soon as I came out of the shower it began.

"Where you off to?" Spalding asked.

He was playing with the piano keys. The Murph was tapping on the wood table with a set of drumsticks. Why he was even in the house amazed me. He only stopped over when Mary Lou was working or visiting the future in-laws. They still hadn't set a date for their nuptials.

"Anyone we know?" The Murph jested.

"Let us know if you get any," sayeth the Spalding.

"Is that all you guys ever think about?" I responded. "I'd love to sit here and chat but I'm late. I'm late, I'm late, for a very important date."

I ran down the steps to avoid the grilling. I put on a casual striped pullover with three buttons at the neck, faded jeans and my best pair of boots. On my way out the door I stuck my head back into the dining room.

"Wish me luck."

"Don't do anything I wouldn't do," quote Spalding.

"Don't catch anything," cautioned the Murph.

"I'll try not to."

I looked at the clock on the wall as I grabbed my Army jacket off the coat tree. It was 8:10 P.M. Fashionably late.

"Here goes," I said to Harold as I walked out the door.

I almost jumped off our porch and jumped on theirs but it didn't feel right. Instead I walked down our sidewalk, across to theirs and up their front steps. It gave me time to catch my composure.

Jennifer answered the door, said "hello" through the screen and just stood there looking at me for a few minutes. I think she was in a state of shock.

"Well..." I finally said, exasperated.

"Oh, won't you please come in?"

"Thank you. Is Michelle in? I think she's expecting me."

"Of course, she'll be down in a moment. Won't you please sit down." She showed me to the couch and then she curtsied, something I hadn't seen a female do since junior high school.

Jennifer retreated to the kitchen. She joined Michelle's other two roommates giggling around the corner. Actually, it was quite humorous and did make me feel a touch less uncomfortable.

I picked up a copy of *The Hobbit* lying on the armrest. It was one of those "must read" books of the 60s that I'd never read, like *Siddhartha*. There were a lot of those type books that I'd never read.

After a few moments, I heard Michelle coming down the steps. Our eyes met and in that instant I realized that I'd done the right thing. No matter what happened the rest of the night, this was perfect.

"Good evening," she said pleasantly.

She was wearing a slinky maroon mini-dress with nylons and casual shoes. It was the first time I'd seen her legs since she'd moved in next door.

"Fine, thank you," I answered a question she hadn't asked.

"Where we going?" she asked, as I helped her put her winter coat on.

"I thought we'd head downtown. Early's playing at the Kove. You going to be warm enough?"

"I'm tough. Are we walking?"

"I thought we were."

"Then I'll put some boots on."

She made a quick change and then stuck her head into the dining room. "Don't wait up," she told her roommates.

I opened the front door for her and we stepped out into the elements. It was a helluva night for a first date. Or to be more precise, a second first date.

Our first, first date had been the previous spring. It was a totally spring romance, begun and finished before summer vacation. A real whirlwind affair in warm, pleasant weather.

This time it was nasty outside. The wind was whipping up the wind chill factor. The snow was falling in large flakes and the drifts were piling up on the road.

We started our uphill climb to downtown with the wind in our faces.

"We must be crazy to be out on a night like this," I said.

"This was your idea."

"I'm glad you came."

"You're right, I must be crazy."

We started walking a little faster in silence. My heart began to race and my lungs were wheezing from the cold. It felt invigorating.

At the top of Depeyster we hit Main Street. There was a stalled car sitting next to the curb. The driver's door was open and a coed was struggling to lift up her hood.

"Should I?" I asked Michelle.

"Be my guest."

We walked over to the damsel in distress.

"What's the problem?"

"It won't start, I might be out of gas."

"That happens to me all the time," I said.

"Me, too," Michelle added.

I went inside the car and pulled the hood latch. It popped up a little. Michelle unhooked the safety and lifted the hood. I was impressed.

"Jump in," I instructed the coed as I unscrewed the air filter. "Turn it on when I tell you and keep your foot to the floor."

"Going to play with the choke?" Michelle asked me.

"Yep. How do you know so much about cars?"

"I had my share of clunkers."

"Floor it," I hollered to the coed.

She did as I instructed. I pushed down the choke and covered the carburetor with my palm, starving the engine for air. It sputtered, then started.

"Keep it going." I told the coed. "Get it to the nearest gas station."

I put the air filter back on and slammed the hood. She took off with a little wave of thanks. We continued on our journey to the Kove.

"Do you really run out of gas a lot?" Michelle asked me.

"No, do you?"

"No, I was just trying to make her feel better."

"Me too."

Something magic was happening and I couldn't quite name it.

We went down to the Kove. The sign out on the street announced "The Hybirds" were playing. I didn't know what to expect. It was a Thursday night and Thursdays were usually pretty crowded in Kent with pre-weekend partiers, but the weather was terrible.

I also didn't expect Early's band to have much of a following. They'd played a couple of high school dances but this was their first chance at the big time. Downtown Kent was like minor league baseball. If you made it here you could go on to bigger and better things. The sky was the limit.

We went inside. The place was jammin'. It wasn't wall to wall but there weren't many empty tables. The Hybirds were playing The Who's "My Generation" and Early was getting down like Peter Townsend.

I looked at Michelle. "Who's he?" I laughed.

"You tell me." She also laughed.

I bought a couple beers at the bar and we walked past the stage. Early saw us, gave us a quick nod of recognition and went back to work. This was no time to bug the man.

We found a table near the back door. It was open to let the fresh air mingle with the smoky interior. You could see the huge wheels of a freight train parked just outside.

"Here's to a new beginning," I proposed a toast with my glass of beer.

"What?" she said. The Hybirds were playing quite loudly.

"Thanks for coming out on such a night."

"Yeah, they sound all right."

Maybe it was a mistake coming to see Early. I just wanted to talk with Michelle and neither one of us could hear what the other was saying.

I just sipped my beer and listened to the music. She did likewise.

"Here, I've got something for you," Michelle pulled an envelope out of her over-sized purse. "Happy Valentine's Day."

I opened a homemade greeting card. On the cover was a hand-drawn Peacock with a peace sign coming out of its mouth like a cartoon figure.

Inside there was a poem by Walt Whitman.

Spontaneous Me

Spontaneous me,
Nature,
The loving day, the mounting sun
the friend I am happy with,
The arm of my friend hanging idly over my shoulder-free.

It was beautiful. It was a work of art. I didn't deserve such an honor. I didn't know what to say. I didn't even know it was Valentine's Day.

"Thanks," I said. "Sorry, I didn't get you anything."

"For what?"

"Valentine's Day."

"Forget it. I was just in a creative mood."

Just then the band took a break. What a relief. We could finally hear each other. Early came over and joined us.

"What do you think?" He turned a chair around and used its back to lean forward.

"You guys are great," Michelle said.

"Do you take any requests?" I asked.

"Like what?"

"Can you play "Far Away?"

It was an old joke but I couldn't resist the opportunity. I didn't want Early getting too big a head.

"You're beginning to sound like the Murph," he said.

"Why didn't those guys come?

"Maybe tomorrow night."

"You want a refill? I get free ones."

"Is that all they're paying you?"

"Just about."

Early took our two empties up to the bar.

"How's it feel having a famous roommate?" Michelle asked me.

"Early's famous all right, but not for his music."

"His lyrics?"

"No, his neatness."

He returned with two beers. "Aren't you having one?"

"I never drink on the job."

"Then how do you get so crazy?" Michelle asked. "Drugs?"

"I don't do drugs," Early looked at me. "Well, just that one time when we got busted."

"Early's on a natural high," I said.

"I played a song on the juke box for you two," Early said. "Here it comes now."

We strained to listen to the words above the noise in the bar.

"What's it called?" Michelle asked.

"'Bridge Over Troubled Water' by Simon and Garfunkel. It's perfect for young lovers. Happy Valentine's Day."

Early smiled at us, stood up and went back to the band.

"How come everyone knows it's Valentine's Day but me?"

Michelle made a strange face that seemed to say, "How am I supposed to know?"

I'd had enough for one night. "Want to get out of here?" I asked her.

"It is a school night."

We bid Early good-bye, thanked him for the song and the beers and stepped outside. The quiet was deafening.

The wind had disappeared and the fat snowflakes jostled to the ground. Michelle took my hand and I didn't feel the cold at all.

Everything was different on the walk home. It wasn't the two beers, although I am easily under the influence. It wasn't the wind at our back or the downhill walk. Something had changed inside me.

Suddenly I was enjoying the winter wonderland. We slid on the ice and tried to catch snowflakes on our tongues under a streetlight. We even grabbed a ride down Depeyster on the back of a car's bumper just like in high school.

By the time we reached our happy abode, I was in love all over again. It felt like spring quarter junior year.

I walked Michelle to her front door.

"You haven't seen The Cave yet."

"Not tonight, some other time."

"My door's always open."

"Good night."

She began to open the screen door, stopped, turned around and gave me a slow, wet kiss. Then she went inside.

It was great.

The guys were waiting for me in the living room, watching television.

"How'd it go?" Spalding asked from the recliner.

"Uh, third base," I shook my hand sideways while hanging my coat on the tree.

"Not bad for a first date," the Murph said.

"I expected better," Spalding said. "It wasn't really their first date."

"Let's hear the details. How was Early's band?"

"Great. Early thinks he's Mick Jagger."

"We got to see him," the Murph said to Spalding.

"Tomorrow night," Spalding said.

"That's what I told him. I'm crashing."

"What? No details?"

"Maybe tomorrow."

"I bet he struck out," the Murph teased.

"Good night guys."

I went down the steps. It was hard to tell. Maybe I did. I

thought things went pretty well but how do you know for sure? Maybe she was just being nice?

I jumped under the covers. I could watch the snowflakes falling from the little window just above ground level. At least everything looked up from down under. I drifted off into dreamland, my favorite location. I would have no trouble scoring with Michelle there.

A short time later I heard a soft knock on the basement door that separated the two halves of the house.

I opened my eyes. *A home run.* I smiled.

Chapter Four:
HAROLD AND SPANKY

Life after Valentine's Day was all downhill. It was like water rolling off a duck's back. Michelle and I were dating while living in the same house. It was better than being married.

We didn't spend so much time together that we got on each other's nerves but if we wanted to see each other we didn't even have to brave the elements.

If we needed some space, so be it. If we wanted to do something together, we were always around. And we had great friends to do it with.

It was almost too perfect. Almost utopia. I was ready to call Depeyster "Camelot."

But even the best of times have a few bumps in the road.

It was still well into the dead of winter when I was sitting in an economics class daydreaming of Michelle. There were five minutes before the bell. I gazed out the window of Franklin Hall on front campus.

The Kent maintenance men were trying desperately to keep the snow off the winding sidewalks. A strong wind was knocking down the drifts as fast as they could pile them back up.

I thought about how spoiled we students were. All these professors, cafeteria workers and janitors worked for our pleasure. All we had to do was read a few books, regurgitate them a couple times a quarter and party our brains out.

Four years later we were thrown out into the real world. But what the hell, until then we had it made. The sad truth was that few of us appreciated our privileged lifestyle. Many students did nothing but complain about their situation.

The economics professor was old enough to retire. I didn't think he knew what he was talking about. He was finishing his lecture on supply and demand, an ancient capitalistic theory.

But it didn't relate to my personal experience. Take drugs for instance. The theory predicted that as more drugs became available the price would go down. Yet the prices kept going up, no matter what.

I wanted to ask him about that but I realized it was an uncomfortable example. Instead I invented my own economic formula: "The Ripoff Theory." According to my theory, businessmen are going to rip you off with whatever they can get away with. It made more sense to me and explained a wider variety of situations.

The bell rang, interrupting my soliloquy. Forget economics, I was supposed to meet Michelle at the library.

I buttoned my Army jacket to the neck and pulled down a blue and gold knit cap over my ears. The walk down the steps from the classroom buildings to the library was always exhilarating.

The library was one of the finest structures on campus. The exterior had the names of famous writers carved in the stone around the top perimeter.

Shakespeare, Milton and Dante lived side by side for generations to gaze upon. Inside, the ornate woodwork and old wooden tables provided a fitting atmosphere to study the great thinkers that lined the bookshelves.

It was the kind of atmosphere they would have felt comfortable in themselves.

It took me awhile to find Michelle. She was sitting in an out-of-the-way window seat in the corner of the second floor. The view of front campus was outstanding.

It would have made for a romantic interlude but I was

burned out. I didn't even unbutton my jacket.

"How's it going?"

"It's going. Grab a seat."

"I think I'm going to head home. It's been a long day."

"Well, I've had enough myself." She closed up a couple of books and put away her notes. I helped her put her coat on.

"You've become a real gentleman."

"Always have been, you just never noticed."

"Oh, I noticed."

We went back out into the winter chill and I realized that it never seemed quite as cold when I was with Michelle. We walked across Lincoln Street, cutting through the Dubois Bookstore parking lot.

Behind it was a house that always fascinated me. Some freak had paneled the front porch with varnished knotty pine, more suitable for an interior den or study. I was about to mention it to Michelle when the house's side door opened and the resident, a longhaired coed, let my dog out into the elements.

"Good-bye Harold," she said.

Michelle looked at me as I whistled for Harold to come.

"What can I say? He has more friends on campus than I do."

"You don't know that girl?"

"Nope." I was being completely honest.

I always wondered where Harold spent his days. "Come here, boy."

The dog ran up to me and started jumping up and down, circling us as we walked, all four legs leaving the earth at the same time.

Harold loved to jump.

I once tried to research his pedigree to explain this peculiar trait. After looking at dog pictures in an encyclopedia, the nearest I could figure was that he had a large lump of Rhodesian Ridgeback in him. It was a breed used in Africa to hunt lions.

Harold was no dummy. In a town and era that stressed

individual freedom he stretched it to the limit. He was like the Tramp in the Disney movie. He traveled a wide circle of friends but knew where to hang his hat at the end of the day. I was always amazed at some of the places I ran into him.

"Someone's glad to see you," Michelle said coldly.

"He always makes me feel wanted." I pretended not to notice her mood swing.

We traveled the rest of the way in silence. In front of Depeyster, I tried to break the ice.

"Want to stop in for a snack?"

"Maybe in a minute. Let me drop off my books."

We each went in our respective doors, Harold following my lead. I left my wet coat and boots by the coat rack. Spalding and Early were sitting at the dining room table sipping cups of coffee.

"Hey guys," I greeted them enroute to the kitchen, throwing my books on the old piano. There was no response. I just shrugged it off to the weather. Everyone seemed a little grumpy in the winter.

I filled a teapot with water, put it on the gas stove and went back to the dining room.

"Why the long faces?"

"We got bad news," Spalding spoke softly.

"Spanky's dead." Early wasn't one to mince words.

"What?" Tears began to form in my eyes.

"The Murph dropped the Chevy off early this morning..." Spalding started to explain.

"Then I was going to use it to go shopping." Early cut him off.

"Spanky was sleeping on the engine to keep warm."

"It happened real fast."

"We already buried him."

My friends were speaking in bullets, practically simultaneously. We were all crying.

Michelle walked in unannounced. The teapot began to

whistle. Harold came into the room.

"What's going on?" she asked in a whisper.

"Spanky's dead," I told her and went into the kitchen to turn off the boiling water.

"Spanky?" She sat down at the table.

I brought in a cup of tea for Michelle and me. We sat around the table trying not to cry, trying to be mature adults. But we were still half-children. Tears kept welling up.

"She was a great cat," Early said. He was the cat lover amongst us.

"I thought she was a he?" Michelle asked.

"We never did figure that out," Spalding said, half laughing between sobs.

"I did." Early said. "He was a she."

"Maybe she was a he-she," I said and everyone chuckled a little.

The tension and sadness began to dissipate.

"Remember when she brought the mouse in our bedroom?" Spalding asked.

"That's supposed to be a sign of affection," Early explained.

"It freaked me out," Spalding remembered.

"I liked the way she slept on your television set," Michelle said.

"It's weird talking about her in the past tense," I said.

There was a moment of silence. Harold came up to me, sensing that something was wrong. Spanky liked to tease him, then jump on the kitchen counter where he couldn't reach her. It was like a member of our family had died.

It helped prepare us for what was to come.

Chapter Five:
CAROL'S VISIT

We were pretty depressed after Spanky's death. Things just didn't seem the same around the old Ponderosa. I especially missed her when feeding Harold in the morning, opening one can of pet food instead of two.

But kids our age were pretty resilient. We just needed an event to shake the winter doldrums and Spalding supplied one just a few days later.

He received a letter from Carol, his steady in Florida, that she was finally coming up north to visit. She wanted to visit in the winter since, like Spalding, she had never seen snow before. Something us Northerners took for granted was truly foreign to her. It amazed us just thinking about it.

It was also a little odd that she'd waited so long. Maybe she thought she'd feel out of place with his "Northern" friends. But I had met her over the previous spring break and she seemed unfazed by our peculiar habits.

Whatever it was, we prepared for her visit like a visit from royalty. We cleaned our rooms, cleaned the kitchen, cleaned the john and tried to remove all traces of Chris' frequent visits. Carol came from a somewhat stuffy, upper class environment and Spalding was worried she might be shocked by our "hippie lifestyle."

She timed her visit for Washington's Birthday, a legal holiday, so there were no classes. We headed out to Cleveland's airport, about an hour ride, straight into a major snowstorm. Cars were stuck on the side of the road but the '57 Chevy drove like a champ.

Fortunately, there was no rush hour. We bought a six-pack of Rolling Rock, cranked up some tunes on the AM and enjoyed the scenic ride through Twin Lakes on our way to the airport.

Twin Lakes was so named because there was a lake on each side of the road. It was surrounded by lovely homes, owned mostly by college professors and administrators.

"Check out the young dudes," I told Spalding as we spun along Route 43 toward the Turnpike.

There were a bunch of high school kids playing ice hockey on a section of the lake that they had cleared of snow.

"Far out."

"You're an ice skater now. Maybe we should join them some day."

Spalding and I had enrolled in an ice skating class for our winter phys ed thrills.

"That'd be great."

"Maybe Carol would goal tend?"

"Is that a shot?"

"Just kidding, old buddy." I popped open a bottle of beer for him. "You going to tell her about Chris?"

"What're you crazy? You going to tell Liz about Michelle?"

"Maybe. Some day."

"We're both in the same mess."

"It's better than when we started the year. Remember? We didn't have anybody."

"You didn't."

"What is that, a shot?"

I opened a bottle for myself. We were pulling up to the Turnpike entrance.

"Hey, hide the brew, will ya?"

A young lady working the toll gate opened her window and handed us a card. The wind blew her hair back away from her face. She was the same one who had warned us about the hitchhikers on the way to Washington D.C.

"Lovely day," Spalding said.

"Isn't it though," she smiled.

"Have a nice day."

"You, too. But you better keep your brews out of sight. You know how Smokie is."

"Thanks."

We pulled away.

"She looks familiar," Spalding said.

"She should. She was doing us a favor. Again."

"What do you mean?"

"She's the same one who warned us about picking up hitch-hikers when we were with Bernstein."

"Oh yeah, I remember now."

"What's with the 'Have a nice day' routine? Are you kidding me? The poor girl's trapped in an icebox passing out senseless pieces of cardboard and all you can say is 'have a nice day.'"

"That's what people say in the real world. 'Have a nice day, have a nice day, have a nice day.' I heard it so many times over Christmas break it about made me barf."

"Then why lay it on the babe?"

"It seemed appropriate, okay. How come you're on your muscle? You better get it out of your system by the time we pick up Carol."

"I just hope we make it."

"Me, too." He looked at his aviator watch. "Three-thirty, she lands at four forty-five."

"We should do all right if they keep the roads clear."

The rest of the trip we just drank and jammed to the tunes, singing along with the radio when we got a little crazy. We pulled into Hopkins Airport's parking lot about 4:30 P.M.

"Plenty of time," I said.

I was wrong as usual. I forgot how long it took to find a

parking spot, how long it took to find the information booth and how long it took to walk to the gate.

"Where's flight 912 from Lauderdale arriving?" Spalding asked the girl at the information booth. We were already panting from speed walking.

"Gate 38. It's right on schedule. That's at the far end of the new concourse."

"New concourse?" I asked her.

"Just opened," she pointed in the correct direction.

I thought I knew the airport pretty well but I was unaware of a new concourse. A new large digital clock above the information booth clicked 4:42.

We had brought a large hand-painted WELCOME CAROL sign with us to greet her when she got off the plane. If we missed her exiting it would be all for naught.

Spalding started running through the crowd with the sign tucked under his arm like a football. I followed in his wake.

The gate numbers grew larger, 31, 32, 33. Time was running out, 34, 35, 36. We were becoming winded. I took the sign from Spalding so he could sprint ahead to catch her.

The gates seemed to stretch further apart. We arrived at gate 38 just as the loudspeaker blared: "Flight 912 from Ft. Lauderdale now unloading."

We leaned our backs against a wall as passengers slowly trickled off the airplane. Spalding held up the sign over his head so she would see us.

The area was filled with pale-skinned greeters welcoming tanned tourists. Families and lovers exchanged kisses. Lonely businessmen snaked through the throng. We regained our breath. The sign grew heavy and I relieved Spalding. Still no Carol.

Finally, the pilot, co-pilot and a couple stewardesses came off the plane, laughing amongst themselves. I let the sign fall to my side.

"Is anyone left on board?" Spalding asked them.

"Sorry, honey," a pretty brunette stewardess answered in a syrupy Southern accent. She turned her head sideways to read the sign. "Better luck next time."

We walked dejectedly past a row of phone cubicles where you could sit in comfort and talk. It was the newest addition to telecommunications.

Spalding took Carol's phone number out of his wallet and disappeared inside a booth. He didn't say a word but I could feel his disappointment.

I gave him some space, walked over to a snack bar and bought a holiday paper. I couldn't believe the headlines in *The Cleveland Plain Dealer.*

STUDY GROUP RECOMMENDS END TO THE DRAFT. I'd been waiting years for this story. But I was shattered as I read the copy. It didn't live up to its billing.

A special Nixon committee recommended eliminating the draft by raising military pay high enough to attract an all-volunteer army. However, it would take at least eighteen months, a full year and a half, to implement.

A lot of good that would do me. I could be walking knee high through the rice paddies by then. I turned my attention to another front page story.

NIXON REBUFFS VIET PEACE SIGNALS. This story was even more depressing. Former State Department Bureau Director Roger Hilsman wrote that 'Vietnamization' of the war, if not actually a fraud, was going much slower than generally believed.

His Washington contacts claimed that Nixon didn't plan to bring most of the American fighting forces home until just before the 1972 Presidential election.

"This is shrewd politics," Hilsman stated, "but the consequences are great" in terms of American lives and money.

"No shit, Shakespeare." I threw the paper into a trash receptacle.

Spalding stepped out of the ultra-modern phone booth.

"What happened?" I asked him.

"She had to work," he said as if he didn't believe her. "She tried to call Depeyster but missed us."

"We did leave early 'cause of the snow."

We began to walk slowly down the same concourse we had earlier ran through.

"And," he paused, taking the sign from me, "I'm no longer engaged."

"What? I didn't know you were engaged."

"It was kind of secret, just between the two of us."

"Did you tell her about Chris?"

"No," he shoved the sign into another trash bin. "She decided we're too young to get married. She wants to join the Peace Corps. See the world."

"You could join together."

"You don't get it, do you? It's over."

We were silent until we got back into the '57 Chevy.

"She didn't meet any Buckeyes by any chance, did she?"

Spalding flashed half a smile. It was a long ride home.

Chapter Six:
TWIN LAKES

The trip to Cleveland Airport did not lighten up the atmosphere at Depeyster as we'd hoped. In fact, it made matters worse.

Spalding walked around all day in a state of shock. The Murph was busy planning his shotgun marriage. Early was having band problems and I dreaded the coming of spring, followed by Elizabeth's return.

I almost hoped winter would last forever. So to celebrate the season I talked Spalding into trying his hand at a sport completely foreign to both of us, ice hockey.

On Saturday afternoon, we borrowed some skates from our phys ed class, bought a couple hockey sticks at the neighborhood sporting goods store and headed out in search of the Twin Lakes games.

It was bitter cold but the sun shone so brightly off the powdered snow we were forced to wear our sunglasses. The '57 Chevy already knew its way through the tall pine trees and leafless oaks to the edge of the lakes.

We found a parking lot for docking boats in the summer and proceeded the rest of the way on foot, trudging through drifts up to our knees.

"You do the talking," Spalding suggested.

We dragged our skates and hockey sticks behind us like the amateurs we were. About ten high school kids were racing back and forth after a black puck on a patch of ice they'd cleared by hand. It was quite a bit smaller than the ice rink we were used to on campus.

We quietly approached the contest, sitting on a large drift made by the artificial snow removal. Most of the kids were fairly good skaters, better than us, but a couple seemed in our league, slow and cautious.

Eventually, one of the larger kids chased the puck down the sideline and an opponent knocked him into our snow drift. We knew it was called a "check."

"You guys looking to play?" the stocky guy asked us, shaking snow from his hair. He had dark hair and a chiseled chin like Kirk Douglas.

"Sure," I said.

"You guys any good?" the thin, blonde skater who had checked him asked. They were a younger version of us, only their body sizes were reversed.

"No," Spalding said.

"We can skate but we never played hockey before," I explained.

"That's okay," the blonde said. "I'll take the surfer." He must have noticed Spalding's permanent sun tan.

"No fair, he's bigger," his partner said. They must have been the two team captains.

"Then I'll take the hippie." He must have been referring to my Army jacket. "He looks meaner."

"Make up your mind."

"You decide."

"I just did, twice."

I pulled a quarter out of my top jacket pocket. "How about we flip for it? Heads I go with you, tails with you."

They both nodded.

Heads. I went with the blonde. He was the natural leader. The other I immediately branded a whiner.

"Hey, let's go," one of their group hollered over.

They went back to the game while we laced up our skates.

As soon as we were ready we just jumped in, trying to remember who was on which side.

Talk about sending lambs to slaughter. These kids skated circles around us. At first it was fun but it soon became frustrating.

We were a bit larger than them, especially Spalding. He could have creamed a couple of my teammates but was too unsteady on his skates.

We didn't score too many points. We mostly raced up and down the ice, passing and stealing the puck, taking a few shots at a reluctant goalie. They looked like the youngest kids on the pecking order.

As we became more confident on the ice, Spalding and I began to play a game within the game. After a couple years of rooming together certain latent hostilities began to build up and a hockey game was the perfect arena to express them.

We began slamming, tripping and checking each other any time we were near the same area of the ice, whether the puck was around or not. At first it was all in good fun but after a while the smiles became more forced.

"I thought you guys were friends," my blond captain asked me after one blatant check.

"We were," I told him, only half-kidding.

Finally, Spalding was actually making a run for a goal, pushing the puck with his stick down the sideline and I crashed him with all my might at top speed. We both hit the ice with a bang. Me on my elbow, Spalding on his knee.

Our bodies were a tangled mess.

"That was a cheap shot," Spalding shouted, pushing at my skates with his stick.

"The same shit you've doing to me all day," I hollered back, hitting his stick with mine.

We began shoving each other as we tried to stand, knocking ourselves back down again.

We came at each other crawling on our knees, trying to

throw punches. None landed. Instead we rolled around on the ice until our two leaders pulled us apart.

"Each of you guys take two minutes in the penalty box," the Kirk Douglas clone said.

"This is a friendly game, take that shit back to college," his friend said.

We got up, embarrassed at being lectured to by a high school kid, and skated over to the nearest snow pile to cool our tempers.

We sat down and chisel chin pulled a six pack of Pabst Blue Ribbon out of a nearby drift. "Maybe one of these will cool you guys off," he handed us the six pack and went back to the game.

For a few minutes we just sipped our beers, staring at the game in front of us, letting our hearts slow down.

"What are you so pissed off about?" I asked. "Just 'cause Carol dumped you?"

"Look who's talking? Wait'll Liz comes back with some Matterhorn."

"That's it, you're jealous."

"Of you? That's a laugh."

We each took another sip of beer.

"A fine example we're setting for these kids," I said, changing the subject. We'd each drawn blood and neither of us wanted to continue. We'd unleashed our aggressions and now a cold chill was setting in.

"You guys ready for more?" the blond captain interrupted.

I looked at Spalding, reading his mind. "No thanks," I said.

"My feet are killing me," Spalding began to unlace his skates. The whole group came over as we began to leave. "Thanks for the beer and the game," Spalding told them.

"You guys live around here?" I asked.

"Yeah," they all kind of nodded. I looked at the impressive collection of glass-faced homes surrounding the lake.

"Must be nice here in the summer."

"Yeah, but the lakes are polluted."

"We can't swim in them."

"That's why we play hockey."

"They're supposed to clean them up."

"Hope they do," Spalding said and slung his skates over his stick like a veteran.

"See you guys," I followed suit.

They all gave us a peace sign as we walked toward the Chevy.

"Good kids," Spalding said.

"Yeah," I agreed. "Come back next weekend?"

"Naw, I think my hockey career's over," he said, rubbing his knee as he walked.

"Me, too," I admitted, feeling my elbow.

We grinned at each other.

Back at Depeyster, the hockey sticks became permanent fixtures above the piano, reminding us that even the best of friends need to air it out once in awhile.

Chapter Seven:
SPRING BREAK

After awhile, winter became pretty humdrum. "Winter was just winter," as Early would say.

It was cold and dreary but Spalding and I began entertaining Chris and Michelle on a regular basis. We became part of the college rut. Going to classes, eating, studying, partying on the weekends.

Winter was a good time to pump up grade averages so you could blow off a few classes come spring. We often discussed how anyone could graduate from college in Florida or California. How could they force themselves to study?

They had to be much better disciplined than us.

Eventually, the bitter cold wore off, the snow turned gray and the wind slackened. February gave way to March. The weather went from miserable to dreary.

That meant it was time to make plans for spring break. Our last spring break. The ultimate highlight of each college year. Party, party and more party.

I'd been going to Fort Lauderdale, Florida, since freshman year. Before I even knew Spalding. Sophomore and junior years he showed me the underbelly of the city, the sections the tourists completely miss.

By junior year, I considered Lauderdale my second home. I was a native, cursing the tourists like the rest of his friends. I could hardly wait for my final triumphant return.

Our plans were complete for the end of finals week. Early would drive Spalding to the airport. He always flew down. His parents bought him tickets so he could spend a few extra days with them.

I would share a ride with someone. There were always plenty of vans heading south, driving straight through. Twenty-four hours later I'd be pulling up in Spalding's driveway, surrounded by sunshine and palm trees.

His family had put me up the last two years and it had been quite enjoyable. The trip was brutal but the result was worth it.

I asked Michelle if she wanted to join me. Instead of staying with Spalding's family we could have rented a place, had a real vacation together.

But she declined, said she had some family matters to attend to. I think she wanted me to visit her over break, but as much as I liked her I couldn't pass up probably my last spring fling. I told her I'd meet the family come spring quarter.

Besides, I needed to prepare myself for the final showdown with Elizabeth. I had no idea what was happening on that front. Her last letter said she was travelling around Europe for spring break.

You couldn't blame her for staying as long as possible. What I wanted to know was whether or not she was travelling with her new friend.

By the time I'd arrived at Spalding's house I felt terrible. I was crashing hard. All we did was smoke and drink and laugh the whole way down. Complete strangers, I never met them before and after we drove back I'd probably never see them again.

But that's the way the sixties were. We shared everything and got along famously.

Except they stuck me with driving the last leg of the trip, when everyone was crashing, including me behind the wheel.

It was one of those trips where you keep nodding out,

then the adrenaline kicks in and you jump up, shake it off and keep going until you begin crashing again.

I was amazed I made it alive. I jumped out of the van around dusk, bid my new found friends farewell and rang Spalding's doorbell.

"Neighbor from the North," I smiled as Mrs. Spalding opened the screen door.

She hesitated a second, she didn't give me her usual "hello." I forgot my hair had grown considerably since the last time she saw me. And I was now sporting a beard.

"Well, welcome, honey, come right in," she quickly turned on the southern hospitality even though I could sense the change in attitude. "Paul's up at the store. He'll be right back."

Mrs. Spalding was a pleasant looking middle-aged lady with gray frosted hair and a permanent sun tan much like her son's. In fact, you could see a lot of Paul's characteristics in his mother.

I placed my backpack by the fireplace and sat down in a chair without being asked. I knew I was welcome despite the electricity in the air. I was confident that once we started talking she'd realize I was the same kid that'd been down to visit the previous two years. The one she'd treated like a second son.

"Would you like a beer?" she offered and I accepted, just to be hospitable, mind you.

"Grown a beard, I see," she said after returning from the kitchen with an already opened long neck.

"Yeah, I thought I'd try it. Where's Mr. Spalding?"

"He went to bed early, he wasn't feeling too good."

"The weather got him down?" I was joking but she agreed with me.

"Yes, we had some bad weather last week," she spoke slowly and deliberately. "Went into the forties. He came down with the flu."

"I guess it's tough when you're not used to it. The weather's beautiful now."

"Yes, it is." She hesitated for a second. "Doesn't that beard and long hair get hot?"

"I don't know, it kept me warm up north. I'll probably shave it come summer."

That was a lie. The more adults were offended by it the more resolved I was to keep it.

"I hope so," she said. "I hear Paul pulling in."

She went to watch for him at the window, like a soldier returning from war.

He entered the room carrying a couple of filled paper bags. "You've seen the hippie, Maw?" he laughed. "By summer I might have a beard of my own."

"You better not or you'll get a whippin', boy," she laughed.

"You need some help?" I asked, following him into the kitchen.

"You can help me chow down a couple sandwiches, you hungry?"

"I guess."

"You need a shower," he held his fingers to his nose. "You know where it's at."

"It was a long trip."

I headed to the shower, cleaned up, came back out and had a light meal fixed by my Southern roommate.

"How come you never cook at Depeyster?"

"'Cause we got Early."

"Where's your mom?"

"She turned in."

"I don't think she's digging me."

"She loves ya. Her whole generation's just crazy."

"Maybe I should look for another place to stay."

"What? She'd be insulted. Besides, we have to run down the boys."

"Who's that? Bones and company?"

"You got it."

Spalding was already finished eating. He ate even quicker in his element than up north, if that was humanly possible. I tried finishing faster myself, just to get out of the house.

Bones was one of his buddies from high school. There were a whole group of them and I knew them from my previous visits.

But before we left I remembered a task I had to attend to. "Hey, Spalding, can I borrow your phone?" I was rinsing my plate in the kitchen.

"Sure, go ahead."

I had to call home and let my parents know I arrived safely. If only they'd seen the group I traveled with, my dad would have had the Big One.

My mother answered the phone. That was a break. She was much more tolerant of my crazy whims.

"Hello, Mom," I tended to talk loudly because I was so far away even though it wasn't really necessary.

"Yes?"

"I'm down at Spalding's. Just called to let you know I'm okay."

"Well, thanks for calling. Don't stay out in the sun too long."

"I won't." *Right, what do you think I came down here for?*

"Here's your dad, he wants to talk to you."

"Okay."

"You're not anywhere near Key West, are you?"

"No, I'm in Lauderdale, at Spalding's house. Why?"

"I just saw a bunch of college kids on television, rioting in Key West. You stay away from there."

"I will."

"And they all had long hair and beards. You better not have no goddam beard."

"I don't." Thank god I was three thousand miles due south. "See you." I hung up.

After talking to my father I had a better idea of where Spalding's mom was coming from. Spalding had just finished combing his hair in the bathroom.

"How's the folks?" he asked.

"Fine."

"And the Big Cheese?" That was his nickname for my father.

"He said 'don't grow no goddam beard'."

"He's in for a surprise."

"I have an idea."

"What's that?"

"Let's go to the Keys."

"Sorry, we got plans for tonight. You can borrow the jeep tomorrow if you want."

"Just kidding. My father says they're rioting down there."

"That's where all the hippies go. You'd fit in perfect."

"Oh yeah, where do all the surfers go?"

"To the disco. That's where we're heading."

I followed him out the front door and we jumped into his open-topped Jeep CJ.

"Disco? What's that?"

"Where you been, man?"

"Let's not start that again."

We took off into the warm spring evening, the cool breeze blowing through our hair.

What a difference from the weather we left behind in Kent.

On our way to the disco we cruised by "the strip," the collection of bars across from the Lauderdale beach that constituted "the scene." Thousands of college kids from up north wandered the sidewalks, acting wild and crazy. On the other side of the road the dark surf roared.

Freshman year the beach scene was heaven. Sophomore year it was fun until Spalding began to show me other sections of the town. Junior year we practically avoided it. This year we just drove past it.

"I don't know how you dated just Carol all those years," I said, eyeing the non-stop parade of beautiful women.

Spalding and Carol were high school sweethearts.

"It wasn't easy."

Just past the strip Spalding pulled into a large parking lot surrounding a two story bar, Diamond Larry's Disco. It was huge. And there was a picture of a bearded Diamond Larry on a billboard outside. He was the only other bearded person I'd seen since I arrived. The hippie movement was slow in reaching Lauderdale. I guess they all went to the Keys.

"This the new hot spot?"

"You got it. He's building these all over South Florida."

We went inside. It was the largest bar I'd ever seen. Two floors packed with college kids and townies, mingling to the sound of taped rock music.

Where was the live band? Disco had invaded South Florida and no one was even aware of it.

It wasn't hard to find Spalding's buddies. They had the best location at the bar, right where everyone had to come to buy a drink. They also seemed to be friends with the bartender, which wasn't unusual. They knew everybody in town.

"Hey Bones," I shook Spalding's high school teacher friend's hand hippie style.

Bones was the local playboy in the Joe Namath mold. He spent his evenings at the bar, picking up different chicks every night.

And to listen to him tell it, he was quite successful at it.

"Hey, buddy," Bones said.

"How's this year's crop?"

"Better every year," he smiled ear to ear as a young lovely walked by.

I tried to shake Ken Johnson, Spalding's construction worker friend's hand also hippie style. He made me shake the old fashioned way.

"Come here, you freak," he grabbed me with a big bear hug. We ended up in a battle of strength, neither one of us letting go of the other's hand. "Not bad for a long haired pussy." We finally let go.

"Give him a break," Spalding said.

"You guys should be in Key West with the rest of the faggots," he laughed.

212

"That's what I told Spalding."

"You don't want to go down there," Bones said.

"Why not?"

"They're arresting people. You've only got one more quarter to go, then you can protest all you want."

Spalding ordered a round.

"How's Carol?" the bartender asked him.

It was a loaded question. I caught Bones giving him a strange look.

"All right, I guess." Spalding passed out the beers. "Actually, not so good," he told his closer friends under the din of the loud music.

"Yeah, we know," Bones made it easy for him.

"How do you guys know?"

"It's a small town."

"Besides, she's here tonight. With a friend."

"Who?"

"Bob Burkheart, Mr. Quarterback."

"I think she's just trying to make you jealous," Johnson said.

"Remember when he threw those three interceptions?" Bones asked.

"The Nova game," Spalding recalled.

"He's a jerk."

"I never liked him."

"Thanks guys. Can't we just forget it."

"Hardly. There she is."

Carol was sitting at the opposite side of the bar. Next to her was a tall, dark, handsome quarterback type.

"Should I go over?" Spalding asked.

"Let her come to you," Bones, the expert, advised.

Spalding caught her eye and raised a glass in her direction. She pointed him out to Bob, then came over by herself.

"Hello, Paul."

"How you doing?"

"Fair to middlin'." It was a Spalding expression that she had borrowed.

"Hi, Carol," the three of us said.

"See you brought the hippie from up north."

"Can't get rid of him. Kind of like a fly on shit."

"What's that say about you?" I gave him a shot.

"Should have brought Bob over," Johnson was looking to create a scene.

"Yeah, we could have asked him about the Nova game," Bones said.

"He doesn't feel comfortable with your type," she shot back.

"Break it up," Spalding said.

"Nice seeing you, Paul," she started to walk away. "You should find some better friends."

"You should find a better pair of tits," Johnson hollered after her.

"That's telling her," Spalding said.

"Spur of the moment," Johnson sipped his beer, grinning. He shot a dirty look to quarterback Bob as he greeted the returning Carol.

"That was fun," I said. "Now what?"

"Drink yourself senseless," Bones suggested.

And that's just what we did. We drank and laughed and watched the beautiful people dance.

Yet something was wrong. Our women were thousands of miles away while we were totally surrounded by hormone motivated young females. I didn't think I could take it. I needed a vacation away from my vacation.

During a break in the action I wandered outside for a breath of fresh air. My ears also needed some relief. In the parking lot I spotted a familiar van with Ohio plates. It was the one I came down with. I walked over. The side door was open and three of the four tourists were sleeping.

"How you guys doing?" I asked them.

They were all anthropology students who roomed together at Tri-Towers, Spalding's and my old digs. I knew most of their life histories after spending twenty-four hours together in the same vehicle. They would have made an interesting anthropological study themselves, especially since they were all freaks.

"We got shut out of our motel room," the only one awake told me. "I don't think they liked our hair," he tugged on his shoulder length locks.

"Bummer. What are you going to do?"

"We're going to sleep here until someone throws us out, then head to the Keys in the morning."

"I wouldn't do that."

"Why not?"

"I heard there's trouble down there."

"I heard the same thing but where else we going to go? Everything around here is filled."

"You guys are my ride home, I don't want to see you land in jail. Let me talk to my friends inside."

I went back into Diamond Larry's and consulted with the natives. Their consensus, crash at Dania Beach. It was slated to be converted into a state park but for now it was unknown territory, used only by local hippies and fishermen.

The more they talked about it the more it appealed to me, too. I felt I was a drag on Spalding's parents, that I'd worn out my welcome.

Camping in the wild on a deserted beach appealed to my back-to-nature sensibilities, especially in my drunken condition.

"Sounds great," I said. "Spalding, how about you telling these guys how to get there?"

He walked me out to the parking lot.

"Listen, buddy, I think I'm going to join them."

"What?"

"I think we need a break as much as anybody. And I won't be embarrassing your parents."

"You're drunk."

"I am but I'd also like to try something new. I've done your house the last two years."

"This isn't because of Twin Lakes?"

"What? Hell, no. But Carol's right. You need a better class of friends."

I punched him in the arm and he punched me back. It hurt. I made a deal with the hippies in the van. I'd help them find Dania beach if they let me crash with them. No problem.

Dania beach turned out to be a godsend, like a week long vacation on a deserted island. We camped, swam all day, caught rays and built a fire in the evening. Completely insulated from the crazies in town.

I read a couple books and mulled over my options from the Vietnam War to Liz and Michelle. Spalding came by and brought his friends to visit around the campfire. His parents didn't have to worry about the neighbor's reaction to housing a hippie.

And best of all, Spalding and I got a break from each other. I guess we were getting on each other's nerves. By the time I headed back up north I was tanned and rested. Ready to take on the world and top off the best year ever with the best quarter ever.

Spring Quarter

"And it's one, two, three,
What are we fighting for?
Don't ask me, I don't give a damn,
Next stop is Vietnam;
And it's five, six, seven,
Open up the pearly gates;
There ain't no time to wonder why,
Whoopie—we're all gonna die."

Country Joe McDonald

Chapter One:
THE PIANO MOVERS

There I was on the steps of the Washington Monument, a half million protesters standing in front of me, awaiting my every word.

"My fellow freaks. I mean Americans. This is a great day in American history. I've just met with President Nixon..."

The crowd went wild, jeering Nixon with a chorus of boos that would have made Brooklyn Dodger fans proud.

"Wait, hold on a minute," I hollered into the five microphones. The television and radio sound guys took their earphones off, cursing me for cranking up the volume without warning them. "Sorry guys," I turned my head from the mikes.

"Give me a second," I pleaded with the crowd. "The President has agreed to our demands. He has seen the light."

The crowd went wild again, this time their jeers turned to cheers.

"The war is over, the war is over," they started chanting. The crowd rushed the podium. I was carried away by the masses as the Beatles played behind me.

I could already read the headlines: VIETNAM WAR OVER, KUBIK SHOWS NIXON HOW.

Somewhere off in the distance a dog was barking. It was Harold. Once again a great dream was interrupted just before its climax. I had to get to him before he woke Spalding and Early or they'd kill me.

Spring quarter I'd gone straight back to Depeyster. No stopping home for this kid. I didn't have the guts to show my parents my new beard and longer hair. Maybe I'd chicken out and shave it come summer, maybe not. I'd worry about that in June.

Early had picked up Spalding at the airport and we all arrived the Friday night before classes started. Spalding and I immediately crashed out, exhausted from our travels.

Early, on the other hand, was full of energy. He was sporting a brand new short haircut, almost like a flat top from our childhood days. As usual, he was ahead of his time.

The early March weather was mild. Cool by Lauderdale standards but pleasant compared to the end of winter quarter.

As we slept, Early had cleaned. He opened the windows, let in the fresh air and generally straightened up. I guess he was pretty exhausted himself by the time he crashed because I reached Harold first that fateful Saturday morning.

Harold was standing on his hind legs at the front window, his two paws on the sill, barking his brains out.

It was an unusual display of aggression. Harold wasn't much of a watchdog. He was so used to the organized craziness of college life that nothing seemed to faze him.

I tried to quiet him because he was my responsibility. Early, the cat lover, disliked dogs and Spalding hated all pets equally. I was always amazed that they didn't bitch about him more often.

By the time I reached the front window I could hear Spalding grumbling upstairs. He must've been looking out his front window at the same time I did because the next words out of his mouth were: "Holy shit!"

Right in the middle of our front lawn was a U-Haul truck. A tall, skinny hippie with long flowing hair was standing behind it, guiding the driver. He was trying to edge it up to our front porch.

Spalding came downstairs, followed by Early, who was hollering "Shut that stupid dog up."

"Get a load of this," I told Early. Since his window faced the back of the house I figured he had not yet seen the spectacle.

I stepped aside so he could take a gander.

"What's going on?" Spalding asked.

"Did we get evicted while we were gone?" I wondered.

"I sent Skerl the rent," Early said. The rent was just one of his many household responsibilities.

We watched as four burly guys about the size of Kent's offensive line exited the truck. They followed their skinny leader onto the front porch.

They began pounding on the door. I was almost afraid to answer it. Early, however, was doing a slow burn. Like I said before, Early was fairly wide himself. He was built like a truck. And his new haircut gave him a mean look.

But all that was negated by his attire. His dress said a lot about his personality. He dressed like an old man. While I was wearing my boxers and Spalding his gym shorts, Early wore a red silk robe and plaid cloth slippers.

"What do you think you're doing?" Early practically ripped open the door.

"We've come for my piano," the thin nerd stated, surrounded by a forest of human redwoods. Only the screen door separated the antagonists. I held Harold in check.

"The piano?" We were totally taken back. We looked at each other in shock.

"Yeah, it's my piano. I lived here last year."

"Come on in," Spalding opened the screen, attempting to be accommodating.

"We got to check this out," I said.

"Check it out with whoever you want but we're taking it anyway."

Once the movers breached the front entrance it was too late to stop their charge. We bid a hasty retreat to the outer ridges of the battle scene. Early called Skerl as they began pushing furniture out of the way.

"Skerl says it's theirs, let 'em have it," he said from the bathtub.

Spalding and I sat in the living room. We had front row seats to the spectacle. Despite their size, the fivesome struggled with the piano.

We might have helped them if they hadn't been so crude and rude in their approach. As it was we enjoyed watching their incompetence.

They managed to push and pull the old beast from the dining room to the front doorway.

"Why didn't you guys take it with you when you left?" Spalding asked.

"I didn't have room for it in my new apartment," the leader explained. "I knew it wasn't going anywhere."

"Then why take it now?"

"I want to take it home before classes start. I'm graduating in June."

At this point they ran into a snag. All the king's horses and all the king's men couldn't coax the damn thing through the doorway. No matter how they pushed, shoved and jostled the piano just would not fit.

"How'd you get it in here?" Early asked.

"I forget," he answered.

After a few more minutes, the leader of the pack suddenly threw in the towel. "Screw it, you can have it," he said. "Let's get out of here."

They pushed it back into the living room just far enough to walk around it and headed back outside. We just looked at them in wonder. Early began to simmer. He was now angrier than before.

But he waited until the big guys were back in the truck before he exploded.

"Hey, how about putting it back where you found it," Early hollered to the leader, who was jumping into the driver's seat.

"Up yours," he hollered back.

"Asshole," Early screamed.

They took off without looking back.

"Way to go Early, now they're mad at us."

"Whatever happened to peace and love?"

Before we pushed the piano back into the dining room we noticed for the first time an abstract painting on the wall. Black, life-sized figures were entangled in erotic poses. Like the piano, they were left there by a previous tenant. The piano had hidden them from our view.

"Check this out man," Early said. He was pulling while we were shoving, so he saw it first.

"Far out."

"I wonder what kind of weirdos lived here before us?"

"Or who'll be living here next year?"

"I think I'll just stay forever," I said.

"I'm sure Skerl will give you a good deal."

"This is going to be some quarter."

Chapter Two:
A BOMB SCARE

Something was wrong, somewhere. The first day of classes came and went and still no sign of either Michelle or Elizabeth.

The girls next door hadn't heard from Michelle, except that she might be a few days late. And I wasn't in any hurry to hear from Elizabeth, hoping to avoid a big showdown.

But I thought she'd at least call and let me know she was back.

What was going on? Maybe they had met each other, compared notes and decided to do away with me completely. Maybe I was a marked man and didn't know it.

The second day of school I was sitting in a world literature class at Satterfield Hall, the main English Department building.

Why I chose to torture myself with such a difficult elective my last quarter beat the hell out of me. I should have taken advanced basket weaving.

It was 11:30 A.M. and my stomach was grumbling. I didn't know if I could make it until the class ended. At least the hunger took my mind off Michelle. I was kicking myself for never asking for her home phone number. Never thought I'd need it.

Right in the middle of a lecture on Andre Malraux a graduate student walked in and whispered something in the professor's ear. He stood up. "Sorry, people. We have a bomb threat. Just pretend this is a fire drill and exit quickly and silently. Don't panic. Follow me. We'll regroup on the Commons."

We fell in line behind our professor, a skinny red head from New Orleans who'd lost most of his Southern accent. Bomb scares were nothing new on campus but it was my first of the new year, 1970.

The previous spring they'd been about as regular as Kent football team losses. Probably some kid who was as hungry as myself couldn't wait for lunch and had a friend call one in to the campus police.

They searched the building as we met under a tree just off the Commons where the rallies were held. A girl's field hockey class had to cease action to accommodate all the students.

"This tree will be our meeting place the rest of the year," the professor decided. "I'd let you go but these bomb scares are starting to piss me off."

Whoa. He emphasized "piss me off." It was unusual talk from a English professor but he succinctly captured the mood of the general campus population.

The rallies, bomb scares and rap sessions were becoming passé. Nothing seemed to make any difference. The Vietnam War kept marching on, soldiers died, civilians were massacred and nothing changed. The war machine kept cranking out casualties.

I started believing what the protest leaders claimed. The war was good for the economy.

"We're going to continue our class right here under this tree, so make yourselves comfortable and prepare to take notes."

This was a radical approach. Once in a great while a prof would take his class outside for a change of pace, but never during a bomb scare. They were always good for an early quit.

As I was about to sit down, my eyes caught a familiar face being dismissed by her professor. Elizabeth was walking away with an unknown female friend.

I immediately jumped up.

"Dr. Naples, there's something I have to do and it can't wait."

"This isn't grade school, Mr. Kubik." He thought I was talking about going to the bathroom.

"This is important, sir."

"You didn't pull this bomb scare, did you?"

"Me? No, sir. I have to go."

I never walked away from a class before in my life but somehow it felt refreshing, like I was saying good-bye to the student life and entering the real world. For the first time I was acting like an adult. The rest of the class stared at me in awe.

I ran to catch up to Elizabeth.

"Elizabeth?" I reached her just before the Student Union.

"Matthew? It's wonderful to see you." She gave me a hug but somehow it wasn't a romantic hug, more like a formal Aunt Bertha type hug. "This is my friend Kathy. She was in Switzerland with me."

"Glad to meet you," I shook her hand. "When did you get back?"

"Oh, Saturday," Liz said.

"Listen, I have to run, you two probably have a lot to talk about," Kathy said, then disappeared inside the Union.

What did that mean?

"Heading home?" I asked her.

"No, I've got another class at the Education Building. Wasn't that bomb scare dreadful?"

"They're becoming old hat."

"I forgot all about them. They don't have anything like that in Switzerland. We're so crude compared to them."

"You must have liked it."

"It was delicious."

Oh, oh. That was the word I loved to hear her pronounce. "Delicious." It was her favorite word. The way she said it turned me on beyond belief.

We walked in silence to the front of the Education Building. I had to build up my courage for the big question.

"You know, I thought you would have called me by now."

"I was going to, Matthew," she stopped and looked away from my eyes. "But things have changed."

There it was. I knew what was coming next.

"Changed?"

"Yes, I met someone over there and he lives near me. He's the one I wrote you about, the guy who goes to Ohio State."

Ah, yes. The Buckeye.

"I understand. I started hanging around with someone myself."

"You did? Who?" She was looking me in the eyes again, surprised by the payback.

"Remember Michelle, the girl living next door?"

"That slut?"

"I thought you liked her? I thought we had an agreement."

"I knew you couldn't be trusted."

She turned and walked away in a snit, like I had done her wrong.

I was standing in a flow of students, flabbergasted.

"Women."

Shaking my head, I started walking downhill toward the flat area of front campus when coming in my direction was the second half of my dilemma.

"Michelle, where've you been?"

"Oh, Matthew." She gave me a hug, a real hug. "I wish you'd came home with me over spring break."

"Why?"

"Because I needed you."

"What's wrong?"

We started walking along the prettiest part of campus. The trees were still leafless but the buds were just dying to burst out. The black squirrels scampered about, digging up acorns they'd buried the previous fall.

"My parents are getting divorced." Tears began to build up in her eyes.

"That's too bad."

"Not really. My dad's an alcoholic. It's been hell living with him. It's just that we're going to lose the farm."

"Damn, I wish I had some money," I emptied out my jean pockets like a clown, hoping to bring a smile to her face.

"I didn't need your money, I just needed your love."

"Oh, oh. You didn't call the Buckeye, did you?"

"Yeah, he was there. He's my friend from home," she smiled through her tears. "But he's not you."

Bingo. That's what I wanted to hear.

I put my arm around her as we walked. "Where you going?"

"Satterfield."

"Satterfield. I just came from there. It might not be open. We had a bomb scare."

"It's starting again."

"Are you scared?"

"After what I've been through at home, this place is easy."

"I know what you mean, I haven't even been home."

"Why not?"

"I don't think my father digs my beard. Or my hair."

"I like it," she ran her fingers through it. "And your tan."

"I wish you'd come to Florida."

"You've got to tell me all about it."

We'd reached Satterfield and they were letting the students back inside.

"See you tonight?"

"I think I remember where you live."

"Depeyster."

"That's right. Depeyster."

Chapter Three:
FARM COUNTRY

The following weekend, I offered to go back home with Michelle. Just for moral support, mind you. And for extra comfort I brought Spalding, Chris and Early.

We always liked taking excursions in the country and with spring in the air, what better time? The weather was still cool, even a bit misty, and the roadside showed the ravages of winter.

Broken branches, brown fields and leftover trash dotted the landscape. Michelle didn't speak much during the hour-long trip to eastern Ohio. You could tell she had a lot on her mind.

Early provided the entertainment with a new toy, a harmonica that he was teaching himself to play Dylan songs on. Spalding and I talked baseball; the girls shared domestic troubles.

Once we pulled off the main highway and began travelling the back roads, Spalding pulled a stunt he'd become famous for when driving the Chrysler. It was the first time he'd tried it with the '57 Chevy.

For some unknown reason, he liked driving on open fields. Maybe he thought he still had his Jeep from back home. Just when the conversation was going stale and Early's tunes began to repeat themselves, Spalding swerved off the road into the first fenceless area he came to.

Talk about your not so subtle wake up call. We all took a pounding, our heads bouncing off the Chevy's headliner. Yet it also made for great fun. We were laughing so hard tears formed in our eyes.

That is, until we got stuck in the mud. Yes, Spalding didn't compensate for the wet terrain. This wasn't Florida sand, this was good old-fashioned Ohio muck.

As he slammed the gas pedal to the floor the rear tire just kept digging itself deeper into the dirt. The laughter ceased and one by one we exited into the middle of an empty field. Luckily, there were no homes nearby. Or maybe it was unlucky.

"Why do you always do this?" I hollered at him.

"It's in his genes," Chris said.

"Then he ought to get a new pair," Early said.

"Not funny. What're we going to do?" Michelle asked.

Spalding just leaned against the car's hood and smiled. "Isn't it great out here? This is God's country."

"Come on, Kubik, let's get some sticks to throw under the tire," Early told me.

We left Spalding with the women and headed toward the nearest clump of trees. "What's he on?" Early asked me.

"Nothing, I don't think. It's just a natural high."

"There's something wrong with him."

"He's just blowing off some steam. You know, spring quarter, graduation, the Army. Not everyone has a far out number."

"I wouldn't mind joining the Army, seeing the world."

"Are you kidding me? There's easier ways to see the world."

"What are the chances you'd get shot?" Early explained. "There's plenty of cake jobs. My old man spent the war at Virginia Beach, fixing Jeeps."

"My uncle saved Alaska."

"See what I mean?"

We grabbed some big, broken branches and dragged them

back to the Chevy. Spalding was entertaining the girls with Early's harmonica. He wasn't too bad.

"I didn't know you could play," Early said.

"You didn't ask me."

"I didn't want you playing and driving at the same time. Look what happened just from listening."

"Good one, Early," Michelle laughed. It was great to see her lighten up a little.

"Go ahead and drive," Early said to Michelle. Mom was taking charge. "We'll push."

"I'll get in with Michelle, for added weight," Chris jumped in the back seat. She had more sense than to help us push.

Spalding and I positioned ourselves behind the back bumper. Early took a couple large branches and placed them under the left rear tire, the one that made the car go.

Michelle looked at us in the outside mirror and smiled.

"Take it slow, just a little gas," Early advised. Spalding and I put all our weight into trying to raise the rear of the car while Early shoved the branches against the spinning tire.

We rocked the Chevy up and down, the tire spun, then it caught all of a sudden. Spalding and I fell to our knees, a branch kicked out and knocked Early on his back.

Michelle pulled a few feet away and then stopped.

"Keep going," Spalding hollered and Michelle stepped on it, splattering us with loose mud. By the time we stood up, the girls and the Chevy were back on the road and we were covered with Ohio's richest soil.

We looked at each other and couldn't stop laughing.

"I don't know if we should let these guys in our car," Chris said once we caught up with them.

"Can't you guys call a cab?" Michelle jested.

We jumped in the back seat and the girls drove. That was a first.

"I hope you don't live too far away," Early said.

"I hope you don't think you're coming in the house?" Michelle said.

"Put 'em up in the barn," Chris said.

"Very funny," I spoke for the guys.

It was late afternoon by the time we reached Cortland, Ohio, on the eastern rim of Mosquito Lake. Michelle's place was a couple of acres of non-working farm with an enormous lake in its backyard.

There was a quaint farmhouse near the road and a barn around back. Michelle beeped when we pulled into the driveway. Her mother Jane and younger sister Marianne came out to greet us. You could see the resemblance immediately. Her sister was almost a twin, except she was shorter, younger and had larger breasts, more like her mother's. Her mother looked strikingly beautiful for her age, she must have been at least forty-five, and she wore her reddish brown hair in a perm.

"What happened to you?" her mother asked.

"We got stuck in the mud."

"Well, come on inside and clean up."

"We could just rinse off in the barn." Spalding suddenly felt responsible for our condition.

"I was just kidding," Michelle said.

"It would be a lot easier," I said.

"You'll catch your death of cold," Marianne said.

"Maybe we could look around before we clean up," Early suggested.

"Yeah, we'll just make another mess," Spalding said.

"Don't you have horses?" Chris asked.

"Yeah, two. Come see them," Marianne led us back to the barn.

Michelle went inside with her mom. We thought it was a good idea to leave them alone for awhile anyway.

Marianne wore her long, blond hair in a ponytail, her striped bell bottom pants and loose purple blouse gave her the impression of a high school hippie.

She took us around back to the barn. The view was magnificent. The lake was spread out before us like a still life painting. A pair of horses pranced around a small corral.

"Anyone know how to ride?"

"Spalding has a horse, don't you Spalding?"

"Yeah, I board one. What kind are they?"

"Buster, here, is a ten year old Appaloosa." Marianne took him by the mane and petted his jaw. "He's a baby. Lightning is a different story."

The young black stallion shook his whole head at the mention of his name. He stayed away from the crowd, prancing with unleashed energy.

"I don't know about him," Chris said.

"Think you could handle him, Spalding?" Marianne asked.

It was weird hearing a high school kid call him, "Spalding." She was obviously smitten with him.

"I'll give it a try," he said, basking in all the attention.

"How about you, Early? Try Buster?" Spalding said.

"I don't know, I never rode one before."

"Go ahead, there's nothing to it," Chris said.

"Then why don't you?"

"I'm not dressed for it," she pulled at the hem of her miniskirt.

"You ever ride one?" he asked me.

"A couple times, give it a go."

Early agreed. Marianne and Spalding saddled up Buster with ease, then Marianne held Lightning back as Spalding buckled him in.

"Can we take them out of the corral?"

"Sure, there's a path along the lake."

Spalding went first. Marianne held Lightning by the bit as Spalding jumped on like the Marlboro man, muddied from top to bottom.

I swung open the gate. Marianne let go and Lightning burst out like he was in the Kentucky Derby.

Spalding displayed his experience, reining in the beast, letting him rise up a few times, then controlling his pace.

Early was next. Marianne brought Buster over to the

wooden fence so he could climb on easier. Early jumped on and Marianne held Buster in check, walking for awhile with the horse.

We followed behind, watching the experiment.

"Ready?"

"Let 'em go."

Marianne stepped out of the way. Buster was a peach. He took a few steps, then stopped.

"What's his problem? C'mon. Giddy-up," Early pulled on the reins and nothing happened. "If I was paying for this I'd want my money back."

Spalding brought Lightning around to see what the hold up was.

"Try kicking him with your heels."

"Won't that hurt him?"

"It'll jump start him."

Early dug his heels into Buster's side, hard. It jump started him all right. Buster leaped up. Early almost fell off and the large animal made a beeline for the barn.

Early held on for dear life, ducking his head just before the top of the barn door separated his skull from the rest of his torso.

Buster calmly trotted into his stall and began munching on his feed. We ran into the barn after them.

"That's the shortest horse ride I ever saw in my life," Marianne said.

Spalding rode up to the entrance and dismounted like Hoss on Bonanza, riding to the rescue. "Is Early all right?" He handed the reins to Marianne who put Lightning in his stall.

"He just turned a whiter shade of pale," I said.

Early's knees were wobbling. "I just saw my whole life pass in front of me," he said.

"That must have been a quickie," Spalding kidded.

"Yeah, how's it end?"

"You guys are funny, real funny."

Early sounded like Barney Fife when Andy Griffith got the

best of him. He walked outside to clear his head. We all followed him down to the lake while Marianne put the horses away.

"Dynamite view."

"This could be our commune, Spalding."

"What do you mean?"

"Her mom's selling the place."

"Why?"

I didn't know how much I should tell them or how much they already knew.

"Because of the divorce," Chris said.

"Her parents are getting divorced?" Early asked.

"Yeah."

"Must be tough."

"I don't know anyone who's been divorced."

"Me neither."

"I had an uncle once. Before I was born."

We were standing by the shore, skipping stones in the lake, when Michelle came out to us. Her black eye liner was streaking down her face. You could tell she'd been crying.

"You okay?" I put my arm around her.

"I'm fine. Would you guys mind terribly if we went back to Depeyster?"

"Hey, no problem."

"It was a great trip."

"We're a mess anyway."

"You should have seen Early play John Wayne."

We walked back to the Chevy, hooking up with Marianne on the way.

"You guys taking off?" she was surprised.

"You and mom can handle it," Michelle told her. They kissed. "Come visit us if you need to get away."

We jumped in the car, Spalding and Chris in front, me, Early and Michelle in back.

"I'm really gonna miss this place," she whispered in my ear as we drove off.

"Me, too," I said.

Chapter Four:
THE MURPH'S MARRIAGE

Spring quarter also marked the end of an era for the Murph. He announced his marriage date, April 4, 1970. He waited until April first to spring it on us. The April Fool, the king of corny one-liners and practical jokes, played one on himself.

No longer would he be living the good life on Depeyster. Mary Lou and he would be experiencing domestic bliss at Allerton Apartments, the married students complex.

The Murph offered to keep paying us his forty dollars a month share of the Depeyster rent but we let him slide. It was our wedding present to him. We knew he needed the money and besides, there was only a little over two months of school left. We'd eat the difference with pleasure.

The wedding's location was Fred Fuller Park, a quaint recreation and nature area on the banks of the Cuyahoga River within walking distance of Depeyster. We often took refuge there when we wanted somewhere off-campus to commune with nature.

There were some baseball fields, playground equipment, picnic tables and an old-fashioned gazebo, perfect for an outdoor wedding ceremony. A covered pavilion stood nearby in case the elements refused to cooperate.

The Murph's luck held out and the day of the wedding was cool and sunny. We were pretty much left out of the planning for the event and it seemed the Murph was, too.

Mary Lou's parents took charge. Their only concession to the wishes of the bride and groom was that it was outdoors, kind of a hippie wedding.

The bride's maids all wore long flowered dresses. The bride wore a semi-traditional white dress, nothing fancy. Although it was loose it still couldn't conceal the fact that she was eight months pregnant. The Murph wore a Nehru jacket that was in at the time but turned out to be the fashion Edsel of our generation. It pushed his neck up into his face like his head was going to explode.

The only real mystery before the big day was who was going to be the Murph's best man.

Would it be me, Spalding, or his roommate Early? I think he didn't want to offend any of us so he chose his brother Tom, our automobile provider.

I guess it's always better to keep it in the family anyway. After June he might not see any of us again but his brother Tom would always be there to crab about how he wasn't picked to be the best man. Marriages were a pain in that sense.

Since we lived so close we arrived only minutes before the ceremony began. Mary Lou, the Murph, the best man and bride's maid, and the family preacher crowded inside the gazebo. The rest of us circled around it.

Spalding, Early and me wore our Sunday best: sport coats and slacks, penny loafers, deck shoes. Early looked good in his new crewcut and Spalding was stylish in his blond curly hair and mustache but my long hair and beard just didn't fit with the collar and tie.

Michelle and Chris wore flowered mini-dresses, as did Renee, Sarah and Jennifer. They were pretty much the style of the day for the female types. The only differences were colors and accoutrements: you know, scarves, jewelry, beads, shoes and purses.

Before the wedding there were the usual introductions and hand shaking, saying hello to the Murph's parents and siblings, who we knew, and Mary Lou's family, who we didn't.

Even though Mary Lou's father was a professor at Kent, in four years I'd never laid eyes on him. It made you realize how big a campus it really was.

After the usual "I do's," the Murph and Mary Lou each read a little poem they'd composed. I wish I could remember the words but I can't. They're lost on the winds of time. A lone female guitarist sang Joni Mitchell's folk song, "Both Sides Now," and it was over.

The Murph was no longer our roommate. Good luck, Mary Lou. At least you knew what you were getting into.

I'd barely known the Murph when he asked me if I wanted to room with him and a couple of other guys our sophomore year. We were all moving from our freshman dorm to a brand new three building set called Tri-Towers.

Life was strange like that. You make a decision on the spur of the moment without hardly a thought and its effects stay with you the rest of your life.

We only had a few minutes to speak with the bridegroom after the ceremony.

"Where's the honeymoon, good buddy?" Early asked the Murph, once we retreated to a spread of food under the pavilion. We hadn't seen much of him before the ceremony to ask such questions.

"Niagara Falls. Pretty bourgeois, eh?"

"Slowly we turned, step by step..." Early put his arm around my waist and we did an imitation of a famous Three Stooges' sketch.

"You got it," he laughed.

"When's Mary Lou due?" Michelle asked.

"May 4th. We have exactly one month of freedom left."

"The first one's always late," Chris said.

"I hope so, about a year late would be great."

"Give you enough time to get your act together?"

"There'll never be enough time for that."

"You gonna graduate?"

"If I don't now, I never will."

"You can say that again. It's hard with a family."

"I bet you guys never thought you'd see me with a family."

"I knew you were history once you got that high number."

"Yeah, how'd you pull that one off?"

"Thee luck of thee Irish, me boddie," he said with a fake brogue. "Thee luck of thee Irish."

"You kissed the Blarney Stone, all right. That's one thing I'll say about you."

"Oops, got to go, guys. The little woman's calling, except she ain't so little anymore."

The Murph signed off with his little hand wave and disappeared into the crowd.

"Hope he has a son," Spalding said.

"No, an Irish lassie," Michelle said.

"Isn't that a dog?" Early joked.

"No, that's an Irish Setter."

"What're you, taking over the Murph's corny jokes?" I asked Early.

"Someone's got to do it."

We waved good-bye as the newlyweds jumped into Mary Lou's parents' brand new Lincoln Continental, en route to Canada. Then we walked downhill to the '57 Chevy, his present to us.

"Wonder if he'll make it across the border," I said.

"Going to Canada's no problem," Spalding said. "If they're smart they won't let him back in."

"Sure, abuse him since he's not here to defend himself."

"We always abused him right to his face," Early said.

"Yeah, I know. You gotta love him for that."

Chapter Five:
SPRING ROAD TRIP

Travel was a prerequisite for any college student in the 1960s. After graduation, you were expected to go to the East Coast, the West Coast or Europe. But we took it one step further.

Each quarter we tried to take a little side trip around Ohio or one of the neighboring states. We'd been to Cleveland, Akron, Detroit, Columbus and so on and so forth. Once we even had a hitchhiking contest to Toronto to see the rock musical *Hair*.

It was a quarterly ritual, kind of like Spalding spending a night in the slammer. It was automatic.

So it wasn't as crazy as it sounds when the first warm weekend in April we decided the ultimate trip to finish off our college career would be a visit to New York City. The Big Apple.

We even had a place to crash. Spalding had a friend studying art at the Pratt Institute, right in the heart of the city.

Besides, our steady dates, Chris and Michelle were tied up at home that weekend. Michelle with her parent's divorce and Chris with a visiting relative. What better excuse to avoid potential in-laws than a spring road trip.

Our grand plan was to cut our Friday afternoon classes, meet at noon on front campus, walk over to Main Street and stick out our thumbs. There was no way the '57 Chevy could make the 500 mile trip, so hitchhiking was our only alternative.

Back then hitchhikers were part of the scenery. They were all over the highways, more common than cigarette butts on the road berm. No one considered it stupid or dangerous like they do today.

Between the two of us, we were carrying about sixty dollars and the clothes on our back for a weekend in the wildest city in the world.

Spalding brought along his new 35 mm camera to catalog the trip for posterity.

In no time at all we were picked up by a suitcase student in a beat-up Ford. Kent had a lot of commuters who drove to classes each day from the Cleveland and Akron areas. They couldn't afford the room and board costs so they studied while living at home with their parents.

There was another contingent who stayed in Kent all week but headed home each weekend for the part-time job or the girl next door. Kent's student population dropped considerably each weekend.

This weekend warrior was also a closet hippie. His hair wasn't very long but as soon as we jumped inside he fired up a joint.

We'd lost our paranoia from our autumn bust but we were still practical enough not to carry any illegal substances ourselves.

"Where you guys headed?"

"New York City."

"Wow, far out. I've never been further than Pittsburgh."

"Come on with us."

"I'd like to but I got to get to work."

"Where at?"

"The Burger Chef in Streetsboro."

"You could miss a weekend."

"Not with *my* boss."

"Oh well, at least you'll be feeling good all day."

By the time we finished the joint we were through Twin Lakes to the intersection of Routes 43 and 303, Streetsboro,

Ohio. Our ride, Jeff, left us off on the corner.

Spalding asked him for a picture so he flashed a peace sign while sucking on a roach. We were still about three miles from the Turnpike Entrance.

A Streetsboro townie provided us with the connecting ride. He was the real deal, a country boy blasting Merle Haggard tunes from the AM radio in his pickup truck. There was a stereotype back then that country folks hated hippies. It came from the movie *Easy Rider* and there was more than a hint of truth in it. Yet this urban cowboy offered us a couple of Strohs beers in the same spirit of friendship as our previous ride.

"Is it true what they say about them hippie chicks?" he asked. "That they'll spread their legs if you as much as look at 'em?"

"Happens all the time," Spalding said between sips. "But it gets old, don't it Kube?"

"Yeah, sure does. That's why we're going to New York, we need a change of pace. These Kent girls are just plumb too easy."

"Man, I go to downtown Kent sometime but I never seem to get anywhere with 'em."

"You gotta grow your hair long, buy yourself a pair of bell bottoms," Spalding suggested.

"Yeah, you gotta give up those cowboy boots. Give them what they want, that's what I say."

"You know, you guys might have something there. Maybe I'll give it a try."

"We're getting off up here, by the turnpike."

"I'll let you off by the entrance ramp. Smokie don't like you boys hitching on the turnpike."

"We hear you."

"Thanks."

Spalding asked him for a picture. He held up his can of Strohs and gave us the finger. "That'll be a big ten-four," he said.

"I guess we're certifiable hippies," Spalding said as he put his camera away.

"To him we are."

If there was any question about it we were given additional proof a few minutes later. A yellow school bus filled with junior high kids drove by. They hung out the windows, flashed us the peace sign and yelled things like "far out" and "groovy."

We flashed them back.

It looked like it was going to be a glorious trip. Two quick rides and we were right on the launching pad to the East Coast.

If we were lucky we might catch one ride going all the way. We weren't very lucky. Car after car looked at us as if we were from outer space. All the college kids were going west toward Cleveland. Only the older generation was going east toward Pennsylvania.

Even Spalding's Cleveland Indians baseball cap, a present from Chris, wasn't doing us any good. My famous good luck had gone sour.

"This is getting old," I said as another country boy lived up to his reputation and threw a beer can at us as he sped by. "How long have we been here?"

"About an hour. How far is New York?"

"About eight hours."

"I've lost my buzz."

"Me too."

"It'll be late by the time we get there."

"I know, I'm starting to worry about it."

"Where's your buddy live anyway?"

"Brooklyn."

"Well that's an okay area, huh?"

"I don't know. Did you ever hear of Bedford-Stuyvesant?"

"They had riots there, didn't they?"

"That's where he's at."

"Why didn't you say so?"

"I thought you knew."

"Shit, I don't want to walk through the ghetto in the middle of the night."

"You want to call it quits?"

"What do you want to do?"

"You make the call."

"He's your friend."

"This was your idea."

"All right, let's forget it."

"Fine."

Just like that we walked to the other side of the street and began hitching in the opposite direction. I let Spalding take the first shift, sticking his thumb in the face of drivers exiting the turnpike tollgates. As he hitched, I noticed an aluminum street light pole filled with graffiti.

It seemed to be a popular spot for hitchhikers, probably on their way to Kent. There were names, residences, destinations, dates and phone numbers written all over it.

My favorite was a series of comments in three different scripts about Kent State President Robert White.

"President White's a jerk," the first writer wrote.

"No, he's not," a second disagreed.

"Yes, I am," a third added.

While scanning the neighborhood I came across another interesting tidbit. A rolled up chunk of aluminum foil. Something told me to pick it up and unwrap it, even though any number of gross items might be contained in the mysterious package.

As I began to unroll it, a little Fiat stopped for Spalding. The driver was around our age, clean shaven, with slightly longish hair. Spalding jumped in the front but when I squeezed into the back I had to push some soldier's stuff aside.

There was an Army jacket like mine, black boots, and green shirts and pants laying all in a jumble. And on top of it all was an infantry helmet.

"Where you guys from?" the driver asked us.

"Cleveland," I answered.

"Florida," Spalding said.

"I'm from Lorain," he said. "You guys are going the wrong way for the opener."

"What opener?" Spalding wondered.

"The Indians game, I saw your cap."

"Naw, it's just a present from a friend."

"The opener's today?"

"Starts in a couple hours."

"What do you think, Fly-boy? We could crash at my parent's house."

"I'm burnt out. We ought to just head back."

"Back where?" the driver asked.

"To Kent."

"That's where I'm heading," he said.

"That settles it," Spalding said.

"It must be fate," I agreed. "You go to Kent?"

"Yeah, if you can't go to college, go to Kent. Bill Schroeder." He introduced himself while making the turn back onto Route 43. "You guys go there too?"

"Yep. Paul Spalding."

"Matt Kubik. What's with the Army stuff?"

"I'm in ROTC. I have to dress up once a month and play soldier."

"Must be tough."

"Other students give you a hard time?"

"Most of them are cool. They realize I had to do it to pay my way. Some of the radicals are assholes."

"How so?"

"You know, they call me a 'baby-killer.' They'd be surprised to know that I'm on their side."

"Who isn't?"

"Well, I know a few lifers who wouldn't like the looks of you two."

As we talked I had a burning desire to solve the aluminum foil mystery. I discretely unwrapped it between my legs. I couldn't believe my eyes. Under all the silver coating was the largest chunk of hash I'd ever seen. It must have been pitched by a hitchhiker about to be hassled by the cops. His loss, our gain.

I considered sharing our good fortune with our ride but the ROTC thing discouraged me. Despite his friendliness, there was no telling how he felt about drugs.

I nudged Spalding's side with my hand, holding open my palm so he could see our good fortune. He turned around and gave me a look that said: "What're you crazy. Put that shit away."

I re-wrapped it and put it back in my pocket.

In the meantime, the conversation had returned to baseball.

"What do you think of the Tribe's chances?" I asked him.

"This could be their year. If the Mets could do it, anyone can."

"They're due," I agreed.

"Overdue."

He dropped us off at the main intersection in downtown Kent, where Main and Water Streets meet.

"How about a picture?" Spalding asked. "For our scrapbook."

"Sure," Schroeder smiled.

He put his ROTC helmet on and gave us a peace sign.

"Perfect."

"See you around."

"Good luck, guys."

"Go Tribe."

"We ought to have a picture of ourselves, hitching," I suggested before Spalding put his camera away.

"Sounds good."

"We'll have to ask someone."

We asked the first coed to wander by to take our picture with our thumbs out in front of the Loft. She thought we were slightly deranged but realized that was what Kent was all about.

"Well, that's it. Our trip to the Big Apple is history."

"One for the record books."

"I had a wonderful time, how about you?"

"Couldn't be better."

"What do you say? The Loft?"

"We're a little early for happy hour but what the hell."

Our failed trip to New York City wasn't the longest or most memorable of our college career. But every time we smoked that hash we told the story about how it was a gift from above.

And a month later the friendly driver from Lorain would be known around the world.

Chapter Six:
EARTH DAY

As April approached May, the campus really began to pop.

Demonstrations were warming up as quickly as the weather. Radical groups were demanding revolutionary changes in all parts of society. Of course, they wanted to end the war, end the draft and dismantle the military industrial complex.

They also wanted to end racism, cure poverty, legalize abortion, limit police powers, increase student power and curb pollution.

The latter was one topic that everyone could agree on. Who could be against cleaner air and water? Many of our lakes and rivers were becoming sewage dumps, while the air over many major cities was unbreathable.

In order to draw attention to this problem, April 22, 1970 was designated Earth Day. All across the nation, young and old alike were planning community projects like cleaning up trash, planting trees and attending teach-ins.

Kent State University's only official act for Earth Day was a speech by renowned consumer advocate Ralph Nader. He already had a national reputation for going after the excesses of big business and big government.

Yet his visit was overshadowed by a group of unknown students who staged their own event. They announced it a week beforehand, so I doubt they even realized it was scheduled to fall on Earth Day.

I was taking a social problems class where we discussed the new wave of free thinkers, everyone from Timothy Leary to Alvin Toffler. And right in the middle of class, in front of a large auditorium, a short-haired, bearded student stood up and announced that the following Wednesday, a group of concerned students were going to napalm a dog on front campus.

The whole class went silent. Napalm was one of those 60s buzz words, like "military industrial complex." It was supposed to be an inhuman means of warfare, as if there were any gentle ways to kill the enemy.

The United States was dumping tons of the chemical on Vietnam and the big complaint was that it stuck to civilians as well as to military personnel. It was said to cause a terribly painful, burning death to the victim.

Napalming a dog was taking the art of demonstrating one step too far. Like the rest of the class, I was shocked.

"Everyone is invited, there is no charge for admission, we look forward to seeing you all there," the student proclaimed.

"Oh my God," a girl next to me sighed.

"You're sick," a dude in a green Army jacket hollered from the back row.

The student put his hands in his pockets and climbed the steps. Everyone stared at him as he slipped out the back door. He didn't come back to class the rest of the week, probably because he was too busy handing out leaflets publicizing the event. It became the talk of the entire campus.

This was one rally I had to attend and I'd have to remember to leave Harold at home.

He could be scarred for life.

The rally on Earth Day was at noon in front of the Student Union. Neither Spalding nor Early nor Michelle could make it for various reasons. I became the designated Depeyster representative.

The crowd was a strange mix. There were almost as many cops as students. And they weren't attempting to hide themselves as narcs. They were in full uniform, helmets, batons, the whole works.

And members of the Portage County Animal Protective League were passing out leaflets, protesting the event.

For once, the students were on the same side as the cops. Torturing a dog to make a point about the war was going a little too far.

It reminded me of "Yippie" leader Jerry Rubin's visit a few weeks earlier. He told about a thousand students on front campus that they should go home and kill their parents. It was hard to take anyone that radical seriously.

The crowd was boisterous while waiting for the "concerned students" to show up. They hadn't really identified themselves as of yet. No Yippies or SDS.

I struck up a conversation with a student standing next to me. He was a couple of years younger than me, with long brown hair and a headband. He introduced himself as Jeff Miller.

"What'd you think?" I asked him.

"This is great."

"Killing a dog is great?"

"Not the dog, the rally. Everyone's getting psyched."

"It's kind of a rough way to stir up a crowd, don't you think?"

"Whatever it takes. They wouldn't be here otherwise. This is such an apathetic campus."

The students organizing the rally finally snaked their way through the crowd.

They were all moderately dressed. They didn't look like the usual crowd of campus rebels.

I saw the student from my social science class pulling up the rear.

Their leader was a tall, dark haired, clean shaven fellow sporting black Woody Allen glasses. He was wearing a white shirt, tie and sport coat. The rest of his entourage clustered around him to protect him from the mob.

His was an unfamiliar face. An outside agitator? I didn't think so. Out of 20,000 students there were quite a few I never saw before.

The speaker attempted to address the crowd with a bull-horn but it didn't work. He threw it down and raised his voice. He was a pretty good public speaker.

He started by explaining about napalm. How it stuck to the flesh like jelly, how hot it got once applied and how one bomb could easily take out the entire crowd.

We were all suddenly very uneasy. What was this guy up to? His rap began to strike home.

Then he talked about the company that manufactured the napalm and how they were conspiring with the federal government, making money by the barrel in a crime against humanity, like the Nazis had done in World War II.

That always made the old folks, especially the cops, angry. Comparing our democratic Army, the one charged with spreading freedom, justice and the American Way with Adolph Hitler's Army of mass genocide rubbed them the wrong way.

The crowd began to boo him.

"If he napalms a dog they're gonna string him up," I told Jeff.

"We'll see," Jeff said.

He seemed to know something that I didn't.

Then the speaker asked the big question.

"Who came here to see a dog napalmed?"

The boos became much louder.

"How many of you are willing to stop me?"

A great cheer arose. We all were.

Then came the kicker. The big speech. There was no dog. There was no napalm.

"Why do you come here today to save the life of one dog but do nothing to prevent the terrible deaths of thousands of our brothers and sisters in Vietnam? I see there are people here from the Society for the Prevention of Cruelty to

Animals. How about a Society for the Prevention of Cruelty to People?"

He'd got us. The crowd was silent. I looked at Jeff Miller. He smiled smugly. He knew all along.

Then a few students clapped, followed by others, a regular standing ovation. The ad hoc student group left the same way they came, in total anonymity.

As the speaker walked through the crowd, followed by his disciples, he was greeted with cheers and pats on the back like a champion athlete.

Even a uniformed cop shook his hand. I shared a hippie handshake with Jeff Miller.

"Going to see Nader tonight?" he asked me.

"Where's he going to be?"

"University Auditorium."

"Maybe I'll see you there."

"Hope so, be cool," Miller said then drifted away.

Everyone went home relieved, especially me. I was looking forward to seeing Harold.

Chapter Seven:
MUD FIGHTS

The week after Earth Day it really started warming up. I mean it warmed up like summertime. And since it was April, it rained too. I mean it really rained.

When you combine those two forces of nature at Kent State in spring quarter there is always the same result, mud fights. Many students thought mud fights were invented at the Woodstock concert but they'd been a part of spring quarter at Kent as long as I'd been there.

Once the conditions were ideal the students poured out of the dorms in cutoffs ready to show off their Lauderdale tans by rolling around in the mud and dragging any helpless victim with them.

In the spring of 1970, there was even more mud available than usual thanks to the construction site in the middle of campus. What was to be the new Student Union next to the new library was just a huge hole in the ground. Great piles of earth were just sitting there waiting to be exploited.

Spalding and I walked right into the carnage after exiting Memorial Gym one fine spring evening. We'd just finished an after-dinner handball match.

Handball was our spring quarter phys ed class. But there wasn't much time to practice during the short one hour class period. We'd decided to take a break from studies and sharpen our skills at the same time.

So far so good. Our mistake was deciding to stop by The Pit at Tri- Towers, our old stomping ground, for a snack.

"Uh-oh, do you see what I see?" Spalding asked as we walked around a clump of trees by Korb Hall. Korb was a lonely orphan dorm out all by itself next to Tri-Towers.

In front of us were about thirty mud-soaked students grabbing victims at random and throwing them in the mud.

"Uh-oh is right, maybe we can slip through the forest."

Even though we'd enjoyed the spectacle in the past, we now felt it was little more than a freshman prank. After all we were seniors; we'd be graduating in a couple of months. We were too mature for such trivialities.

At least those were the thoughts that went through our minds at the time. We were forced to make a split second decision. Join in the festivities or book. We decided to retreat. It was perfect training for Vietnam.

Except our shortcut backfired. Our escape route was as disastrous as General Custard's Last Stand at the Little Big Horn. We went from a fire fight to a full scale battle.

There must have been a hundred kids in front of Tri-Towers rolling in the mud.

"What do you think?" I asked Spalding.

"I just washed these jeans," he said.

"I'm with you, let's get out of here."

It was then that we made our fatal mistake. Rather than act upon our instincts and turn tail we stayed and watched the spectacle below, hypnotized by the carnival atmosphere.

Students were dropping plastic bags full of water from the dorm windows on unsuspecting students. Throwing water balloons at motorcycles.

A car surrounded by attackers with buckets of mud opened its windows and shot back with a fire extinguisher. Of course, it was all in great fun. Especially when watching from afar.

The frat guys liked to prey on the coeds, especially women in fancy dresses. The coeds went after the guys who seemed willing to go down easy. Some were ready to throw themselves into the muck with only a little gentle persuasion.

We figured we were safe. Then I heard a familiar voice. "What about those two? They seem awfully clean."

It was Elizabeth, covered head to foot in mud, commanding a small army of loyal jocks like an Amazon queen. They came out of the trees like Robin Hood's gang of Merry Men.

She pointed in our direction. We took off down the hill like long-legged Gazelles chased by a pack of lions.

We didn't have a chance. It was open field running without a blocking line. They tackled us easily and we skidded through a couple puddles. It reminded us of our adventure on the way to Michelle's.

"This is getting old," I said to Spalding after they let us up.

"Join the party guys," Elizabeth said, running up to us. She had a mud-covered accomplice with her.

"Is this anyway to treat an old friend?" I said.

"Paybacks are a bitch," she countered.

"How do I always get involved in your domestic squabbles?" Spalding asked, picking mud out of his ears.

"What about Earth Day? You guys are raping the environment," I argued with Liz.

"That's what I told her," her friend laughed.

"Who's your partner in crime?" I asked.

"Sandy Scheuer, meet Matt and Paul."

"Charmed, I'm sure," she shook our hands with one as muddy as our own.

"How'd Liz rope you into this?"

"The same as you guys," she laughed.

"You have a weird way of making friends," I told Elizabeth.

"Me and Sandy go way back. What was it, freshman year?"

We'd gotten up and began walking together through the organized chaos.

"Yeah, you short-sheeted my bed."

"After you put flour in mine."

They both laughed.

"You're proving my point," I said.

"Which was?"

"Your strange way of making friends."

"It's worked fine so far, right Sandy."

"That's why I like her."

"Well, we got to go," Spalding said.

"So soon, won't you stay and play?" Liz begged.

"We're too old for this," I said.

"What'd I tell you, Sandy. A couple of stuffed shirts."

"A couple of muddy shirts," Spalding said.

Sandy laughed again. Her laugh was contagious.

"Don't mind him, it's his second time," I explained.

"See you later then," Liz said.

"How's the Buckeye?" I had to ask as we walked away.

"The who?"

"Your boy friend from Ohio State."

"Oh. He's fine."

"The Buckeye? I like that," Sandy laughed.

"How'd you like to be a Buckeye?" Liz said and attempted to wrestle Sandy back into the mud.

We took off, leaving them to their follies.

"Talk about strange friends, you've got more than your share," Spalding said.

"You're proof of that," I shot back.

Chapter Eight:
NIXON'S SPEECH

Despite all the craziness going on spring quarter I still had classes to attend and homework to finish. Even though I was winding down my college career I still wanted to make halfway decent grades.

All of us at Depeyster felt the same way. Throughout our student lives we'd been taught to do the best we could and it was hard to stop studying even with all the diversions.

But the diversions were coming at us fast and furious.

On Thursday evening, April 30, 1970, I was sitting at my desk pounding away at the keys of my portable typewriter. I had a mid-term paper due for abnormal psychology.

I could have picked almost any subject around me: my roommates, student radicals, the Kent football team, even Harold. Instead I chose recent American Presidents.

And as if to prove my point, Early started hollering at me from the top of the steps.

"Get your ass up here!"

"What's going on?"

"Just get up here!"

Early had a habit of over-reacting at times so I finished the paragraph I was working on and strolled up the steps.

"What's the big deal?" I asked.

Early and Spalding were staring at the television set. A gray-skinned President Richard Nixon was addressing the country.

"Nixon's invading Cambodia," Early said.

"What?"

"He's nuts," Spalding said.

We couldn't believe it. Nixon had been telling the country that he was winding down the war in Southeast Asia. In fact, there was a plan in place to withdraw 150,000 troops within the next year. Yet the attack on Cambodia had already begun, two hours earlier.

"This is not an invasion of Cambodia," Nixon was saying as I took a seat on the couch. "Once enemy forces are driven out we will withdraw."

He estimated the military action would last from six weeks to two months. He justified the move by explaining that the North Vietnamese Army was being supplied by strongholds in Cambodia.

"We take this action not for the purpose of expanding the war into Cambodia but for the purpose of ending the war in Vietnam and winning the just peace we deserve."

"Yeah right," Spalding said.

"What an asshole," Early gave him the finger.

Spalding walked over and turned off the set before the television news commentators did their thing.

On the surface Nixon's speech sounded plausible, maybe it was even proper military strategy. The problem was, he'd lied to us too many times in the past. No matter how he tried to justify this latest round in the Vietnam War, it looked like he was expanding the conflict instead of ending it.

"Now the shit's going to fly," Spalding said.

"What're Russia and China going to do?" I wondered aloud.

"I'm glad I got a high number," Early said.

"Yeah, thanks for reminding us."

It wasn't hard to sense the mood of the country. You could feel it in the air. With one public relations blunder, Nixon fanned the flames of dissent that had been smoldering for most of spring quarter.

Four Days In May

"There's something happening here,
What it is ain't exactly clear,
There's a man with a gun over there,
tellin' me I've got to beware.
I think it's time we stop, children, what's that sound?
Everybody look what's goin' down."

Buffalo Springfield

Chapter One:
FRIDAY, MAY 1st

PART ONE: The Protesting Blues

Nixon's Cambodia speech was it. It was what the SDS, the Weathermen, the Yippies and every other radical group had been praying for all year. And the timing was too good to be true.

Each day the weather seemed to be warming from spring to summer. Perfect for outdoor rallies and protests.

And as if on cue, four SDS leaders from the previous spring takeover of the Hearing and Speech Building were let out of jail. They'd spent almost a year in prison for assault and battery and inciting to riot.

This gave local radicals a cause to celebrate. Graffiti sprouted around campus like the crocuses, reiterating their four demands from 1969.

1) ABOLISH ROTC
2) END LIQUID CRYSTALS
3) CLOSE THE CRIME LAB
4) DISARM CAMPUS COPS

Abolishing ROTC was a given. It was an easy target.

The Liquid Crystal Institute was another target associated

with the defense industry, the military industrial complex. The radicals claimed it was funded by the Department of Defense, using high tech to fight the Viet Cong.

Ditto for the Crime Lab. It was part of the campus law enforcement major, another easy target. It helped identify student radicals as well as criminals.

And of course the campus police didn't need guns. No student carried a gun back then. It was unheard of. Even airports didn't have metal detectors yet. The four demands were written with chalk on sidewalks and with spray paint on bus shelters. They were everywhere but no one knew who put them there.

The day after Nixon's speech, another rally was planned for the Commons. This one was almost as interesting as the Invisible Dog.

A group of graduate students in history vowed to bury a copy of the U.S. Constitution in honor of May 1st, Law Day. This was to protest the undeclared war in Vietnam.

Despite all the thousands of casualties and millions of dollars spent in Southeast Asia, the spineless Congress never had declared war on Vietnam. It was still considered a "police action" prompted by the executive branch of the U.S. Government, the President of the United States.

Michelle and I decided to go to the rally together. What better way to spend a warm spring afternoon with your girl friend?

It was scheduled for noon so we met at Depeyster for an early lunch.

As I picked up the dishes she told me that she had to go next door for something. "Fine," I said.

I met her on the front lawn. She handed me a brown paper shopping bag, smiling in a curious manner. What was she up to?

I pulled a Spiro Agnew hardhat out of the bag. What a treat!

Agnew, Nixon's Vice-President, loved calling college protesters strange names like "left-wing commie pinkos." He was a national joke to the hippie generation.

I tried it on, adjusted the inner band and off we went. I'm sure I looked quite strange, my long hair flowing out from under the white hardhat, my bearded jaw jutting forward.

Hardhats were another symbol of the 1960s. Shorthaired, clean-shaven construction workers in New York City had taken it upon themselves to stage counter-protests at the same time the long-haired hippies were protesting the Vietnam War.

They'd marched wearing their hardhats, displaying the American flag and carrying signs like "AMERICA: LOVE IT OR LEAVE IT."

The two sides symbolized the deep split in American society between generations and classes as the 1960s came to a close. There seemed to be no common ground between them.

All of which combined to make Michelle's present so unique. Or so I thought.

As we walked up Summit Road holding hands I recalled all the changes that had occurred since the first day of classes when we'd taken the same walk.

Who would have believed that in nine short months we'd rekindle our love affair? That the Murph would be married and almost a father? That someday we'd actually grow up and graduate?

We were part of a large group of students heading toward the Commons, like salmon rushing upstream. Our hormones were out of control. It was spring and we had a lot of steam to blow off.

"Looks like it's going to be a good one," I commented as if talking about a football game.

"Should be the best," Michelle agreed. "More and more people are realizing how screwed up society is."

"It's not really society," I begged to differ. "It's just the war."

"It not just the war, it's everything. It's the war, it's pollution, it's black power, gay rights, women's lib. It's the whole oppressive political system."

"Come on, you don't have it so bad," I argued. "The system's all right, there's just some losers running it right now."

"How can you say that?"

"I just did, didn't you hear me."

She was mad. I could tell by the way she stared straight ahead as if she didn't know me. We'd walked across front campus and were nearing the student union. The Victory Bell was ringing.

I should have let the argument die a natural death but I had to prove my point. I was at odds with her radical friends on a number of points. Just because they were right on Vietnam didn't mean I had to buy into the rest of the program.

"Try holding one of these rallies in Russia," I said as we hit the outer fringes of the Commons.

She stopped, turned around and got in my face.

"I don't believe you. You sound like Archie Bunker."

It was true. The Spiro Agnew hardhat was affecting my brain. I was beginning to sound like my father. Or worse yet, Archie Bunker, the star of the most popular show on television. He was a middle-class working stiff, always arguing politics with his hippie son-in-law, Mike Stivic, affectionately known as "the Meathead."

Back in Cleveland I was the Meathead, defending my generation against my elders. Now in Kent I became Archie Bunker, arguing the conservative side against my peers.

Where was this coming from? My Catholic school upbringing? My inner-city bias against the spoiled suburban brats I felt were naive as hell?

I was hot. I decided to go for the jugular.

"Oh yeah? Well how can you be against the war and for abortion?"

It was a question I'd wanted to ask her since we'd been sleeping together.

"Because we're the ones who have *your* babies," she pushed my chest with her finger.

"Right on, sister," a girl in the crowd piped in.

"Who asked you?" I turned on the stranger.

"Ah, screw you and screw Spiro Agnew," a male protester came out of nowhere.

We were attracting a crowd and I was becoming the object of their wrath. "You long-haired hippies are all alike," I borrowed a line from my father.

"If you can't dig it, split man," the hippie was now sounding like a hardhat.

I looked at Michelle. Her arms were crossed and her lips clamped tight. I had dared to question the leftist gospel of the 1960s. I was now an outcast. A man without a country.

"Ah, screw you and screw your protest," I threw my Spiro Agnew hardhat at Michelle's feet and stomped up Blanket Hill.

"Liberal," she hollered at me.

"Fascist," I hollered back.

I walked to the top of the hill, stopping on the sidewalk in front of Taylor Hall, the journalism building. The offices of the Daily Kent Stater, the student newspaper, were right behind me. I was blocking their view of the spectacle below.

As I caught my breath, a television news team came out of the Stater office. It was the first one I'd seen since the previous spring's takeover of the Hearing and Speech Building.

Their presence meant the anti-war movement was becoming news again. One thing I'd learned the year before, what I saw happening in front of me and what appeared on the six o'clock news often had little in common.

The camera gave the protesters more clout than they actually had on campus. I watched with curiosity as the news team took close-ups of the U.S. Constitution being buried.

It made for an interesting photo shoot.

A Vietnam vet took advantage of the opportunity to burn his discharge papers. It was a nice touch. The camera kept rolling as Michelle joined a ring of freaks, holding hands, dancing in a circle. I wondered what Archie Bunker would think of that scene as he ate dinner in front of his television set that evening.

"Where the hell's this going to end?" I asked no one in particular.

The graduate student took the bullhorn and stood on top of the brick casing holding the victory bell.

"We'll have another rally right here again on Monday, May 4th at noon," he announced.

FRIDAY, MAY 1st

PART TWO: Working the Parking Lot

Once again Michelle was messing with my head. I sleep-walked through my classes. But by early evening there was no time left to worry. I had to meet Spalding for our latest attempt at joining the work force.

The Murph had turned us on to a job opportunity that sounded too good to be true. I was supposed to meet Spalding in front of the Towne House, a local bar on the corner of Main and Depeyster.

But I arrived before he did. And while waiting, I noticed a classmate of mine panhandling in front of the laundromat next to the Towne House. He was a tall, thin political science major with wild, bushy brown hair, wearing a tank top.

He was leaning against a brick wall, holding a tambourine filled with change out in front of him. I remembered him from a medieval political thought class and I'd heard he was from a fairly well off family. Maybe his parents had disowned him.

"How you doing, Sam? You fall on some bad times?" I asked him.

"Naw, just waiting for my clothes to dry," he said. "How you doing?"

"I'm hanging in there."

Spalding showed up and rather than interrupt us, dug deep into his pocket and threw some change into the tambourine.

"Thanks, friend," Sam said to Spalding. "Help yourself," he pushed the tambourine in my direction.

"What?" I asked.

Spalding looked at me as if we had a scam going on.

"I've been giving away slightly more than I take in," Sam explained. "It's a little experiment in supply and demand."

"This is my friend, Paul Spalding. He wouldn't be too happy if I took his money."

"No problem, take it back," Sam pushed the tambourine in Spalding's direction.

"No thanks, it's all yours."

"Hey Sam, we got to go check on a job."

"See ya."

We disappeared into the cool, dark atmosphere of the Towne House.

"What's he on?" Spalding asked me.

"A pre-law major," I explained.

Joe Sanitelli was the owner of the Towne House. The Murph had described him to us so it wasn't hard to spot him working behind the bar. He was short and muscular, wearing a red banlon casual shirt. He poured us a couple beers as we talked.

"You know those two parking lots out back?" he asked us.

"Two?"

"The one behind us and the one next to the Blind Owl."

"Oh yeah."

We often used the alley between the two as a shortcut from Depeyster to Water Street downtown.

"Well, it's not the Blind Owl's parking lot anymore. I bought it. We're going to charge two dollars to park in them but you guys will give the driver one of these cards worth two free drinks in here. Capiche?"

"Sure."

"Sounds good."

He handed us a stack of 3x5 inch index cards. Hand written in ballpoint pen on each card was: REDEEMABLE FOR

TWO DRINKS AT THE TOWNE HOUSE LOUNGE.

It wasn't hard to figure Joe's rationale. The Towne House, Blind Owl and other bars closer to campus were taking a beating the last few years by the popularity of "the strip," Kent's answer to Ft. Lauderdale.

J.B.'s, Orvilles and the Kove were the new hot spots down by the railroad tracks.

On weekends, downtown Kent was jammed, parking was at a premium and Joe hoped to attract some of the non-students coming in from Cleveland and Akron. Once he had them inside the bar for a few free drinks he'd try to keep them there.

At worst, they might buy a few before heading to the strip and perhaps stop again before heading home.

Easy money, we figured.

"How much are you paying us?"

"Two bucks an hour," Joe looked at his watch. "It's seven o'clock now, you should be done by midnight. An easy ten spot."

"Each?"

"Of course."

It seemed perfect. As we walked outside through the Towne House's back door there was only one lingering doubt in my mind.

"These cards don't look very official, do they?" I asked Spalding.

"I know, we should have a uniform or something like they do at the hotels in Miami."

We surveyed our new territory. Both parking lots were empty, the sun was setting over a nearby hill and happy hour was just breaking up. A sprinkling of inebriated students fell out of the Blind Owl.

"You ever been in the Blind Owl?" I asked Spalding. It was a one-story box like structure, painted white, hidden away from any main roads.

"I didn't even know it existed."

"I used to go there freshman year. Why don't we stop inside."

"Are you crazy? We just started this job."

"It'll be awhile before anyone shows up. This is our last quarter, we got to go for the gusto."

"What if Joe's looking for us?"

"So we get fired and stay in the Blind Owl all night. Big deal."

"That don't sound like you. What's going on?"

"Come on in and we'll talk."

I'd coaxed him to the Blind Owl's entrance. We grabbed a couple of bar stools and were immediately attracted to the luscious bar maid in cut-offs. On the back wall a slide show of snapshots from spring break in Lauderdale clicked automatically. "Make you feel at home, buddy?"

We had to turn around on our barstools to study the beach scenes as we sipped our quarter draft beers.

"Can't beat this job," he smiled.

"You going to miss this place when you go back?"

"Sure, aren't you?"

"I mean the north."

"Oh yeah, but I'll get over it," his smile broadened. "So what's been going on that has you bent out of shape?"

"Want to hear some surfin' songs?" I changed the subject. I wanted to get at least one beer in me before I spilled my guts.

"Here," he handed me a couple quarters. "Play some Beach Boys."

As I walked over to the jukebox a redheaded coed in a mini-skirt breezed past me on her way to the ladies room. I could smell her sweet perfume. She smiled and I smiled back. That was the way Kent was. Everyone said "hi." Everyone was friendly, as if we all lived in Mayberry.

I played "Surf City" and "Let's Do It Again" for Spalding. I added "Louie, Louie" by the Kingsmen and "Good Day Sunshine" by the Beatles. I was beginning to feel better.

I took my time making my choices hoping the redhead

would return. She did. She walked by, took a quick glance at the jukebox, touched a song, then kept walking without saying a word.

"Sorry, I'm all out of change," I yelled after her. I was tempted to chase her, hesitated, and was about to go back to the bar when I noticed her opening her purse.

She came back. "What's it take, quarters?" She asked me.

I nodded. She gave me one and walked away again.

"But you get two songs," I informed her.

"Surprise me," she smiled, then wiggled her mini-skirt back to her friends.

I looked at her request. "Bridge Over Troubled Water" by Simon and Garfunkel. It was Michelle's and my song. The one Early played for us on our first date. That hurt.

It ruined my mood but I got over it.

I returned to my barstool.

"Took you long enough," Spalding teased. He'd witnessed the entire scene.

"I was detained."

"You devil."

I took a hit of my beer. It went down easy.

"What'd you play for her?"

"'Light My Fire' by the Doors. Is that too obvious?"

We reminisced about spring break and had another round. The records played but not in the order I selected them. The redhead and her friends stood up. She came over.

"I didn't hear my song," she said.

"You'll have to stay awhile longer."

"Can't, my friends are leaving. Which one was my surprise?"

"Louie, Louie," I lied.

"That's a good dance song."

"You like to dance?"

"Yes," she said, demurely, shaking her long red hair.

"We could meet you later," I offered. "This is my friend Paul."

"Pleased to meet you. We're going to J.B.'s."

"We have to work until about midnight. Will you be out that late?"

"Probably."

"Then we'll look for you."

"See you later," she turned and left.

"So, Mr. Smooth, what's her name?" Spalding asked me.

"Damn," I said.

"What's Michelle going to say about this?"

"That's what I was going to tell you. We had a pretty good fight at the rally today."

"Did you break up?"

"I don't know. We really got into it."

"Is this going to be a regular spring thing?"

"She just pissed me off. She's too radical. Too women's lib. She probably doesn't even believe in marriage."

"I thought you were the one who didn't want to get married."

"Not now, but maybe someday."

"How about the redhead?"

"How about the redhead."

By the time we went back out into the parking lot it was a warm dusky, summer-like evening. The sun had disappeared but there was still some light in the sky.

Only a couple of cars had parked for free while we were in the Owl. No problem, we'd make up for them in no time.

The next car to pull in was a late model Buick in the Towne House lot. It was a double-dater, couples in both the front and back seats.

"It's all yours buddy," Spalding said.

"Thanks."

I walked up to the driver's side window.

He was just rolling it up and had to roll it back down again.

"What's happening?" the driver asked me. He was the clean cut type. I could tell by his clothes that he was probably a working class youth who just came to Kent for some weekend excitement.

"I hate to tell you this," I said with absolutely no authority, "but it's going to cost you two dollars to park here now."

"What? It never did before." He looked me up and down as if he wondered if I was for real.

"Well, you do now."

"I came early just so I could park here," he argued.

"I know but the Towne House just bought the lot. You do, however, get two free drinks for your two dollars." I flashed him the 3x5 inch index card.

"That's bullshit, I'll just park in the street." He punched the car in reverse, almost ran over my foot, then sped off, his rear tires flinging gravel at us from the cinder parking lot.

"I knew these cards were going to be trouble," I said to Spalding.

Once the side streets began filling up and parking became scarce the two dollar fee became less of a hassle. We began running from car to car, servicing both lots. Things ran pretty smooth until a VW bug pulled into the Blind Owl lot.

I ran over to collect our ransom.

Out of the little car emerged a pair of guys large enough to be sumo wrestlers. They wore black leather jackets, dirty jeans and biker boots. Their long hair was greasy and in pony tails.

"It costs two dollars to park here now," I stammered, almost apologetically.

"Says who?" the driver asked.

"This is the Blind Owl, it don't cost nothing to park at the Blind Owl," his partner said with a twang.

"Well, you see, you get one of these here cards and they're worth two free drinks at the Towne House," I tried to match his country accent.

"We ain't going to the Towne House," the driver ripped the card into little pieces.

They started standing uncomfortably close. For a brief instant I was ready to panic.

"Well, you should have said so in the first place," a friendly voice came out of nowhere. Spalding had seen my predicament and rushed to my rescue. "My partner gets a little confused sometimes."

"Anybody can make a mistake," the driver looked at his compatriot.

"Don't let it happen again," he pushed his large finger against my chest, causing me to fall backwards. I could imagine what his fist would feel like.

They disappeared into the Blind Owl.

"Is that a biker bar?" Spalding asked.

"It is now," I sighed. "I owe you one, buddy."

We took a break, sitting on a stone wall that held up part of the Towne House lot.

"How about a bottle of Pineapple wine?" Spalding suggested. It was a peculiar addiction we developed over spring break.

"Those Lauderdale slides get to you?"

"I'll buy if you fly."

"It's a deal."

I walked over to the nearby beverage store. By the time I came back Spalding was still sitting on the short wall, rolling a joint.

"You're getting to be the bold one."

"I thought about what you said. It is our last quarter."

"Any more customers?"

"I think it's about played out."

We drank our wine and hit our number in silence. It was a peaceful, golden evening. Our pockets were full of cash, we caught a good buzz and we'd be off work in a short while.

"While you were gone I called Chris," Spalding said.

"You did?"

"I told her to meet us at J.B.'s. Do you mind?"

"Why should I?"

"The redhead might get back to Michelle."

"Maybe it'll make her jealous."

Spalding checked his watch. "Almost midnight. Time to go."

"Great."

We turned our cash over to Joe and he doled out our ten dollars each.

"Have a beer," he offered. "You guys did a nice job, the joint is hopping."

"No thanks. We got to meet some girls."

"Well, stay away from the strip."

'Why's that?"

"I heard they're having some trouble down there."

"Okay," we said but as soon as we got out the door we headed straight for the strip to meet Chris.

As we turned the corner of Water and Main, we encountered an unbelievable street scene. There was a riot going on. Some students were running away from it. Some, like us, were walking toward it. Others were piling out of the bars into the melee.

"Holy shit," Spalding said.

A gang of rowdies had taken over the street. They looked like the two guys who gave me some shit at the Blind Owl. Biker types.

Kids were jumping up and down on parked cars. There was a fire in a barrel in the middle of the street. Some couples were dancing. Traffic was at a standstill. The bikers were doing wheelies.

"Let's get out of here," Spalding suggested.

"What about the redhead? And Chris?"

We watched the riot grow in strength like a hurricane off the Florida coast.

Someone broke a window. Then another one. A police car pulled up, flashers shining. A beer bottle bounced off its windshield. It retreated.

Out of the mess, the Murph appeared. He wasn't boasting his usual smile. Instead he looked a bit worried.

"What's happening, guys?"

"You tell us."

"Mary Lou's getting ready to pop."

"No shit."

"I was bartending at J.B.'s. She called, she's having con-tractions."

"Did you see Chris?" Spalding asked.

"No, it's a madhouse in there. The cop's are throwing everyone out."

"How about a redhead in a mini-skirt?"

"I would have remembered her," the Murph laughed. "But no."

More police cars appeared. Lights and sirens. Kids scream-ing.

"Time to get out of here," I said and we began walking back toward Depeyster.

The Murph was moving at a fast pace.

"You need us to help out?" Spalding asked him.

"No thanks. We got it all planned."

"The best laid plans..." I said.

"Don't say laid to a guy with a wife nine months preg-nant," the Murph joked. He broke into a jog. We left the mad-ness behind.

"You guys need a ride."

"Don't worry about us."

"Where's your car?"

"Down by the train station."

"We could be home by then."

"Let us know what happens."

"You're on the top of my list."

"Be careful."

"Peace, brother."

We split up, going our separate ways. The throng was fol-lowing us like a slow moving creature, breaking windows in its wake. Police cars passed us, going the opposite way.

We jogged up Main Street toward the Towne House, final-ly slowing to a fast walk to catch our breaths. Just before we turned the corner on Depeyster a campus bus passed us. Something was not right. They didn't run that late on a Friday evening.

"Look at that," Spalding said.

The bus was filled with cops in riot gear, sitting very still like androids in a science fiction movie.

"Reinforcements," I said.

"They look like the Highway Patrol," Spalding said.

We ran full speed downhill back to Depeyster. We were scared shitless. This felt different from the Moratorium in Washington D.C.

Washington was the nation's capital. There were supposed to be protests and soldiers there.

This was Kent, Ohio. Mayberry, U.S.A.

Where was Barney Fife with his bullet and Sheriff Taylor with his down home common sense?

We walked into Depeyster panting. Early was sitting on the couch, watching television with Michelle's sister Marianne.

He shot us a goofy grin. Marianne flashed a peace sign.

"I ran away from home," she said.

"There's going to be big trouble," Spalding said in half-breaths.

"I'm not going back," Marianne said emphatically.

"Not you. Downtown. There's a riot going on."

"No shit?" Early asked.

"Where's Michelle?" I asked Marianne.

"In her room. I don't think she wants to see you."

"Too bad," I said.

I walked right in her front door and up to her bedroom. She was laying in her bed reading with her headphones on. She didn't know I was there.

I was tempted just to watch her in her nightgown but was afraid of scaring her. She jumped when I took her headphones off.

"What are you.."

"Shhh," I put my finger to my lips. "We have to talk."

"About Marianne?"

"No, about us."

HIPPIES

I told her about the riot. I told her about the parking lot. I didn't tell her about the redhead. She told me about the six o'clock news, the riot at Ohio State, the eleven o'clock news and Nixon's reaction to the turmoil on the college campuses.

We made up. We made love. We forgot all about Cambodia, Laos and Vietnam. We had each other.

Chapter Two:
SATURDAY, MAY 2nd

PART ONE: Town vs. Gown

Saturday morning was marvelous. I woke up late, revived and refreshed. I vaguely remembered Michelle slipping out of bed very quietly, not wanting to disturb my slumber. She probably had errands to run.

No one else was around either. I had the place to myself, except for Harold, my ever faithful companion. When I went to feed him I discovered the cupboard was bare. We were not only out of dog food but also other necessities such as coffee, milk, juice and sugar.

I decided we'd better stock up for the coming revolution. I made a list and ventured over to the Sparkle Market that was conveniently located catty-corner from our abode.

Harold tagged along for the exercise. It was such a pleasant morning that I'd just about forgotten the riot from the night before. Unfortunately, no one else did, especially the local town folks.

As I instructed Harold to "stay" outside the Sparkle Market's automatic doors, an elderly lady was having difficulty pushing her full shopping cart over the hump between the doors.

"Having some trouble?" I smiled and began pulling on the

front of her cart.

"No thank you," she replied gruffly and about ran me over once she pushed past the hump.

I received similar cold-shoulders from the produce manager, a mother with two toddlers and a teenage stock boy. Kent was no longer the friendly small town it had been just two days earlier.

The generation gap was widening at the speed of sound.

At least I could strike up a conversation with the long-haired Kent student standing behind me in the checkout line.

"I don't think they like us here anymore," I said.

"It's the beard and long hair," he agreed.

"Were you downtown last night?"

"No, but now we're all rioters."

That was it. The famous guilt by association that small towns practiced with great zeal. Even my favorite cashier, the young brunette who I often joked around with, had a different attitude.

She gave me my change without her usual smile and "have a nice day." I figured our romance was over before it ever began.

It was a huge relief to step out of the hostile environment, into the fresh open air and Harold's waiting paws.

Across the street from the Sparkle Market there was a doctor's office that did not open on Saturdays. I saw my housemates standing in the middle of the empty parking lot.

Harold and I wandered over. Spalding and Early were on their knees, playing marbles. They were shooting aggies from outside a large chalk circle. Michelle, Renee and Marianne were standing behind them blowing soap bubbles. There were traces of a hopscotch game already concluded on the black asphalt.

"What's going on?" I asked, putting the grocery bags down, much to Harold's chagrin.

"Marbles," Early said with a slight degree of irritation. "And keep that dog out of the way."

"Don't bother him, he's shooting," Michelle advised.

"Early takes everything so seriously," Marianne said, as if she knew him all his life.

Early let loose his attack and like a chain reaction three different marbles jumped outside the chalk circle. He stood up and collected his winnings, jealously guarding the little pieces of glass in his large hands.

"Isn't college great," he laughed.

"The weekends are," Spalding also stood up.

"What else do you have in the bag?" I asked Michelle, who was standing next to a huge plastic bag with Zayre's stamped on it. Marianne picked up the bag as Michelle displayed her wares.

"We've got kites, we've got squirt guns, we got a couple Frisbees, we even have a rocket launcher."

"Far out."

"Isn't it neat," Renee said.

"We went shopping for socks and came back with this stuff," Michelle said.

"You girls are really earning your keep around here," I kidded. "Now if we could only get you to cut the lawn."

"Don't laugh, it's already done."

"Yeah, but we did it," Early said.

"Only because we nagged you into it," Renee added.

Marianne pulled out a Frisbee and we began tossing it around the street, Harold trying to catch it in his mouth. As we played like young teenagers I watched Michelle's graceful moves, her long body stretching for the Frisbee as her blond hair flowed in the wind.

I realized what a lucky guy I was, having such a far out lady and groovy friends. Who cared about the war and the riots and the politics of it all?

"Did anyone hear from the Murph?" I asked.

"False labor," Spalding said.

"What's that?" I asked.

"It's like a false fire alarm or a bomb scare," Michelle

explained. "It feels real but nothing happens."

We spent the rest of the day playing around the house and yard, staying away from the campus radicals, the outside agitators and the upset townies.

Maybe that was the best road to travel. Tune in, turn on and drop out.

Only it was easier said than done. The campus kept drawing us back like a magnet and we had little resistance to its force field.

SATURDAY, MAY 2nd

PART TWO: Saturday Night Fever

Saturday night the local authorities vowed not to let another riot occur downtown. So they basically shut down the place, slapping an 8 P.M. curfew on everyone off-campus.

The only problem was that almost as many students did not know about the curfew as did. It didn't really matter to us anyway because we already planned on going to Kent's annual experimental film festival.

These were the kinds of activities the University officials were encouraging. Nice wholesome, clean fun as opposed to rioting and burning.

I guess they never watched any of these films. My favorite was *Airplane Glue, I Love You*, about an adult forced to re-take the sixth grade. You can imagine his favorite hobby.

Anyway, Michelle and myself, Spalding and Chris and Early and Marianne all walked over to the university auditorium that was located inside the Administration Building.

The crowd inside the auditorium was as playful as we had been that afternoon. Students were flinging Frisbees and bouncing beach balls before the films began.

The sampling of independent films made mostly by university professors ranged from gross to funny to stupid. Another of my favorites was shown right before the intermission.

It detailed the reaction Christ would receive if he suddenly appeared on a modern college campus as a long-haired hippie freak. It was actually a comedy, but the irony was hard to ignore.

Once the lights came back on the beach balls and Frisbees reappeared. Spalding needed a smoke so we left Early with the women. We walked along the second floor of Merrill Hall that was connected to the Administration Building.

Spalding found an open window and lit up a Winston. The cool spring air smelled sweet but there was also a peculiar odor in the air, like burning wood.

"You must have a stale pack of smokes," I told Spalding.

"It's not me, take a look," he pointed. The scene below was even more eerie than downtown the night before. As we were watching strange movies inside the auditorium someone had set the ROTC building on fire. Flames were shooting out from its windows.

"This is too much," Spalding nervously puffed his cigarette.

"Let's get a better look," I suggested.

"What about the girls?"

"We'll come back for them."

We ran down some steps and came out on the Student Union side of the Commons. It was filled with demonstrators chanting "DOWN WITH ROTC."

A fire engine pulled past us with its siren roaring. Three firemen jumped off the back of the pumper wearing black rubber outfits and dark helmets. Two of them pulled a hose off the back of the truck as the driver jumped out and began turning knobs on a control panel.

The fourth fireman seemed to be the boss, barking orders.

"Lay out that line, let's get some water going."

The two workers dragged the nozzle close to the ROTC building's window and waited for the limp line to fill with much needed H20.

But before they could begin attacking the fire a couple demonstrators appeared out of nowhere and tried wrestling the nozzle out of the firemen's hands.

It was too much for me to take. My uncle was a Cleveland fireman. As much as I hated the war and the old, decrepit ROTC building, my instincts took over and I went to the firemen's aid, tackling one of the protestors.

Spalding followed my lead and after a brief struggle, rolling on the Commons lawn, we chased the protestors off. But others followed, attacking the hose with pocket knives, puncturing it and trying to cut it up.

There was no police protection, so once the fire engine started pumping water the fireman turned their hose on the students, including me and Spalding. Us long hairs all looked alike.

We were soaked. As the firemen were forced to waste their valuable time on the protestors the ROTC building built up heat. The flames burst through the roof and live ammunition inside began to pop.

"Let's get out of here," the fire boss shouted.

They threw their hose on the back of the pumper and began to back away.

The crowd cheered "BURN, BABY, BURN."

Spalding and I started walking back to the movies.

"Remind me never to go anywhere with you again," he said, shaking the water out of his hair.

"You kept bitching how hot it was in there," I said.

Behind the Administration Building there was an ancient little courtyard, a throwback to the days when botany professors planted exotic ferns from far-off lands around intricate brickwork.

It was one of the most pleasant patches of Kent's campus. As we approached the courtyard a vague apparition appeared out of the misty smog and smoke from the burning ROTC building.

Two columns of National Guard troops were marching right toward us in full combat dress, their M-1 rifles against their shoulders, shiny bayonets pointing skyward.

We stood back and let them pass, feeling like we should salute them or something. I looked in their faces, they weren't much older than we were.

"Is that how I'll look on my way to Vietnam?" I wondered.

We hurried back to the auditorium. The news had already spread.

"Where were you guys?" Michelle demanded.

A faculty member on the auditorium stage began making an announcement.

"The rest of this evening's program has been cancelled. The ROTC building is burning, the National Guard has been called in and Kent is now under a state of martial law. Please avoid the Commons on your way home. Be careful, we care about your safety."

"Let's go," Early said.

"What happened?" Chris asked.

"Why are you so wet?" Marianne wanted to know.

"You're not going to believe it," I said.

Michelle wanted to go over to the Commons but we talked her out of it. Spalding and I told our story as we walked back to Depeyster.

On our way down Summit Street we were interrupted by a voice from above. It was like God telling us to go home, that we were breaking the curfew commandment. Except the order was blasted over the sound of whirling helicopter blades.

The chopper came in low, shining a light on us brighter than anything I'd ever seen before. The darkness changed to noontime. For a few brief seconds we experienced the same terror felt by the civilian population of Vietnam.

We scattered for fear of our lives. Michelle and I ran through a couple of back yards before finding our way home.

When we finally regrouped, safe and warm under our Depeyster roof, I never felt such a great sense of relief.

The revolution had come to Kent.

Chapter Three:
SUNDAY, MAY 3rd

THE CALM BEFORE THE STORM

Sunday morning was warm and lazy. We didn't realize just how wild Saturday night was until we read about it in *The Cleveland Plain Dealer*.

Kent was moving into the big time.

After a late breakfast Spalding, Early and me went out in the front yard to enjoy the summer-like sunshine. A Crosby, Stills and Nash album could be heard from the back speakers.

No one felt like doing anything. We were pretty much burned out from the weekend's events.

Then a familiar car drove into our driveway. It was Michelle's mom Jane.

"Looks like you're in big trouble," Spalding said to Early, who was lying on his back in the front lawn, eyes closed, catching some rays.

"Me, what'd I do?" Early slowly pulled himself up.

"Harboring a fugitive."

"Who?"

"Marianne."

"Uh-oh," he saw Marianne's mother.

"Hello, men," she smiled, looking bright and vivacious in a short dress she must have borrowed from one of her daughters. "Is Michelle home?"

"I think so."

"Actually, I'm looking for Marianne," she whispered. "Michelle called and told me she was here."

"I think you can catch them both."

"Has she been any trouble for you guys?" Spalding and I both looked at Early.

"Not for me," he answered. "How about you guys?"

"I think she's just a little mixed up right now," Jane explained. "You know, the divorce."

"We're sorry to hear about that."

Jane walked into the girl's side without knocking. We heard Marianne screech, then some loud words were exchanged, then everything quieted down. Spalding and Early stretched back out on the lawn while I remained on the porch steps.

"What do you feel like doing today?" I wondered aloud.

"I'd like to go for a swim," Early said.

"The Lauderdale beach'd be great," Spalding added.

"I mean really."

No response. No one ever wanted to make a decision.

Jane, Michelle and Marianne came out of the girl's side of the house.

"I'm going back to Dullsville," Marianne announced.

"That's probably a good idea," I said.

"It's getting too crazy around here," Spalding agreed.

Early said nothing.

"What did I tell you," Jane said to Marianne, pleased by our support.

"Marianne wants to see the ROTC building first," Michelle said.

"You mean what's left of it?"

"You guys want to come along?"

"We're not doing anything."

"I'd like to see it, too," Early said.

We jumped into the back of Jane's Chevy station wagon with the wood trim on the side. She went up Depeyster to

Main Street, then took a right, driving toward campus.

Driving around with the windows open felt great. It was like we were little kids in the back seat going on a Sunday drive, wearing our t-shirts, shorts and tennis shoes.

The few students on the streets seemed to be moving in slow motion. No one was in any hurry to get anywhere. Everyone seemed pretty laid back until we reached the edge of campus.

Then everything changed. Sitting right in front of the Main Gate, the old "clean it with your toothbrush, freshman" entrance way, was a dull green Army combat tank. Its cannon was pointed directly at archaic Rockwell Library as if to say, "Be careful what you read in there."

It was intimidating. Suddenly the mood changed from mellow yellow to uptight baby. Troop carriers, Jeeps and soldiers were moving in every direction like an ant farm.

It was as if there was a war nearby but no one could find the front. Groups of students walked aimlessly amidst all the activity.

We parked in the parking lot next to Taylor Hall on top of Blanket Hill. From there we could look down upon the Commons and the smoldering ruins of the ROTC building.

It was a circus atmosphere and we joined in the festivities. The National Guard provided the entertainment. It wasn't that often that a college student could inspect a real live tank next to his dormitory.

"Let's go down closer," Marianne insisted.

From the top of Blanket Hill we could still see smoke rising from the blackened rubble. Spalding and I retold our story from the night before as we approached the ruins.

"The firemen didn't appreciate our effort," Spalding complained.

"They were probably scared," Jane said. Having an older person with us changed our perspective completely. There wasn't the usual agreement we were so used to from students our own age.

Other parents took pictures of their kids standing next to Jeeps or sharing cigarettes with the National Guardsmen.

"We were about over here when the ammunition started to blow," I explained, standing on the grassy flat land of the Commons.

"I can't believe they stored that stuff on campus," Michelle said.

"Are their guns loaded?" Marianne asked. No one was able to answer her.

What was left of the ROTC building was roped off. Only a blackened file cabinet withstood the fire's effects. National Guardsmen stood at ease surrounding the area.

"Tough night, eh?" Early asked one of the Guardsmen.

"What'd you mean? This is fun," a baby-faced soldier responded. He was leaning forward, both hands folded on the rifle's nozzle. His slender frame strained to support his heavy uniform. His blue eyes were half covered by his helmet.

"Yeah, my wife thinks this is great. She ain't seen me in a week," his much stockier companion added. His rifle was strapped over his shoulder.

Together they reminded me of Laurel and Hardy in a World War I movie.

"I thought you guys just got here last night?" Early said.

"Yeah, but we came straight from the Teamsters' strike in Cleveland," Laurel said.

"And last weekend we were at Ohio State," Hardy observed. "They really know how to riot down there, you guys are amateurs compared to them."

"See the world, that's why I joined the Guard," Laurel joked.

"Are those guns loaded?" Jane asked for Marianne.

"Yes, ma'am, the M-1 rifle, fully automatic," Laurel picked up his rifle and held it across his chest.

"A soldier's best friend," Hardy took his rifle off his shoulder and put it's butt on the ground.

"They are?" a girl with long, brown hair and deep, brown

eyes interrupted us. She was with a thin male companion with long hair himself, stuffed under a floppy hat.

The National Guardsmen just nodded. They were tired of answering the same question.

"Don't I know you?" she said to me.

"Maybe an English class," I took a wild guess. I'd seen her around campus but I didn't think I really knew her.

"Allison Krause," she introduced herself. "And this is my boyfriend, Barry."

We all exchanged pleasantries. "Didn't you two go to the Moratorium in Washington?" Barry inquired.

"Yeah, far out," I looked at Spalding.

"We were there," Allison became excited.

"I knew I saw you guys somewhere."

"It didn't seem to help much," Barry motioned toward the Guardsmen.

"I know what you mean."

Our conversation was interrupted by a weird sight. A short, blonde coed with a basket full of yellow daffodils was walking past the Guardsmen, putting the flowers in the gun barrels of the ones who would let her.

Laurel smiled and obliged her. Hardy put his rifle back on his shoulder before she could plant one in his.

We gave Laurel a round of applause. He flashed us a sideways peace sign without taking his fingers from the tip of his gun barrel.

One of the Guard's officers caught Laurel's antics while sitting on a nearby Jeep. He jumped down and ran over to us.

"What are you doing with that flower in your rifle, soldier?" he screamed.

"Nothing, sir," Laurel and Hardy both snapped to attention.

"Then get it out of there."

Laurel gave the daffodil to Allison.

The officer walked back to his position.

"Flowers are better than bullets," Allison hollered after him.

He just kept walking.

Chapter Four:
MONDAY, MAY 4th

Monday morning, May 4th, 1970, was perfect. You couldn't create a better morning if you could control the weather. There was just the right mixture of sunshine, blue skies and light breeze.

My first class was an 11 A.M. abnormal psychology in Merrill Hall on the top of front campus. It was strange walking to class with the National Guard posted at every intersection, on the lookout for outside agitators.

But life went on for most of us. We figured they'd eventually tire of playing soldier and just go home. Just as we hoped the U.S. Army would do in Vietnam.

Walking across lovely front campus was invigorating. The dogwoods and fruit trees blossomed pink and white flowers. The oaks and elms revealed the fresh vibrant traces of green leaves, just beginning their summer-long battle against the elements. The clear blue sky provided a flawless backdrop.

The steps from Rockwell Library to the Administration Building were my favorite part of campus. The Ad Building had a columned façade front that resembled an ancient Greek temple. As I climbed the steps its grandeur drew me in. I felt like Socrates on his way to debate the great philosophers of the Parthenon.

Then, to top off an already aesthetic experience, I found a

Greek goddess sitting on the stone ledge next to the Administration Building entrance.

Michelle was sitting there with her legs crossed, her eyes closed and her head bent back to catch the sun's rays. Her long, blond hair almost touched the ground.

I imagined her wrapped in a white tunic with a ring of flowers in her hair. I quietly snuck up to her and kissed her smack on the lips. The other students waiting for the bus snickered.

"I knew it was you," she opened her eyes.

"How's that?"

"I could feel your presence."

"I used deodorant this morning," I tried to smell my armpits.

"You going to the noon rally?" she changed the subject.

"I wasn't planning on it. Are you?"

"Of course."

"I'm burned out on rallies."

"Yeah, well you were there Saturday night while I missed it."

"Sorry. They keep having rallies and more rallies but nothing never changes."

"Well, I don't want to miss the action."

The campus bus pulled up. It was the famous one, the same bus used at the end of the movie *The Graduate* where Dustin Hoffman and Katherine Ross in a wedding dress jumped aboard on their way to living happily ever after.

Kent State was proud to add it to their fleet.

Michelle picked up her large purse and pile of books and stood in line behind the other students. I kissed her again. It wasn't like me. Usually I deplored public acts of affection.

I'd just had a strange feeling since I first woke up.

"Be careful," I told her.

"I will," she said.

"Maybe I'll see you there."

My abnormal psych class was half empty. Maybe it was

the weather, maybe it was the scary weekend, maybe it was the upcoming rally.

The professor dumped his planned lecture, suggesting instead that we go to the noon rally and study the crowd behavior. We could apply it to an upcoming section on group psychology. Like the rest of us, he was unaware that Ohio Governor James Rhodes had outlawed all campus gatherings.

He let us out of class early. I hoped to take advantage of the early dismissal to beat the noon crowd to a bite to eat at the student union.

I walked through the quaint courtyard behind Merrill Hall where Spalding and I first saw the National Guard Saturday night. That already seemed like an eternity ago.

In the daylight I noticed the stone benches, drinking fountain and twisted walkway. It made me yearn for the good old days when colleges were Ivory Towers again.

When was that anyway? Freshman year?

The Student Union was already crowded. The Ohio National Guard had a large contingent around the burned-out ROTC building.

The Victory Bell was ringing. Someone had painted the word "STRIKE" on its brick casing. Students were flocking to fill up the Commons.

An even greater crowd of spectators filled the perimeters, like football fans waiting for a game to begin.

The Hippies versus the Guard. Step right up and get your programs. You can't tell the players without a scorecard.

I forgot about lunch. I decided to go down closer to the speaker, hear what they had to say and look for Michelle.

The noon chimes pealed from the Administration Building. Classes were being dismissed. More students were being drawn to the Commons like lemmings.

Everyone seemed to be there. Al Bernstein, our Washington ride. Jeff Miller from the dog napalming. Bill Schroeder, our ROTC ride from Streetsboro. Allison Krause and her boyfriend Barry from the day before.

It was like some sort of weird class reunion. We were trading hippie handshakes and chanting slogans, laughing and making fun of the National Guard.

For a while it was a Mexican standoff. Both sides sizing each other up. Then the National Guard's patience ended.

Four soldiers jumped in a pale green open-topped Jeep, a driver, an officer with a bull horn and two rifle toting Guardsmen in the back seat.

They drove right toward us and the crowd parted like the Red Sea for Moses. The officer barked through his bullhorn.

"ATTENTION, ATTENTION. THIS IS AN ORDER. DISPERSE IMMEDIATELY. THIS IS AN ILLEGAL ASSEMBLY."

"NAPALM KENT," we shouted back. "ONE, TWO, THREE, FOUR, WE DON'T WANT YOUR GODDAM WAR."

The lines were drawn, neither side seemed willing to back down or compromise.

The National Guard wanted to show they meant business. About forty of them donned their outer-space looking gas masks, shot a volley of tear gas and charged right at us.

We broke ranks and fled up Blanket Hill toward Taylor Hall. A couple of bold students picked up the still smoking tear gas canisters and threw them back at the Guard.

The crowd was cheering us on. I felt like a football hero. I began looking for Michelle again.

Instead I found Elizabeth. Her face was half-covered with a red railroad bandanna.

"Matthew, Matthew," she laughed, tears running down her high cheekbones. "Isn't this fun, isn't this delicious?"

She had a few of the same group with her that were at the mud fights.

"Having a good time?" I wiped the tears from her cheek with the end of her bandanna.

"This is wonderful. The Guard's retreating," she tugged at my arm. "Let's go back down."

"No thanks, I'm looking for someone."

"Paul?"

"Yeah, him too."

Her friends dragged her back to the middle of the Commons where the students were regrouping. I was left standing by the Stater offices in front of Taylor Hall.

Meanwhile, the Guard went over the top of Blanket Hill, on the other side of Taylor Hall. I followed them and in the process finally found Michelle.

She came running up to me. "Am I missing all of the action again?"

"I don't know, it might be over. Where were you?"

"My history prof tried to keep us after class. He didn't want us over here."

"He can't do that."

"That's what we told him. We finally walked out. What's going on?"

We were following the Guard as we talked. They seemed to be chasing one lone protestor across the practice football field.

I squinted my eyes in the sunlight. Damn, if it wasn't Al Bernstein, hauling ass with the Ohio National Guard in full pursuit.

"Remember my trip to Washington?" I asked Michelle.

"Yeah."

"There's our driver." I pointed at Bernstein.

"The SDSer?"

"You got it."

Bernstein dove under a cyclone fence out of sheer terror.

"Right on, Al," I raised my fist to cheer him on. The crowd roared its approval.

"What're you hollering about?" a familiar voice asked. Spalding arrived in the nick of time.

"Hey buddy, that's Bernstein diving under the fence," I told him.

"You got good eyes," he said. "Hi, Michelle."

"Hello Paul. Where's Early?"

"Back at Depeyster. He didn't want any part of this."

"Chickenshit," I said.

"He's probably smarter than we are."

The Guard, thanks to Bernstein, had marched itself into a dead end, blocked by fences on three sides. About half of them took a break, shedding their gas masks.

Then this longhaired protestor, wearing a jean jacket and headband, began taunting the Guardsmen with a black flag on the end of a stick. As if he was daring them to do something about it.

"That guy has no brains," Spalding said. "Let's get out of here."

"What? You don't have no guts either?"

"Remember Washington?"

"I'm staying," Michelle said.

The Guard finally had enough of the taunting protestor. About ten of them, still wearing their face masks, dropped to one knee, shouldered their rifles and took aim at the Che Guevera look alike.

My heart skipped a beat. Spalding halted in mid-sentence. Michelle dropped her books. The protestor froze in place. All of Blanket Hill became silent.

Nothing happened. The Guardsmen stood up. The flag-waver let out a war hoop and raced back into the crowd, a hero to his peers.

"It's over," Spalding said.

I looked at Michelle. "He's right. Let's get some food."

The Guard came back up the hill, right towards us. A lonely voice came out of the mass of spectators. "Throw down your rifles and go home. You're surrounded."

The crowd laughed and applauded.

We ducked under the shadow of a concrete Japanese pagoda to make way for the approaching Guardsmen. They were obviously going back to the Commons to join up with the rest of their unit.

"I guess you're right," Michelle said.

We turned our backs on the Guard and walked down to the Prentice Hall parking lot. Sandy Scheuer, Elizabeth's mud fight partner, was walking next to us.

"You look a lot better after a shower," I joked.

"Don't bug me, I'm late for class," she laughed and walked ahead of us.

"Who's she?" Michelle asked.

"A friend of Spalding's," I said.

Suddenly there was an eerie silence, followed by a strange popping sound. It reminded me of the Fourth of July.

For thirteen seconds everything stood still, like a dream sequence in an art film.

"Did you hear that?" Michelle asked.

"Yeah, firecrackers," I said.

We turned around, just to make sure.

At 12:22 P.M. on Monday afternoon, May 4th, 1970 at Kent State University in Kent, Ohio, the Ohio National Guard shot and killed four college students: Sandy Scheuer, Allison Krause, William Schroeder and Jeff Miller.

At 1:04 P.M. the same afternoon, Mary Lou Murphy gave birth to a seven pound, six ounce baby boy: Patrick, David, Paul, Matthew Murphy.

"And in the end, the love you take is equal to the love you make."

The Beatles

PHOTO CREDITS

SONG LYRICS CREDITS

Peter Jedick's above photo is from his hippie stage circa 1970. Jedick graduated from Kent State University cum laude with General Honors but he feels more comfortable working on a railroad track gang than hobnobbing with intellectuals. He has been a freelance writer since graduating from Kent and works as a Cleveland fire fighter to pay the bills. He is the author of *League Park*, a history of the early home of the Cleveland Indians, and *Cleveland: Where the East Coast Meets the Midwest*. Jedick is married and has five children who believe his stories about half of the time.